BRIDE OF THE KRAKEN

A DARK MFFM MONSTER ROMANCE

FOR THE LOVE OF TITANS
BOOK TWO

CASSANDRA MEDCALF

LOVE OUT LOUD PRESS, LLC

*For everyone whose definition of love
is different from the movies.
Be the change.*

CONTENT WARNING

You thought the *last* book was wild?

Well buck up, Buttercup. Cause I've got another list of triggers and tropes a mile long.

Please remember as you read that this is a work of fiction. Art and stories are safe spaces where humanity can explore their deepest, darkest fantasies—but not every story is for every reader. This is a story of finding oneself and battling with inner demons. If these topics are hard for you right now, that's okay. Find a book that fills you up.

But when you're ready to let loose and be rung dry of every last drop... come find me 🌚

Triggers and Tropes:

Pregnancy
PCOS/fertility issues (mention)
Miscarriage (mention)

CONTENT WARNING

Nonconsensual sex (not with end-game partners)
Dubious consent
Enthusiastic consent
Generational trauma
Non-generational trauma
Bisexuality
Hypnosis
Magical manipulation
Mind-break
Breeding kink
Edging
Biting
Cock rings
Orgasm denial
Cucking
Pain play & injury play
Erotic asphyxiation
Forked tongues
Misandry
Sapphic sex
"Straight" sex
Group sex
Lactation play
Greek mythology b-sides and discussions of Edith
Hamilton
Cephalopod shifters
Tentacles. Like, so many tentacles.
Bi awakening
Polyamorous awakening
Talking swords
New York accents
Live birth
The use of orgasms as pain management

Interspecies relations/monsters
Vikings

If you read through this and discover I'm missing something, please reach out to me at cassandra@cassandramedcalf.com.

Godspeed!

PROLOGUE
TIFFANY

"Lillian, Wait!"

"No, I–I..."

My best friend's breath catches in her throat, and I freeze. Her shoulders are heaving as she sits on the ground, lips quivering while she tries desperately to fill her lungs.

Not again.

"Lil, shhh, it's okay," I whisper, kneeling down beside her and wrapping my arms around her. Her skin is clammy, either a result of the humidity of the day or her incoming panic attack. When I rub her arms to try to comfort her, she pushes me away.

"Air!" she gasps, and I flinch.

She's hyperventilating. I don't know what to do.

"Just, um... count the breaths." I scour my memory for what she said her therapist told her to do in these situations. I also back away a few inches to give her space. "In, one, two, three–"

"H-hold, wuh-one...t-two..."

She rocks herself back and forth, knees trembling as she pulls them out of the mud and up to her chest. Tentatively, I reach a palm out to rub her back. She closes her eyes, and I count with her in series of fours, mimicking the square breathing with her until she can inhale and exhale without shaking.

"It hurts," she whispers, sobs still wracking her shoulders. "It hurts so much."

I thought a hike through the evergreen forests surrounding the beach of Lake Superior would give us both a change of scenery. A chance to breathe in fresh, oxygen-rich air and breathe out the stress and angst that have been plaguing us lately. Lillian might be plus-size, but she's active, and has always loved hiking and swimming. It's part of why *this* is our annual vacation spot.

But it's been a pretty wet trip this year at the lake cabin. It's rained three of the four days we've been here. The trails are way more slippery than they usually are this time of year, and poor Lillian slipped on a pile of leaves and slammed right into a huge puddle.

She's already been close to tears for the past three months as she dealt with her breakup and the miscarriage, but as soon as I heard her ass hit the ground, the dam broke.

Poor thing. I just wish I could help her. But it's like everything I do is making her more miserable.

She shudders out a breath on a four-count, and we start again.

"Why can't I—just get better?" She chokes out, and tears sting the backs of my eyes.

My attempts at comfort die on my lips. What else can I

say that I haven't already said? What relief can I offer her? I don't know what she's going through.

It's not like anyone would ever want to have kids with me.

My friendship with Lillian is the longest-lasting relationship I've ever had. She's my person.

But where *I* have only dated casually as an adult, Lillian's been clear from the get-go that she wants to get married and have a family. Too bad her asshole ex was never honest with her about his intentions. He never fucking deserved her—always acting like he was doing her some big favor by mooching off of her all these years.

I wish she'd realized it sooner. Before he ruined her life.

Why can't she see that she deserves so much better than that?

"It'll get better, Lil. It'll be okay," I say softly, letting my hand rest on her shoulder and squeezing.

In, two three four…

After about five more minutes, she stops shaking, but her face is swollen with tears. Her nose is running something awful, and I know her whole backside has got to be covered in mud and wet sand.

"I'm gonna go back to the cabin to change. I'm cold."

"I'll help you make a fire–"

"No, Tiff, it's fine. I just want to shower and be alone for a little bit. You should finish the hike. I don't want to ruin your trip anymore than I already have."

"Lillian–"

But she's already shrugging me off, climbing up from the forest floor and trudging back to the cabin.

Away from me.

"Goddammit," I mutter when her silhouette disappears beyond the trees.

This is nothing like I thought it would be if Lil and I were ever single at the same time again. The dreams I had of admitting my feelings for her fade away with each day I watch her struggle, as I realize once again that I'll never be enough. Not for her, not for anyone.

Hey, at least she's leaning on you for help, I tell myself. But that sentiment rings more and more hollow every day that my "help" does diddly squat to get her out of this depression.

I continue up the lakeside path, making my way towards a scenic overlook that's marked on the little trail map we picked up at the convenience store on our way here. Supposedly it's one of the places where there have been lake monster sightings in years passed.

Given how the rack of ghost stories was one of the first things Lillian had expressed interest in in weeks, I thought that going on our own little paranormal adventure might lift her out of her funk a little bit.

Sigh. So much for that.

As I climb the steeper, rocky outcropping, the trees around me thin, and slowly the unimpeded view of Lake Superior stretches before me. White foam splashes against the pebbly beach below, the inland tide slapping against the larger rocks and creating a spray that tickles my face.

The overcast sky is the only thing keeping the picture from being perfect. That, and the lack of Lillian beside me.

My throat works, a lump forming that I can't swallow away.

I just want my friend back. More than anything, for her to get through this. Be that hilarious, gorgeous beam of sunshine in my life again.

My person.

"Please, God," I pray—fucking *pray,* I'm so goddamn desperate, "just lift her grief away. Give my friend her happiness back, I will trade anything…"

Tears pool in my eyes as I realize it's true. I'd give just about anything to get my best friend back. To see her actually smile again. To go back to the way we used to be, when–

A flash of lightning cuts through the clouds, seeming to hit something on the shore of an island across the lake. The entire sky lights up, and thunder crashes so loud around me that I almost lose my footing on the slippery rocks.

"Ah!" I gasp as my heart rate ratchets to a hundred, splaying my arms out to my sides to catch my balance. *That could have been really bad.*

The water below me churns darkly. Unnaturally dark— the usually clear shallows swirl inky black below as the froth of the surf intensifies.

What the…

A figure rises from the lake, and my heart stops. An enormous, *stunning* woman slowly grows from the water, revealing a silver crown atop a head of snake-like hair, a perfectly symmetrical face, and a naked, pale green torso with the most gorgeous set of boobs I've ever seen.

I blink. It's like the wind's been knocked out of me—I can't do anything else.

"Anything?"

The woman—*goddess? monster?*—speaks, and her voice envelops me like a mother's embrace. Air expands in my lungs, and from nowhere a smooth, muscled limb scoops me up from behind and lifts me closer to Her perfect face. A dull, hypnotic buzzing fills my head as I take in Her form, warmth pooling in my belly.

Who is this creature?

"Ha haha," Her laughter is at once like the tinkling of windchimes and the rumble of a dragon. **"Oh sweet human. I am the goddess to whom you pray."**

"G-goddess??" My mouth goes dry. I can't tear my eyes away from Her. "Y-you—"

"I have the power to take away your friend's grief," She says, loving sympathy filling Her silvery eyes. **"Lillian, is it? She is in much pain. More than I thought a mere human to be capable of."**

"Please!" I gasp, still practically dumb in Her presence. "I'll do anything—"

"So you say."

The lump in my throat returns, and I gulp. She's appraising me now, pulling me closer as she raises an eyebrow. The muscle around me flexes, and I look down. That's when I realize what's holding me.

I'm in the grasp of a giant tentacle.

Tentacle?!

Oh fuck, oh fuck, oh *fuck...*

"Calm yourself, Tiffany. You are in no danger. At the moment." She pauses, peering into my eyes as if She can see straight into my very soul. The silver orbs glow and pulse, and I can't even blink anymore as I follow the swirling eddies within Her irises, filling my head with the sound of the inland sea...

"My price is steep. But I, too, know what it is to lose a child. I take pity on your friend.

"I will lift the pain from her mind, if you agree to pay the debt of your ancestors. Give me your first-born child, Tiffany, and you will get your friend back."

"I don't have any children," I blurt out stupidly, struck honest by the powerful aura radiating from the goddess.

Everywhere She touches, my skin scorches with electricity, sizzling up and down my nervous system and leaving me powerless to resist Her. "I'll never be able to pay you."

"We will see about that."

I shake my head. "No, Goddess... you don't understand. I'm not the motherly type, okay? I'm..." I pause, memories that I thought I'd processed and moved on from coming back in a rush.

But this goddess doesn't need to know about my baggage. Doesn't need to understand just how bad a fit I'd be as a mother, how hopeless the idea of me ever having a perfect little family is. But it wouldn't be fair to get Her hopes up for nothing.

"...on birth control."

"Hush, human." Her eyes glow brighter as She steals the words from my mouth. *"I know what I ask. If you never quicken with child, then our debt will simply go unpaid."*

"Really?"

She raises me to eye level, and I shudder as Her supernatural gaze meets mine.

"Really."

We hold there for an unbearably long second as She waits for my response. Shaking, I lower my head once in a nod.

I don't know what else to do.

As quickly as She appeared, She retreats. Her tentacle unfurls, depositing me back onto the overlook before She slithers back into the water. The inky swirls among the surf fade once more into the crystal-clear waters of the lake, and the clouds miraculously clear away. The goddess sinks into nothingness, and the fog clears from my head.

As She retreats, Her voice echoes in my mind.

Swim in my waters by the light of the moon. Lillian's grief will disappear by morning.
I'll be watching, Tiffany.

CHAPTER 1

DEAN

I can hear my dad now.

"Now remember, Poindexter. First: analyze the situation. You've got brains, use them. Don't just barrel in there without thinking."

Guess I really bit the horn on that one.

You could say I've been preparing for this my whole life. Decades of training, followed by three years of watching Tiffany and Lillian like a hawk, knowing that someday they'd lead me right to the monster.

Truth be told, I had all but abandoned the "hero's birthright" my father had hammered into my psyche from birth before I met Tiffany. Growing up in the Apostolos household, reminders of our Greek heritage were everywhere. And I don't mean moussaka and crucifixes. All that *My-Big-Fat-Greek-Wedding* hoopla and community was about as far from my upbringing as you can get. No, *my* childhood was filled with an overbearing father trying to isolate me and my mother from the rest of the world. Filling the void with pagan myths and morality tales, stories of heroes like Hercules, Achilles, and of course our family's ancestor: Perseus.

Slayer of the Medusa. Athena's chosen warrior. Savior of women.

Now, I know what you're thinking: all that high-falutin' Olympian upbringing must have gotten me *all* the bitches.

Yeeeeeeaaaah, no. The life of a Greek hero in training is not nearly as glamorous as the movies make it out to be. Every evening and weekend was spent strength training or survivalist camping with my old man. When I wasn't at school, I was learning ancient Greek and the history of *my people:* The Olympians.

Whenever I *did* get a spare second to breathe, I was playing video games. Don't get me wrong: convincing Pops to get me a PS2 back in the day wasn't easy. He hated how much of a nerd I was. How skinny and lanky I've always been—even after puberty hit and it just seemed to make me taller. Seeing his son become a nerd was probably the biggest disappointment of his life, and he wasn't about to be supportive of my "Poindexter hobbies," as he called them.

Until I showed him the trailer for *God of War* and he realized some of them might help me appreciate my heritage a little bit more.

But that never really happened. The more I learned about the Olympians from sources other than my old man, the more I hated them all. Especially Zeus, my million-greats grandfather. What a fucking prick!

When I put midwest suburbia and my family in the rearview the day I left for college, I thought I would finally be done with all of that. Get my comp-sci degree, lock down a software engineering gig somewhere, and move on with my life. I vowed to never make my kids suffer the way I did, with the literal weight of the world hanging over their shoulders like Atlas their entire childhoods, with parents trying to convince them it was their job to carry on the legacy of the mighty heroes of old.

And then I met Tiffany. And everything I *thought* I'd processed in therapy came rushing back in a blink.

I could smell it on her: that strange scent of salt and ozone that called to my very DNA.

Titan.

The most beautiful girl in the bar had tangled with an honest-to-Zeus Titan.

And after a lifetime of training followed by years of trying to get away, I had the opportunity to finish the job my ancestors started.

I would have loved to walk away from her right then and there: truly stick it to my destiny and choose my own path that night. The path I chose for myself. To be a regular, clock-punching software engineer, and just forget all that hero nonsense.

But then I saw her face.

I guess you could call me a sucker. Say it's a tale as old as time. But the second I saw her, I knew. She was the one for me. Love at first sight. And then I met her best friend, Lillian, and between the two of them? I thought I was the luckiest man in the world. Somehow, the gods had smiled upon me, delivering me into the lives of these amazing women.

Only to get tangled up in their brush with the mother of Medusa.

While Keto's scent is what brought me to Tiffany, I believe the Fates would have led me to her with or without the Titan's curse. She was in trouble, locked in a deal that she couldn't possibly understand the ramifications of. Our threads were destined to intertwine long before I stumbled in that bar, and once I found her, I couldn't let her go.

I accepted my destiny and followed her to the ends of the earth, only to beef it up big time at the first sign of danger.

I lift my head, neck aching from the weeks I've been strung up and shackled to the wall of Keto's underwater cave. Across from me, Tiffany's chin brushes her chest, soft snores sending bubbles drifting from her nose. She looks thin, even thinner than usual, and I worry if she's eating enough.

Pssh—duh, Dean, of course she isn't eating enough. You've both been surviving on boiled deer carcasses and fish scraps from your jailor for the past twenty-odd days.

The temperature of the water around us rises, and I know She's approaching. Keto.

Shrunk down to Her more human proportions, though still giant, She glides up to Tiffany. But of course She does. She always zeroes in on her first.

Her, and the baby.

My fiancé doesn't wake just yet. She's been sleeping more lately, a result of the pregnancy's toll on her body. I'm not thrilled with the fact that the only thing we have to eat under here is meat, seeing as I know she needs more nutrition than venison alone can deliver. But I'm sure the enchantment Keto has us under probably enhances the resilience of our gut biome. I mean, I hope so.

Gods, I hope the baby is okay.

Little baby Percy. To be named after my some thousand-greats grandfather, the original Greek hero. Pop's idea, of course.

I reached back out to him after Tiffany and I started dating. Faced with the thing he'd always warned me would happen, I didn't know what to do. For generations, the Apostoloses had kept the dream alive that someday our ancestors would call upon us to finish the job of defeating the last of the Titans. Hunted for the remaining beings, scoured the earth for signs of them. The ones that got away.

But, come on. It'd been hundreds and hundreds of years. Greek mythology had been relegated to just that: *myths*. Legends. Made-up stories that were more fodder for paranormal romance plots and 90's archeological adventure movies than any actual source of history. Generation after generation of Apostolos searched and searched for any sign of them and every time, came away empty-handed.

But even I couldn't deny the pull of my blood once I got a scent. *Seek the ancient ones.* Find Keto; destroy her once and for all.

And for that, I needed my dad's help.

So I started training again. Visiting my parents on weekends, even bringing Tiffany home for Christmas to learn a little about the family. Not *everything*, obviously—I didn't want to scare her away. But enough that someday, she might understand. Understand why I had to lead her into danger. Why I had to follow her on this trip. Why I had to convince her to push Lillian into...

Gods. I can't even think about it. The plan Pops cooked up to get us here.

"Get her to let you tag along. It's been two years that you've missed this opportunity, are you really going to let a third pass you by? Are you really going to take that risk, when she's got the family heir on the line?

I should have known it wouldn't work. I should have been stronger, more resistant. Protected Tiffany—and Lillian—better than I did. Convinced them instead to forget the lake cabin and try taking their girls' trip somewhere, *anywhere* else...

But how could I have known the deal that Tiffany made? Sure, I knew she'd been touched by the gods, but I didn't know the details of the bargain, made before we even met. Tiffany didn't even know that I knew about Keto. Why would she think to bring it up to me?

Regrets upon regrets, piled as far as the eye can see. If I'd have only been more honest with her about my family's history. About what I'd scented on her. If she'd only told me about the deal. If, if, if...

I want to look at her so badly. Take in the curve of her cheek, the soft rise and fall of her chest as she breathes unnaturally in this underwater cave. But if I show any sign that I'm awake, it'll start all over.

Keto's torture.

Part of me suspects She knows. Realizes that the blood I carry in my veins is the same that murdered Her children all those millenia ago. Medusa. Polydectes. Monster after monster. Felled by the mighty Perseus.

And my family's been hunting the remaining Titans ever since.

It would almost make it easier to accept the way She tortures us, if She knew who I was. But that seems a stretch. The torture She's subjecting us to isn't the kind She would if She *actually* hated us. No. It's far... kinkier than that.

I pretend to be asleep, suppressing the shiver that tickles my spine in Her presence. I don't know if I can handle another session with Her teasing me in front of Tiffany, only to edge me until I'm just about to burst, before turning away and making me watch as She brings Tiffany to orgasm over and over again. I don't know what's worse, honestly. Not getting to come, or being forced to.

I hear her sob herself to sleep whenever the Titan leaves us. All I want is to reach out, cradle her head in my arms, tell her it's all going to be okay.

But that's bullshit. Nothing about this is okay.

In the sliver of vision beneath my mostly-closed eyes, I see Her approach us. I stay perfectly still as the long-clawed, green hand of the Titaness skims the skin of Tiffany's bare belly.

Fire burns in mine.

The urge to protect my fiancé is overwhelming. This is beyond me playing hero. This is the woman I *love*, goddammit. I've failed her enough already. I'm not going to let Keto play with her anymore.

Get away from her!

"Oh?"

The monster turns, and the heat in my stomach flares with that all-too-familiar ache that always burns in Her presence. This is the thing that, even with all of my training, Pops *didn't* prepare me for.

Titans are...sexy. Like, *inhumanly* sexy. As in, when you're in their presence, your body just *does* things outside of your control. They use it to their advantage, too, in some truly fucked up ways.

It's why Tiffany succumbs to Keto's demands to scream Her name when She makes her fall apart. Using Her mouth and hands and tentacles and snakes and all the other magical limbs at Her disposal. It's why I get hard everytime I see Her.

I mean, I'm *already* a pretty horny guy. Let's be real: I was a lonely kid with no friends aside from video game characters. Forced to suppress and hide my sexuality for my entire teenage-hood, because my dad was training me to be some Greek hero. I figured out I was bisexual in college, but lacked the social skills to really start dating until after I graduated.

Search *any* guy's google history with an upbringing like mine and you're going to find some kinky shit, okay? I had to live vicariously through porn for most of my life. I can't help what I'm into.

And Keto? *Fuck,* man. She's like every hot Dark Souls boss blended into one terrifying sex goddess.

Watching Her fuck the love of my life, while her best friend mates with the *other* tentacled titan next door? Terrifying, absolutely.

But also the hottest hentai wet dream you've ever fucking read, let's be honest.

Except for the fact that none of us asked for this. Tiffany certainly didn't. And the shame and guilt and fear that swirls in my stomach everytime She approaches is proof that this is *not* a dream. It's a nightmare.

And I don't want to sit through another second of it.

You slimy sea witch. You're disgusting.

She chuckles, Her silver eyes darting to my erection.

"Believe your lust is my fault if you will, Dean, but I can assure you it isn't. If I was trying to seduce you, you'd know it."

Suddenly, She is in front of me, stirring my dick to life with a feather-light stroke of Her sharpened claws. I gasp, clenching my muscles tight to resist Her allure, but it's no use.

Fuck her. She's *absolutely* seducing me.

I'm starting to think my ancestor battling the Medusa was playing on easy mode. He couldn't look at his prey for fear of turning to stone. Whereas I?

I'm forced to take in every godly curve of my captor. But

instead of turning my body into stone, the only part of me that turns rock-hard is…

Well. You get the idea.

"Fu–argh!" I cough, as She continues to tease me. Bubbles burst from my mouth at the curse, and another sinister laugh reverberates through the dark cave where She's keeping us captive.

This has been Her game ever since Lillian disappeared. Pamper Tiffany. Torture me.

"Your body is so eager, Dean. I'm not sure I can choke this cock any harder."

She lowers her lips down my body, licking a trail of hot kisses all the way to the base of my shaft, which is wrapped ten times over with golden rings. She blows a kiss, and I feel another ring, the tightest one yet, manifest above the one from yesterday.

Yep. She's got me in a sleeve of metal cock rings. It started with one the first night She captured us, and She's added one every time She finds me awake.

Please! I beg, as Her strokes and kisses make me swell painfully, pushing the sensitive skin into the biting metal. *I can't—I don't–*

"Oh, don't tell me you're giving up our game already?" She stares up at me from under Her navy blue lashes, silver eyes gleaming with mischief and Her flushed, emerald lips curling forward in a pout. **"It's only been twenty-one days, my tasty human. Surely you can't be so desperate for release?"**

Tiffany stirs, waking, and I tense painfully. *Fuck,* I can't control it. Can't let her see me like this… not with *Her…*

The goddess's hand grips and tightens, surrounding the exposed inches to an excruciating squeeze. I yell out in ecstatic pain, and if Tiffany hadn't been awake before, she is now.

Let go of him!

No! I beg her in my mind, but it's too late.

Keto has already turned from me. But not before I saw the silver flash in Her eyes.

It's what She's been waiting for. Another bargaining chip in Her twisted game.

"Sweet Tiffany," She purrs, and I see the jolt zip through her spine at the sensual sound of the titan's voice. My hips jerk forward instinctually, and a whimper escapes my lips.

The power She has over us is unreal.

You're toying with us. You have your brood now, you've got your children—why do you insist on torturing us?

"I don't have my children yet," She snaps. **"They are growing. Just as I grow...bored."**

That sounds like a you problem.

My heart seizes. My fiancée is a gods-damned *menace.* She's the real hero between the two of us. Meanwhile, I'm one giant failure. A disappointment to the whole Apostolos clan. Can't even protect my fiancé or our baby from the monster I was trained to fight from birth.

Still. Tiffany hasn't run out of fight. Hasn't given up. And I gotta admit, I've never found her sexier than when she's talking back to a Titan.

The pain in my dick swells, and I choke on another gasp. Fuck!

Well, at least *that* arousal—the kind I get from Tiffany —is natural.

"Oh, it's no problem. After all, as you so helpfully pointed out, I have two new toys to keep me entertained.

"Let's play a game, shall we?"

CHAPTER 2
TIFFANY

I don't care how powerful and sexy this goddess is. She needs to get her claws off my man.

I don't want to play games, Keto.

She pouts at me. Like a cute toddler begging for a cookie. Like a friend might, jokingly, when twisting your arm to go to an anime convention with you. In the last few days, Keto's adopted the demeanor of a gal pal. As if, now that She has everyone I love in Her captivity, we can be *friends.*

I haven't seen Lillian since she agreed to pay my debt. Do the unthinkable: play surrogate to the titan Keto and her lover, Phorkys, and become pregnant with an entire clutch of demigods.

My very soul aches at the thought of her, alone and in pain, as she struggles with the demands of a supernatural pregnancy. At what memories it must be bringing up for her. At the unfairness of it all.

Lillian sacrificed herself to save me. She is currently pregnant with thousands of monstrous children, and I'm...

I glance down at the swell of my belly in the dark before

staring daggers at the titan who can't seem to resist torturing my fiancé and me, despite Lil's sacrifice.

But she's always sacrificed for me, and I was never grateful enough. Maybe this is my punishment for all I put her through over the years.

I remember once, in college, when I dragged her to a yoga class on campus because I was trying to bang one of the girls who always went to the Saturday morning sunrise sessions. She was *pissed* at me for waking her at 5:30am to make it to the fitness center by 6:00 on a weekend, but she still did it, grumbling all the way. Neither of us were sporting the Lululemon leggings and sports bras of the other girls; we stuck out like sore thumbs at the back of the mirrored room in sweatpants and baggy tees, stifling our laughter at how pretentious the names of the poses were.

I don't even remember the name of the hottie I was trying to impress, or in what terrible and careless way she left me hanging—as my romantic interests always did in college. I was having too much fun at the back of the room with Lil, holding in our farts until we ran out of the room as fast as we could at the final gong. We hightailed it to the dining hall for breakfast and a metric fuckliter of coffee to make up for the early morning. The two of us crop dusted the entire quad, Lil cursing the whole way for making me, quote, "crunch her fart muscles before last night's dinner had digested."

Six years later, in Chicago, I convinced her yet again to join me for another ridiculous fitness class, only this time it was pole dancing. Lillian was with her ex then, but she and I were still shacked up in a shared studio apartment in the southside, and this was a rare foray uptown for the two of us. The cost of the class for the two of us would usually be close to half our rent, but I had an in.

A burlesque dancer I'd hit on at a show had personally invited me to the class, and Lillian was playing wingwoman. About a half an hour in, she and I had both fallen on our butts—and *almost* our heads—a handful of times during a few tragic attempts at inversions, and the teacher finally kicked us out for laughing too loudly and distracting the rest of the class.

Afterwards, sipping on smoothies at Jamba Juice, Lillian was re-enacting the overreaction of the instructor when I almost face-planted on the platform, and a lock of her hair fell out of her messy bun and into her face. Wheezing, I reached over and brushed it away, and for the shortest of seconds, my fingers lingered on the curve of her cheek.

That was the first inkling of it. The feeling that, if I'd just been honest with myself from the start, I'd have realized what was lying dormant even before the Post Yoga Crop Dusting Streak of Junior Year.

I was in love with my best friend.

God, I miss her.

Why couldn't I have just been a better friend?

Keto tilts Her head at me, clearly eavesdropping in on my internal lecture. It's no wonder She's confused. She can't possibly know what love is. What friendship is.

I scowl at Her, knowing She's reading my thoughts, and She huffs.

"Do not claim to understand me, child."

Dean, the other victim of my bad decisions, looks at me questioningly. I haven't been able to look him in the eye the entire time we've been held captive—not that I've had too many opportunities. Keto's been keeping me in an artificial sleep for most of the time we've been trapped here in this underwater cave of Hers, separating me from my fiance by keeping us on separate walls of the giant space, his face barely visible over the wide expanse of lake grass and water.

I miss you. I call out to him, mind to mind, the only way we're able to communicate here.

I miss you, too, Tiff.

His eyes glow with so much emotion, I can hardly parse them all. Pain. Love. Regret? He's a deep-drilled well of feelings, and I can't afford to belay all the way down there. Not with Keto in our heads.

I try to block my thoughts from Her, but it doesn't come easy. It's like trying to meditate in a yoga class—something I was *never* good at. How do you think of nothing? Doesn't the natural state of having a brain mean you just have thoughts running through your head all the time? How am I supposed to think of nothing??

So instead, I just close my eyes, block out Dean's face, and repeat a singular sentence in my head while She stares at me.

Stop engaging Her. Stop engaging Her. Stop engaging Her...

"You refuse to speak to me?"

I open my eyes, adopting a glare as I lock eyes with Her. The goddess tilts Her head and raises an eyebrow at my expression.

It doesn't matter if I refuse to speak or not, I retort, attempting to look down my nose at Her despite the fact that Her massive body takes up the majority of the cave. *You'll just read my mind anyway.*

And I really am shit at meditation.

She laughs, a full-bellied, joyful sound that is so out-of-sorts with this whole goddamn situation. She bends in a shallow dive and propels forward until Her face is mere inches from mine, and traces a finger down my cheek, before digging Her claw into the bottom of my jaw and pushing my chin up. She meets my eyes.

"I must say, when I kidnapped the two of you I really thought you'd be more fun. Phorkys is having the time of his life with those two in the other cave. Whatever happened to the promiscuous couple with the delightful collection of sexual toys? The Tiffany who dreamed of bedding her best friend at their little cabin on the lake? Or the Dean who fantasized of threesomes? Has this baby–" She splays Her hand over my belly, rubbing it up and down until the pad of Her thumb brushes against the underside of my breast. I shiver. *"–really changed you both so much?*

"What prudes."

Her fingers tense, and a flutter of arousal tickles low in my belly, mixing with the shame that bubbles up at her words. She traces the sensation with Her index finger as it travels to the apex of my thighs. I moan involuntarily as She presses into the seam below my mound and the pleasure intensifies.

Fuck you! I want to scream, writhing in the weedy binds that secure me to the cave wall. It feels good, and I hate that it does. Guilt spirals in my stomach at the blossoming arousal, both feelings building simultaneously as She plays with me.

She smirks, stroking Her finger deeper until it grazes my clitoris, and Her supernatural touch becomes just shy of unbearable. My heart is racing. My body approaches climax unbelievably quickly, legs shaking against their ties.

Ah! I hear, and glance up to see Dean also writhing against his restraints. My eyes travel down his body, and then widen in shock.

His dick is hard as nails, straining against a collar of rings that climb from its base up to just a couple inches below his head. They look to be made of solid metal, gold in color and, if the purplish hue of the exposed skin is any indication, are causing quite a bit of discomfort.

She's kept us apart, hiding most of his body behind the lush grasses of the cave, fastening our wrists and ankles to the cave walls. I haven't been able to see how much She's been torturing Dean. He hasn't told me, either. Everytime I wake, he's only concerned about how I'm doing.

And right now? I'm furious.

She isn't just playing with me. She's playing with both of us. I know She's made me come dozens of times over the course of our imprisonment. How many times has She assaulted Dean in the same way?

What are you trying to—oh, God!

I start to question Her, but an orgasm overtakes me. She's sunk below my waist: a dangerous position, as there She can use *all* of her supernatural parts to drive me to the edge. Her thumb rubs my clit, fingers splaying me open, while Her tongue licks teasing strokes along my lips. One of the snake-like tails trailing from Her living hair penetrates me steadily, too. It wriggles inside me: a motion that's as disturbing as it is incredible.

Admit it. No man can love you like this. No human.

No...

I know if She wants to, She'll keep me on the edge like this for hours. Now that I've come once, She knows I'm like putty in Her hands. Her arms. Her tails. Even Her hair.

She is a literal goddess of pleasure. And I can't help it when my body gives in.

Who is the only one who can make you feel this way, sweet Tiffany? Who is the goddess of your pleasure?

I—I can't–

Tell me! Say my name!

At once, all of Her tentacles still in their assault of my body, filling me inside and out, stretching me to my limit, to the point of pain. I can't move, I can't fight—and frozen on Her limbs like this, I can't come either.

And She knows it.

This is Her game. What it always comes down to. Scream Her name, or pass out from pain instead of pleasure.

K...Keto...

SHOUT IT!

"Keto!"

Water fills my mouth and lungs as I shout, and Her entire body moves as one within me.

My head bows as my entire body clenches and unclenches around Her, waves of pleasure overwhelming me. Through squinted eyes, I try to find Dean—but even that small rebellion fails as my vision goes white with the sensations spiraling from my core. Eventually, I just succumb, choking on my orgasm, closing my eyes as I surrender all emotion to sensation.

It doesn't end. The titan unties my legs from their bonds. Her tails wrap around my legs, holding me open once my own muscles grow too weak. I lose track of which part is doing what: snakes, eels, fingers, tongue, tentacles—what does it matter? My body isn't even my own anymore. It's Hers.

That's right, Tiffany. You're mine. You've always been mine. You'll always be mine.

The longer it goes on, the louder Dean's cries echo in my head and the tighter I close my eyes, praying to wake up from this nightmare. His voice ringing in my head is the only thing keeping me tied to reality.

My brain is mush. My arms and legs are twitching helplessly, my core is on fire, and Keto's words are a mantra in my mind. Is She trying to hypnotize me? Does She want to keep me here forever?

What about Dean?

It isn't fair to be so close to the man I love and yet unable to touch him.

That's the thing about threesomes, I think in a guilt-ridden daze, some cloudy moral lecture forming in the floatiness between my second and third orgasm, *they're never as fun as you think they're going to be. And in the end, you ruin whatever relationships you had going into it.*

You can only belong to one.

Begging without begging, I wish I could come up with an appeal to stop it all. Instead I just scream, again and again, endless pleas dropping from my silent lips. Praying for a way to get Keto to leave us both alone.

But I can't think of anything. Too overwhelmed by the excruciating pleasure and guilt rocketing through my body, until I black out.

CHAPTER 3
KETO

Both of my human captives have fainted by the time I'm done toying with them. Tiffany, fragile that she is, can usually only withstand a dozen or so climaxes before her body gives out. And Dean...

It isn't orgasms that I torture him with. No, the games he and I play are far more interesting.

Killing human males has been a pastime of mine ever since the crash that tore Phorkys from my side. That tragic accident was the beginning of hundreds of years of loneliness. Naturally, I found a way to entertain myself.

There was no shortage of human warriors sailing into my domain in those days. Tattoos and scars adorning their body, seeking conquest and glory and battle, only to be sucked into a storm and find themselves at my mercy. Oh, how I enjoyed drawing out their screams.

It was a few hundred years before I learned to use my powers to give them gills. Keep them trapped in my lair. Without their pesky need to breathe above water, I could torture them for *ages*. It became something of a game.

I remember the first one to react to my violent administrations with lust. His manhood wasn't nearly so enticing as Poseidon's, the only lover I'd known to have a human-like cock. But it was intriguing, bobbing between us, growing more and more swollen with every cut of my claws across his skin, each lash down his back.

His favorite game was when I'd wrap my tentacles around his neck, closing off his gills, asphyxiating him until his eyes bulged, red and veiny, mirroring the reaction below his waist.

At first, it took merely a graze of one of my tails to make him erupt; slimy strings of white film shooting from his penis like a cannon. A new game emerged: how long could I tease him, torture him, play with him, before he burst?

After he perished, it didn't take much for me to learn how to elicit similar arousal from my human prisoners *intentionally.* Just because my perverted little warrior had finally succumbed to death, didn't mean my erotic games needed to end.

The jewels and adornments I once wore as queen regent of the seas had been going to waste for centuries. I soon learned to reuse the precious metals for a better purpose; I crafted rings that could allow a man to resist climax for days—weeks, even—more than long enough to find another victim to pass the time.

I didn't have the highest hopes for Dean when I first captured him and his darling Tiffany. I decided to be gentle with them both. The female, of course, I have a soft spot for...she and Lillian both have suffered and lost much in their short lives, as only women ever seem to do in this cruel world.

The games I play are merely a feather added to even the scales, weighted against female kind for all of history.

And yet, Dean proved heartier than I would have

expected. I've only had one prisoner to withstand my torture longer, and he claimed to be a member of his nation's elite armed forces.

Perhaps there is more than meets the eye with this skinny mortal...

A current whispers through the water around me as I admire my prey, finally ridden unconscious from my games. If Tiffany's already stirring, I must have been playing with him for longer than I realized. Five or six hours, at least. Might be a new record for him.

Good morning, sweet minnow.

Stop...looking at him like that...

I turn to face her fully, obscuring her view of the man, hiding the scratches on his chest and the reddish bruises circling his neck from my tentacles. It is best if she doesn't know the full extent of mine and Dean's adventures.

Sweet dreams? I ask. She shudders, eyes clouding as her mind spins. Too quickly for me to pick out any specifics— just memories of the various failed relationships through her life. Longing. Regret. Guilt. The familiar wheel of emotions I've come to expect from her recurring night-mares. **No, I suppose not.**

Get out of my head.

I grin, her response so typical. Humans always feel so violated, so betrayed, to know you're reaching into their minds. What hypocrites. Every man I've met has prayed ceaselessly to his god to save him from my torment. Yet when I, a true goddess, seek to know their true desires, they're infuriated by it?

So fickle are you humans. So embarrassed by your own dreams and fantasies. I stroke a clawed finger down the delicate line of her jaw, cheeks more hollow than they were when we first descended to this cave of mine. Her body vibrates in response, and I can almost feel the shiver rolling from the crown of her head down to the tips of her toes.

It must be magnificent, as a mortal, to be touched so sweetly by a goddess. More flashes of her lingering dreams flicker behind her eyes, and I latch on to a particularly tragic tryst with a lesbian couple from her past. ***Always wanting what you cannot have…***

I only wanted to protect my friend and my family.

Hmm. Is that so?

Her steely gaze falters under my steady one. Too quickly, her eyes dart away, and I move closer, stroking my other hand up and down her naked hip.

Is it true that your lover Phorkys, that he… impregnated her?

My suckers latch onto her legs, spreading her thighs apart slowly. I savor her slight gasp as the cool water climbs its way up to the entrance of her sex. Enjoy the way her eyes hood when two of my tails wrap low about her waist, squeezing slightly to ease the burden of her heavy stomach.

My lips move to her shoulder, her neck, her jaw. My claws scrape against her scalp, my snakes flicking their forked tongues sensuously across her delicate, pale skin.

Yes.

How?

She's breathing more heavily now as I stroke a tentacle up and back across her lower lips. I can see when her mind drifts to imagining it—Lillian, in a position just as compromising, as a tentacled beast spreads her limbs apart and a shadow approaches her open, weeping sex.

My jaw tenses at the idea of Phorkys being that shadow. Of *my* consort, bedding another woman. A *human,* at that.

He used his vessel. The ancient one. From the shipwreck.

Memories of a long, slim boat, manned by oars, crashed

at the bottom of the lake amongst crags of jagged rock. I project the image into her mind, and she gasps.

What–

My consort would not lower himself to bed a mere mortal like Lillian. He took the form of the human, Erik, her male companion. I do not like him or his clan. They attacked my first clutch in these waters many years ago.

More visions: the wild lightning storm, high waves, and me, wrapping the sad remains of the Viking ship in my arms and crushing it as easily as I would a lump of clay; dozens of men and women clutching the rails, flying across the deck, falling to their deaths...

Then the true tragedy: my clutch of eggs, smashed to bits by that same ship. The crime for which I wrought my vengeance.

I share every picture from my mind to Tiffany's. So she can understand the *real* reason she and Lillian owe me this debt. What their people, their species, took from me.

My children. Once again slaughtered by humans.

A swallow bobs in her throat. *But now a human gives them life.*

I hide a snort. Her face, impossibly, grows paler.

So it would seem.

I remove the visions from her head, and she wilts in relief. For a moment, the only sounds between us are the sloshing of the gentle currents between my tentacles and her skin as I brush the sensitive area at the apex of her thighs. Her heart rate increases, her eyelashes flutter, and just as I think she's about to fall off the edge–

Is she in pain?

I freeze. Her eyes lock with mine as she holds her breath.

No. Not yet. But childbirth is painful for every woman.

She exhales, closing her eyes. Suddenly, I don't feel like playing with her body anymore. Perhaps I've overextended myself. How long have I been cooped up with these mortals this time? Eight, nine hours? Practically an entire night.

I withdraw, untangling my tentacles and tails from her weak body as I prepare to hunt for their breakfast. These creatures are so needy. I am truly a merciful goddess to keep them alive this long.

I feel like I remember... did Phorkys say something about her feeling... pleasure?

Her voice is practically a whisper. I could ignore it, but I hear the faint glimmer of hope in her voice. As if, maybe, her friend's fate is not so monstrous as she believes her own to be.

Heat builds in my chest at her lack of gratitude.

I believe you are more than knowledgeable regarding the pleasures our kind is able to provide.

I feel the shiver race down her spine. That same cocktail of emotions threaded through it: regret, guilt, *fear*.

She should be afraid. They should all be afraid. Cautious, always, of just how helpless they are compared to me.

Don't you, Tiffany? Don't you know just how ecstatic the heights I can build inside you? The pure, unadulterated, bliss...

I descend on her in a flurry: winding arms encase her shoulders, snapping her bonds and pushing her back until she's prone flat on the lake floor, knees bent and legs open enough for my entire body to press against her. My snakes and eels tumble forward, framing her face in a sheet of hissing privacy, their forked tongues slithering out to tickle her jaw, her neck, her collarbone. My tails splay her limbs aside as I take four fingers and thrust them inside her, my other hand clutching just tightly enough against her throat to tease the edges of her gills.

Yes. *This* is the pleasure I love to deliver.

Tinged with pain. With guilt. With shame. Watching my victims suffer as *I* have suffered...

Her eyes flutter closed, and I feel every thought racing through her oxygen-starved brain.

The panic.

The arousal.

The *fear*.

I jerk my hand free of her sensitive pussy, and her eyes burst open—mouth gaping on a silent cry. I replace it with two of my tentacles, curled and wrapped about themselves until they resemble a giant phallus, larger than that of any human male.

Yes, you feel it, don't you? This is what your friend desires. What she goes wild for. That male seduced her with a body much like this one, you know. Brought her to the peak of sexual satisfaction. She loves her monsters, that friend of yours. Shall I show you what drove her most crazy? What she desires most?

I remove my hand from her throat and grasp her wrists, thrusting both of her hands towards me until they're cupping my firm breasts. I drag her thumbs across their firm peaks, already beginning to grow swollen and sensitive as my milk comes in to nourish my brood. I see Tiffany's eyes widen as they settle there, finally taking in the beauty of my body, letting herself yearn for it.

That's right, Tiffany. Embrace it. Lillian did. You are being consumed by a titan. Let yourself enjoy it!

There's arousal building in my stomach now along with hers. Her fingers sink into the heavy flesh of my breasts, kneading in earnest now. She flicks and plucks her thumbs at my nipples, and I arch up, removing one hand from her body so I can play with my own. I rub under my tentacles as I thrust inside her, bolts of sensation darting between her hands and mine through my body.

I know the pleasure is building inside her, too. I can feel it, as her pussy squeezes around me, her grasping hands growing more frantic as I lower my head to hers and thrust my tongue into her open mouth.

I can bring you pleasure beyond anything Phorkys gave them, I whisper in her mind, sucking her orgasm out of her mouth with a moan. Her nails dig into my breasts, and I return the favor, letting my claws dot the curve of her ribs with little indentations.

Oh God, your tongue is forked, too, she thinks, and I smile as I flick the points of it across her lips.

That's right, little minnow, I hiss, lowering myself until my mouth is merely a breath away from her nipple. *I'm your God now.* I coax a rumble from her chest when I dart my tongue out like a snake and flutter it across the turgid peak.

That's the thing that tips her over the edge. Her juices seep around my tentacles as she clenches down on me, a soundless cry echoing in my head and hers as I draw out her pleasure as long as I can.

Which, as a goddess, is a very, *very* long time.

Please, she begs. I can feel her mind struggling to process the ache settling into her body, the slight zing of pain that accompanies every thrust inside her, the burn and sting of my fangs on her nipples, my claws on her skin.

And woven throughout the haze of her mind, the idea of Lillian feeling these same feelings. Her back arching, her breasts aching, her lips parting for her own monster lover.

How that image sends her careening into climax yet again.

Yes, sweet minnow! Submit to me! Embrace that height, that pleasure not even gods can withstand!

Her spine arches. Her legs shake.

Again, and again, and again.

I can feed her later. For now, it is *my* turn to feast.

CHAPTER 4

TIFFANY

"You're up early."

Denise finds me in the kitchen of her and Sylvia's gorgeous apartment in the city. I can't imagine how I ever got so lucky to have Denise as a friend. She was a senior in band with me when I was a freshman—the only other bisexual person I knew. I reached out to her when my parents kicked me out sophomore year and she took me in, no questions asked. Even after she got a girlfriend.

They took me to my first Pride, helped me apply to schools. Helped me learn what it was to be queer. I went to their wedding last summer, right before I left for college.

They're both like sisters to me. Well, not exactly sisters. What's a word for something that's like role models, teachers, and best friends all rolled into one?

Or I guess, after last night... more than friends.

I'll admit, I haven't been able to see them much since starting college. It's been almost a year now that I've been away: making my own friends at college and experiencing true freedom as an adult.

But we still text almost every day. I missed them so much,

Denise especially. We've been so close ever since she took me in, but there was always that barrier between us when I was still in high school. When we arranged for me to visit this weekend, I was so excited.

Finally, I'm meeting them on an even playing field. We're all cool, independent adults now. Finding our way in the world.

And then when the two of them suggested we all fool around last night... it was like it was meant to be.

Denise comes up behind me, resting her hand on my hip and her chin on my shoulder, turning her head to press soft kisses up the curve of my neck.

"I thought I'd make the three of us coffee."

"That's so sweet, Tiff. You don't have to do that." Heat rises to my cheeks, and she kisses them too, giggling at me blushing. She tucks a strand of hair behind my ear. "You're so beautiful. Last night was... amazing."

Isn't that an understatement?

I can't hide my grin as I nudge her away to fill the coffee maker. Once I snap the lid shut and we can hear the water percolating, I turn back to face her.

She nuzzles back into me, and I breathe in her coconutty scent, wrapping my arms around her.

"You know, I haven't found a place to stay yet for the summer. I was thinking, now that you, Syl and I..."

She stiffens in my arms, which makes me trail off. I pull away to see her face, which looks... surprised. "What? What's wrong?"

"You... haven't found a place? I thought you had that new friend—Lillian, right? Didn't you two get the same internship? Weren't you going to rent a studio with her?"

"I mean, we talked about it. But that was before..."

I shrug, giving her a shy smile. Before the three of us had sex, *I want to say. Before I realized the two of you wanted me.*

But something is off. She doesn't meet my eyes or flirt back, and instead she turns away from me and starts pulling out mugs.

She puts two on the island, then lets out a sigh.

"Tiffany... about that. Syl and I... well, we are so happy for you. And we're so excited for your new life. Your first year at school has gone so well, and we wouldn't want to hold you back now that you're finding your way."

"Hold me back?" I lift a hand to my sternum, rubbing at a sudden tightness in my chest. "Denise, you two could never. I wouldn't even have gotten into college if it weren't for you! You guys are my whole world. How could you even think that?"

"You seem to really like your new scene. Sounds like you're making good friends. Dating. You've really found your way."

"Thanks to you," I say, stepping forward to touch her arm. "I never could have done it without you."

A pop from the coffee pot makes both of us jump. I check it, but it's just the hot plate heating up. A few seconds later, the scent of fresh beans wafts over us as the piping hot coffee starts to drip into the carafe.

I turn back to Denise, but she's avoiding my eyes. Finally, she takes a deep breath.

"Syl and I, we decided we want to start a family. We're looking into it right now, what our options are."

Finally, she looks at me. Questioningly. Guiltily.

The tightness in my chest squeezes hard, so much so that my breath stops. My mind starts to race, but I do my best to shut it down.

This is Denise. My... whatever she is, my closest person.
And she wants to have a baby!
I smile wide, shoving down the weird mix of shame, regret,

and humiliation burning inside me, trying to show her my support. Her lips curl up a bit at the corners, and some of the tension eases from the room.

It's always easier when I push my feelings down.

"Denise, that's amazing!! Congratulations! You two are going to be such good parents!"

"Thanks," she says, eyes lighting up as she gets a sentimental look on her face. "It's something we've always wanted, you know? We're ready for it."

Wow. A baby. No wonder she seemed so nervous. That's huge.

My chest is still tight, but I ignore it. Denise looks like she wants to say something else, and maybe this will be the moment when she asks me what I think. If I want to be part of something more than just a relationship, if maybe I'd ever considered—

"But that also means... we don't really have room for another adult living here anymore."

Oh.

Shut it down. Don't let the negative feelings spill over. Not yet.

I nod, blinking rapidly.

There's no way I'm going to let her see me cry. Of course not. Not when she's kicking me out. Not after the three of us spent the night together, and I convinced myself it meant something way more than it did.

Stupid Tiffany. They're married. They want a family.

I'm not family. I'm just some teenager that some cool twenty-somethings took pity on once upon a time, and now that I'm old enough to take care of myself, they can get on with their lives.

"We had so much fun with you last night."

Her words, close—whispered into my shoulder. I was so focused on holding in my emotions that I didn't realize she'd come in for a hug. My arms rise automatically to grip her shoulders back, and my head bows into hers like it always does.

She's so tiny. So short and spunky and cool.

And now she's going to be a mom. She and Sylvia. Together. Without me.

"Yeah... yeah, me too."

"Do you want to stay for breakfast, before you head out?"

Before I head out. As in, not stay the rest of the weekend.

Because they've moved on already. They didn't save a place for me when I went to school. Why would they?

"No, no, that's okay..." I blink, looking about the room for some kind of excuse I can give, but all I can see is the two mugs on the island. Only two. "I, uh. I gotta get going anyway. Lillian and I should start searching for sublets. It's almost summer!"

I have to get out of there. Have to leave before she sees how wrecked I am. How stupid, for thinking they loved me as much as I loved them.

"Okay, but before you go, Tiffany–"

No. I need to get out. Just let me go.

"Tiffany."

Her hand grasps tight around my wrist. My other wrist. My ankles.

Let me go!

"You didn't actually think we loved you, did you Tiffany?"

I'm trapped, bound and strung up in their apartment, unable to move...

"We never loved you. We're already happy, just the two of us. There isn't room for you."

Then let me go!

"Foolish, selfish, Tiffany..."

Let me go!

Tiffany!

Dean's voice ringing in my ears wakes me from my

nightmare. Every night since Keto caught us, my subconscious has been streaming reruns of Tiffany's biggest relationship failures.

And through it all, the same, cruel voice in my head telling me how stupid I am. How desperate, how detestable. How I deserve to be treated this way. How it's all my fault.

And it's right.

Tiffany! Can you hear me?

I let my head float upright, grateful for the buoyancy of the water. After three weeks trapped in this cave, my muscles are sore and weak. I need to move. Before my whole body wastes away.

Yes.

Oh thank God. After you passed out... He pauses, the steadiness in his voice wavering a bit in my mind. *Well, regardless, Keto just left a little bit ago to get food.*

He pauses for a minute, maybe longer—it's hard to tell how much time is passing with my body drifting in and out of sleep. *I'm gonna get us out of here, Tiffany. I promise.*

The urgency in his voice spikes my heart rate. I squint across the cave, trying to take in the expression on Dean's face, but I can't make out much. Without Keto's natural glow illuminating the cave, all I can see is his eyes. They shine with an almost manic energy as he desperately meets my gaze.

We need to talk, Tiff.

What?

Panic grips my chest as he says those words. How many times have I heard them in the past few weeks alone? Playing on repeat in my nightmares, everyone I've ever loved telling me that it's been fun, but they never intended anything serious with me. Never wanted to try.

And with how much trouble I am? Who can blame them?

It's time I came clean. About my past—my real *past.*

Huh?

I don't know what you're talking about. Fear is replaced by confusion, and the adrenaline spike fizzles out, likely because my body is too weak to sustain it. The words exit my mind at a crawl.

I'm so weak, so tired from fighting my own body and mind. So exhausted from the endless nightmares, both waking and sleeping. From worrying about Lillian, about Dean, about our baby. Wondering if any of it matters, or if I should just give up entirely.

My family. I should have told you about them, about me, forever ago. I know you met them last Christmas, and that you think they don't like you, but it isn't true. It's my fault. I took way too long to introduce you to them. It's just that, when I met you, at first, I...

I wince. Dean's family is crazy. The type of people that are obsessed with where they come from, and how perfect their ancestors were. And like, I get it, that can be important if your people have been marginalized or oppressed or something, but the history of the Apostolos clan is *painfully* white.

Still. They're Dean's parents. I wanted so badly to impress them.

I've never done well with families. It's one of the first things Lillian and I bonded over, one of the reasons we always did holidays together. Because neither of us felt like we wanted to, or could, go home.

I never told you, but... my family, we're—we're not just Greek. We're like, super Greek.

Yeah, no, I got that, Dean.

How could I not, when their home was covered in old maps, pottery, and books that looked like they were rescued from the library of Alexandria?

I start to tune out. I'm already barely hanging onto consciousness. I love Dean, but sometimes he overthinks things, usually when he's excited or nervous. I guess it would make sense that he'd rant when he's scared, too. But I'm too tired to try to make sense of it right now, not when we have more important things to worry about. He keeps talking, but I'm not really hearing it anymore.

Like, descended-from-Greek-gods Greek.

God, I'm so hungry. How long has it been since Keto fed us?

...what I'm trying to say is, our lineage goes way back. All the way to...

Is Lillian okay? Is she being fed? Is she safe? Has she... has she had the monsters yet?

You look pale, are you okay? Dean pauses, and the silence is enough to draw my attention back to the concerned look on his face. *You don't look so good. Is it the baby? Are you—*

I'm hungry, I answer honestly. I'm also terrified and plagued by nightmares whether I'm awake or asleep, but I don't tell him any of that. We've both seen better days.

He cuts off abruptly when I answer, and his eyes soften in sympathy, looking less wild.

How long ago did She leave?

Not long, he answers softly, like a caress. It makes me miss him even more. The only partner who's ever stood by me. The worst part of all of this isn't just how scared I've been—it's how Keto has kept me apart. From Lillian, from Dean.

I'm so lonely.

How is he so strong right now?

I wish I could touch him. Whenever words fail me, physical affection always helps me express the things I can't say. Sex is always what I've been best at. What all my partners have wanted me for.

Maybe that's why the best friendship I've ever had is crumbling. Because I don't know how to tell her how I feel with words alone.

This is the first time She's left us alone when we're both awake.

There's something urgent in his tone that pushes me out of my spiral. I blink, shaking off the fuzziness of hunger and sleep, my vision clearing slightly.

I can make out more than just Dean's face now. I take inventory of his body, his narrow shoulders, deceptively strong arms, and long legs. He's staring at me intently, and I wonder if I missed something important. What was he saying about his family? Was there a point to it?

What's wrong, Dean?

I...It's my fault we're in this mess, Tiffany. Where we are now, this situation, it isn't an accident. I knew you were connected to Keto, back when we first met. I was supposed to defeat Her, to fulfill my family's destiny. I followed you to Her on purpose.

I blink.

This is even worse than the other nightmares. I must be so delirious that my brain finally started spinning the kind of nonsense dreams I've always wished for, instead of the endless stream of bad memories and lifelong regrets.

I have to wake myself up.

You're not dreaming, babe. I know it seems crazy. Hell, I grew up being told all the old legends, the myths, and even I thought they were all just a bunch of stories until I met you. But... it's time that I admit it to myself. That I own up to my destiny. I know it sounds crazy, Tiff, but I… I'm a hero. Like the Greek heroes—Perseus, Hercules, all of them—they're all real, and now I have to finish what they started.

His eyes are wide as they bore into mine. I hold his stare for a long time, neither of us speaking. His words are so ridiculous, I think my brain has actually short-circuited. For once, my mind is entirely blank.

Dean. *My* Dean. The adorable, horny computer nerd who's squishier than a cinnamon roll. The one obsessed with video games. Who goes home every weekend to visit his parents. Who, ever since I got pregnant, works himself up into a nervous tizzy when I leave the house without him.

Is he actually trying to tell me that he's some kind of legendary hero? Like in a fairy tale?

The longer I look at him, the weaker he looks: just a skinny nerd, the literal antithesis of a traditional hero. I mean, sure, he's got enough muscles to toss me on the bed every once in a while, but he's talking about taking on a *titan.* He's not strong enough for that.

My judgments are only supported by the sucker-shaped bruises along his legs and neck, pink scratches that cover his arms and chest, and the collar of gold rings obscuring most of his dick. *Fuck,* he looks awful. Now that I can see him, I don't know how I was ever able to sleep through whatever our captor has been subjecting him to.

While Keto's been torturing me with endless orgasms, it looks like She's been *literally* torturing him.

I don't know all the details. It all happened while I was passed out. But taking in all the marks covering his body, I know Dean is having a far worse time here than I am.

I wish I knew Her endgame, why She's doing this to us. He's in even rougher shape than I am trapped at Keto's mercy. There are circles under his eyes, and his skin is getting pale. Neither of us can take this for much longer.

What did She do to you? I ask, the gears finally turning. Maybe the torture actually *has* been too much for him, and he snapped. He's gone so nuts from orgasm denial he thinks Disney's *Hercules* is a documentary. *How long have I been out of it?*

Too long. You need food. We both do, he says, not answering my real question. *We can talk more later, after we eat. When you passed out, I told Her that you needed sustenance. That you couldn't keep...*

He winces, cutting off the thought with a downward turn of his lips. But I know where he was going with that sentence.

A phantom shiver permeates my spine as my body replays the sensations from Her last visit. The scaly slide of Her tails slithering up my thighs. Her surprisingly rough tongue playing at the seam of my lips.

Playing Her game? I spit out what he's afraid to say. His cheeks turn red, and I don't miss the way he shifts his hips uncomfortably. *Looks like She's toying with you, too, whenever She's done with me. What are all those bruises? And those rings around your–*

It doesn't matter. He shutters his expression, breaking eye contact as he cuts me off. *You should rest. Just know that I'm working on a plan, okay? I'm gonna get us out of this. I'm gonna save you. Us.*

Dean, I–

I promise. For now, just sleep, okay? I'm sure She'll wake you when She gets back with breakfast.

His eyes linger on my belly, then drift up to my face, pleading.

That's right. I need to pull through this. Not just for

Dean, or Lillian—but for the other life that's depending on me.

I nod. One thing is for sure: whatever Keto's done to him hasn't changed how protective he is of me. He's clearly worried about the baby.

He cares for me, too, I remind myself, even if the voice in my head is screaming that no one could ever really want me just for me.

I love him. Truly, I do. More than I've ever let myself love anybody.

I don't know what I did to deserve him. Until he and I started dating, only one person in my life had ever loved me and accepted me unconditionally.

Yeah, and you've finally ruined that relationship. As disastrously as you possibly could.

I want to ask him if Keto's mentioned anything about Lillian. If he knows anything more. If she's okay. If *he's* really okay, or if his hallucinating Greek mythology fanfiction is a sign of a deeper psychotic break.

But I know he won't be able to focus on anything else until I'm fed and rested. And I *am* so tired...

So I let my eyes drift close once again. As sleep overtakes me, my mind plays its greatest hits album of intrusive thoughts.

Your friendship with Lillian is over...

No one's ever really cared about you...

Dean's parents hate you. He's only staying with you for the baby...

A fictitious image of Dean swirls to life in my brain, his face contorted in concentration, bronze armor shining in the sunlight as he levels a sword. Gorgons, hydras, and a beautiful titan monster with hypnotizing silver eyes draw forth to do battle as my subconscious slowly succumbs to my fiancé's crazy fantasies.

CHAPTER 5
KETO

Oh, Erik! Yes, yes—yes!

The woman's cries of ecstasy echo through the entire lake as Phorkys and his humans play with each other. The ichor and hormones swirling through her veins must be driving her insane with lust. I cannot escape the sounds of their constant lovemaking. Despite the distance between their cave and mine, my hearing is too powerful. The only thing that can drown out the sound of Phorkys enjoying his humans is the cries of my own mortal hostages.

But alas, with Phorkys preoccupied in keeping his consort riding the edge of sexual gratification, I must hunt. Despite losing so many children, I find myself once again in the position of having an abundance of mouths to feed.

These prisoners are a hassle. As are these senseless mating rituals. If it weren't for the fact that I need my children to seize back my power, I wouldn't bother with it.

Yet here I am, skirting the shore and snatching *mammals* from the surface because Lillian's and Tiffany's fragile bodies cannot risk digesting raw fish. Because too much sea life risks them poisoning their young with minerals. I have to boil squirrel and venison and anything else I catch in the lake, all because if I do not, they risk squandering their pregnancies.

It is painfully tedious.

Whatever god created these silly humans and their means of reproduction is a fool. Their bodies are too frail to incubate even their own young, never mind *mine*. Even now, I can feel the human Lillian drawing upon my strength to keep herself alive.

My Tiffany wastes away as the tiny human parasite inside her feeds upon her strength reserves. I must feed her constantly—sometimes even more than once *per day*—and her pathetic mate is hardly hardier. They are impractically fragile.

But it *is* fun to test the limits of their bodies. Tiffany is particularly delicious when she falls apart.

Lillian's body, of course, is fortified with my own magic. I will not risk losing another brood to the shortcomings of their mortal species.

Growing my children in her tiny human body cannot be easy. In my midnight explorations, I've snuck into the entrance of their cave to drop off meals and observe the incubation of my young. My sweet, sad Lillian tosses and turns in her sleep as the eggs mature inside her. Salty sweat saturates the water around her; her body strains to contain the magic within her. When she wakes, I imagine the pain of her rapid growth must be nearly unbearable.

It is only the pleasure that Phorkys delivers that keeps enough dopamine and adrenaline flowing through her to keep her alive. That, and the sustenance that I provide to fuel her expanding body.

I leave my offering of boiled venison at the entrance of her nest, and swim away.

My human guests are slightly less demanding. Although they lack the gratitude that Lillian expresses. Her blissful exaltations ring out with every single orgasm.

Tiffany and Dean, meanwhile...

As I pierce and slice up a generous dinner for the two ungrateful whelps, I recall the fury on their faces. Her vicious words.

Fuck you!

I will never understand why humans insist on using the same words to curse as they would to seduce. She hardly enjoys it when I fuck her. So why would she claim to fuck me?

I shouldn't waste my precious intelligence attempting to make sense of them. This is the same human who is carrying a child despite her fear of commitment. Who brought that child directly to me, while simultaneously petrified that I would take it away.

She is full of contradictions. None of her motivations make sense, except for where her beloved friend is concerned.

Where's Lillian? she asked me during our last encounter. *Is she okay?*

"Your friend is floating in never-ending bliss," I snapped, annoyed.

Tiffany could be enjoying her imprisonment, too. Could be enjoying me, and everything I give her. I could also enjoy these humans and their pleasure, if they would simply let go of the pretense of their disgust.

I am the Queen of the Seas.

Yet they reject me.

Pin bones and blue blood mist in the water around me as I tear them from my fishy victims. Humans don't eat the bones. Their fussiness is exhausting. It reminds me of the Olympians.

Always bickering and throwing unnecessary feasts. Fiddly foods, endless adornments.

"Why do your females dress in jewels?"

It seemed so unnecessary to me, to decorate the face of a goddess in shiny stones and metals. The golden eyes of my mane frame my face in a halo brighter than any crown.

"Keto, my dear, it is because their beauty is more frail than that of the Oceanics." *Poseidon reached his strong fingers forward to cradle my chin, and I let him. They weren't webbed or clawed like the hands of my brethren. Nor were they covered in glittering scales. He looked so plain, despite being imbued with all the magic of the seas.*

My betrothed. Despite his simple demeanor, he was handsomer than his father, Kronos, before him. More powerful, too— especially after the uprising.

He was to be my husband as a gift from Zeus the Usurper. As the strongest of the remaining oceanic deities that stood with the Olympians in their coup of our fathers, my claim was unchallenged, blessed by Hera. Our union would unite the old gods and the new into a mighty pantheon.

"Perhaps you want a frail, decorated wife for yourself," I teased. His eyes, bluer than the deepest trenches, sparkled. "Like your brothers and their tiny goddesses. Hera is particularly waifish."

"Keto..."

I shake myself from the memory, as clear in my mind as the waters before me. The meat is cleaned and cooked. I can feed the humans now. I do not need to dwell on the thought of Poseidon's kisses. His sweet words.

His ultimate betrayal.

I wonder if Dean's cock is ready for another ring.

CHAPTER 6
DEAN

The weeds binding us are stronger than they look.

Maybe it's the density of the water, which prevents me from creating enough torque to rip them open. But eventually I resort to feeling out the strength of the knot instead of testing the weeds themselves.

If I can just free one hand...

My right wrist bends over itself and I stretch my fingers down to the ties holding me. The teachings of my father come back like it was only yesterday.

"Knots will save your life one day, boy!"

His voice bounces off the trees as he drops my canoe into the river. I'm strapped to the bench seat, heavy rope knots tying my hands to a double-sided oar. Instantly, the current twists around me, and the aluminium sides bob precariously in the white-flecked waters.

"Dad, I won't be able to swim!" I cry out, watching him grow smaller and smaller as the river sweeps me away.

"You will once you free yourself, boy! Make me proud!"

One last view of his gleeful smile, before the rapids obscured my vision. I paddled for my life, wondering if I'd ever see his face again.

I blink at the memory: the summer of my eighth year. The first year of hostage training. Or as Father called it, "resourcefulness practice."

I can still taste the roasted trout we had for dinner that night at the campsite, a celebration of my Houdini-esque escape. No meal has ever tasted as sweet.

Facing your mortality will do that. Make you savor every moment.

A natural, he called me. Another fated hero for the Apostolos clan.

The nail of my middle finger catches the seam of the knot and I wedge it between the loops. My cheeks stretch as I smile—an unfamiliar sensation after two weeks in this prison.

I'll be out of the bindings by nightfall.

Not that I know what time it is. I can only judge the passage of time by the meals Keto brings us. Breakfast and dinner for Tiffany, only dinner for me. Whenever She leaves to hunt, it feels as though She's gone for about an hour. Rarely is She gone less than half that time, but whenever She is, She's in a particularly foul mood. That's when Her torture is worst, as if by making us suffer She can relieve whatever's annoying Her.

She's a sadist.

I wince as I shift against the bindings to ease the wrapping higher along my forearm, giving my hand more space to work. Everytime I shift, the metal rings around my dick clink. Though they aren't as tight when I'm not aroused, they're just snug enough to chafe whenever I move.

Fuck. By the time we get out of here, I won't be able to have sex for a month.

I spare a glance for Tiffany, head still lolling against her chest, fast asleep. The little bit of light that shines from the entrance at the top of the cave casts a thin ray crossing her chest like a seatbelt, illuminating her body.

She's changed so much since I met her.

Her boobs have gotten bigger with the pregnancy, even as she's gotten skinnier over the last few weeks. It's hard not to notice, with the shifting light underwater high-lighting the fuller curve of them, her brown nipples. It's one of the few places on her body that looks healthy.

My chest squeezes as I take her in, wishing I could hold her. Her long eyelashes, fluttering over her cheeks. Her glossy, red-brown hair that shines like copper at sunset, drifting lazily in the water. Her full lips, cracked and broken from how much she's likely been biting them from worry, a bad habit of hers. Her stomach, rounded with our baby.

Our baby.

I still can't believe it. For years, I was always afraid of having kids. Of passing down my stupid family curse onto another generation. But when I think about having a family with Tiffany—with Lillian, too...

I know that she had a miscarriage before I met them, and that it messed her up. Is it weird that part of me thought the two of them might get closer when Tiff got pregnant? That maybe we could do something different than all of our parents did?

I've been around the two of them long enough to know that none of us are too keen on the way we were raised. We could do it differently. Families don't have to look like the 1950's ads anymore. We don't have to mess our kids up like our parents did us.

Maybe after all of this, now that Keto spilled the beans and it's all out in the open: the crush Tiffany's been harboring for Lillian all this time that she refused to fess up to, *my* secret attraction to the idea of being with both of them...

Once, I brought up the idea of a threesome. It was about a month after Tiff and I started dating, and it was so obvious to me that their friendship was something more than just that. But Tiffany claimed up and down that Lillian was straight, that even suggesting it would ruin their friendship. And I would never dream of pulling them apart.

Not when, *together,* they would clearly...

Mmf. I grit my teeth as the rings squeezed tighter. *Fuck.* I should know better than to let my mind linger too long on the two of them while my balls are literally trapped in a chastity collar.

God, why am I such a pervert? Am I crazy, thinking that maybe this would all be easier if the two of them just admitted their feelings to each other instead of keeping it bottled up? Break up that sexual tension and just–

Gah!

Okay, okay! No more sexy thoughts. Think about knots.

I picture the Boy Scouts handbook my father gave me on our first ever camping trip, and the page of different knots. Clove hitch, rolling hitch, timber hitch, bowline, taut line...

I let out a breath as my penis shrinks back down.

I focus back on the task at hand, wiggling my middle finger until I bury it up to the first knuckle.

Don't think about burying your knuckles anywhere else, Dean...

Not like it's easy, when this entire imprisonment of Keto's is one fucked-up kink exploration after another. This whole "orgasm denial" thing She's doing to me right now —while it *could* be fun if explored in a safe, consensual environment—is *not* a good time. It's almost enough to make me jealous of the treatment She's giving Tiffany: orgasms first thing every morning and to tuck her in at night.

Except for the fact that I've seen what it does to her. Every time she comes, she spins deeper into a tornado of guilt. She already feels bad enough for what Lillian's going through. I can hear her calling out to her in her sleep, the nightmares getting worse and worse every time she passes out.

I need to get her out of here.

Back and forth, back and forth my finger digs against the tightly wound weeds. I think I have some leverage now. Just a little more...

The tip of my finger pushes through to the other side, and I stifle a cheer.

Yes!

First loop is the hardest. Now just to–

No sooner do I think it, does Keto propel Herself into the cave. I yank my finger out, lifting my shoulder slightly so my wrist doesn't pull on the weeds and undo all my hard work. Luckily, Keto seems distracted this time—ignoring me completely—and doesn't notice the slight bulge in my tie.

As always, She approaches Tiffany first. She carries with Her a sack of fish and venison, which She's chopped into bite sized pieces for us.

My chest tightens as I watch Her lean Her face into my fiancé's, kissing her awake with a brush of Her emerald lips. A dark tongue darts out and licks a line up her cheek, and I hold back a groan. Tiffany shifts, and I can imagine the shiver that passes through her body when she sees those silver eyes staring at her.

"Dinnertime, humans."

Thank the gods.

The mane of snakes hisses as Keto whips her head around and sets Her silver eyes on me. One eyebrow is raised on Her sharp-featured face, and She takes in my prone body hungrily.

"I am the only god you should be thanking, boy." She spits the last word, then approaches me. As Her tentacles writhe and drag Her upper body forward, She grows in size, filling the cave and blocking my view of Tiffany completely. By the time She's floating inches from my face, I'm dwarfed by Her shadow, and only the shining eyes—golden in Her snake hair and silver in Her face—light the space between us. *"You ought to brush up on your history."*

Ha, if you only knew—I start, only to shutter my thoughts as quickly as they come to me.

I have to block off my mind. As long as She doesn't know who I am, we have an advantage.

"What's that?" The titan tilts Her head, listening. My heart rate climbs as She leans in, examining my face. Despite the pounding in my chest, I keep my face as passive as I can.

I'm not sure how successful I am. If we weren't under-water, sweat would be running from my temples like a river.

"I can't hear you…"

An almost human finger points from Her webbed hands, tipped with a sapphire stiletto of a claw that presses into my scalp before scratching its way down my hairline. In a flash, She captures my head in Her hands, fingertips digging into my skin as She tilts my face this way and that, those bright eyes studying me intensely.

A slow smile cuts its way across Her lips. A terrifying smile.

A swallow bobs in my throat.

She taps my temple. ***"You're blocking me out."***

I–I don't know what you're talking about. I'm barely even able to think, I'm so hungry. Can you please–

"Quiet!" Her eyes glitter menacingly. ***"You are stronger than you look, aren't you? Not quite what you seem?"***

And then She surprises me entirely.

She lowers Her head to my sternum, and *sniffs* a line up my center until Her face is level with mine.

Close enough to bite.

My heart is beating a million miles a minute, and it's everything I can do not to vomit. Her eyes glitter like diamonds as She narrows them, Her crown of snakes hissing at me in a disturbing chorus.

"Oh, Dean... why didn't you say something? I wasn't aware I was in the presence of royalty."

A weak gurgle sounds from across the cave.

Stop teasing him...

That terrifying smile is back, and this time it's wide enough to reveal a crescent of shark-like teeth.

"He never told you?" She's addressing Tiffany, but Her eyes—including the yellow ones of all of Her snakes—are just for me.

Fuck. This is what I was trying to tell her earlier, but she was too out of it to make sense of it all.

How was I supposed to give her my whole fucked up backstory when she could barely keep her eyes open?

And now it's too late. If Keto tells her, if she doesn't hear it from me, she's going to think...

Tiffany, let me explain–

"Your fiancé is an Olympian." Keto interrupts, sniffing me again. She settles Her head at the base of my neck, licking a long line up to my earlobe and nipping it. I can't hold back a shudder. ***"Well. An Olympian, 2647 times removed."***

Whatever sour mood She had when She entered the cave is long gone. Now, She's nothing short of euphoric.

Which can't possibly mean anything good.

"Tell her, Dean. Tell her all about your old ancestor, Zeus."

TIFFANY

What the fuck is this monster smoking?

Jesus, no wonder Dean was spouting off about Greek heroes and all that nonsense earlier. Keto's been whispering delusional sweet nothings into his ear while I've been passed out.

I can just barely make out Dean's face past the swirling snakes of Keto's hair, his cheeks turning a dusky pink in the dark cave. Blushing. He's blushing right now—like the sweet guy he is. He's a fucking software engineer for Christ's sake. Smart, sure, but he's a lover, not a fighter. He doesn't even go to the gym regularly. He's a momma's boy who still visits his parents three times a week to help them with their email and mow their lawn.

There's no way he's an *Olympian*.

Dean... don't listen to her. She's driving you crazy. We both need food, we need sleep, we–

Keto floats back, sweeping the oilskin bag of meat off the ground with a tentacle. She shoves a piece of venison into my mouth before preening Her tails and settling on the floor of the cave. Her eyes bounce between us as She fishes out a chunk of flesh and gobbles it down like popcorn. My view of Dean is now unencumbered, and he shifts his legs a little, looking uncomfortable in his bindings.

I tried to tell you, Tiff, but...

I stare at him, but he won't meet my eyes. *Tried to tell me what?*

And then I remember. Visiting with his family at Christmas, seeing all the ancient pottery and tapestries decorating the walls. I thought they were just eccentric. Proud of their heritage. Greek, like he said.

"Go ahead, Dean. Tell her about your greats-greats-grandfather, Perseus."

Perseus. Was that the one that killed the minotaur? Charybdis and Scylla? God, it's been *years* since studying Edith Hamilton's *Mythology* in high school, and dusting off the unused "useless trivia" file in my brain takes a minute.

Regardless, it doesn't matter. Because it isn't real. I mean, titans are one thing, but mythical heroes?

Even as I try to rationalize it all, the argument falls apart in my head.

Dean, I think to him, disbelieving. *She's joking, right? You're joking. Perseus isn't real. The Greek gods aren't real. They're myths. They're–*

"Who do you think I am, child?" She interrupts, swimming up to my side and shoving a hunk of meat into my mouth before I can answer Her. **"Who Phorkys is?**

"To call us "Greek" is an insult. We are gods of all of Earth, plain and simple. He and I existed long before those flashy Olympian brats, and will survive long after their spawn eventually betray and destroy them, as they destroyed their parents and children and everyone who got in their way. It is the prerogative of those usurpers."

She scowls at Dean then, and I begin to piece it all together. What was that She said, all those years ago...?

My children were tricked and slaughtered by the children of the Olympians. Greek heroes, seeking glory, mercilessly hunted and murdered them one by one...

Perseus, Perseus...

Medusa. Perseus killed Medusa. The terrifying monster with snakes for hair and–

Oh fuck. Oh, *fuck.*

Keto... Even in my mind, my question trembles—my inner voice as weak and afraid as if I had to force the words from my throat. *Was Medusa your... daughter? Was Perseus the one who killed your children?*

A snake drifts before Her eyes, hiding Her expression. But before She can speak, a panicked voice bubbles into my mind, attempting—and failing—at bravado.

Dean.

Some all-powerful goddess you are. Couldn't even protect your own daughter from a half-human like Per—mmph!

Despite the fact that he doesn't need his mouth to mind-speak, the surprise of Keto swimming up to him and shoving a fish tail into his mouth is effective in shutting him up. His face shines bright in the cave, and I realize it's the reflection of Her eyes, glowing with power.

"Silence, you buffoon!"

She whips around, Her terrifying gaze recentering on me, and with a start I remember the power of Medusa, of the Gorgons. They were the monsters that could turn men to stone with a look.

Does Keto share that power? Can She turn people to stone?

"Very good, Tiffany. It appears as though you're finally figuring it out."

Her shark-like teeth glitter when She smiles. Her whole body emits light down here; it's the only thing providing any sort of illumination now that night has descended and sunlight doesn't filter through the breaks in the cave wall.

Are you going to turn us to stone?

"Turn you to stone? Why would I do that? Then we wouldn't be able to have any fun."

You don't want to have fun. You just want to torture us.

"You love my torture, Dean, admit it. You're a traitor to your entire family line..."

She approaches him, and panic laces his face. I want to stop it, stop it all, so I can think clearly. But I don't even know what's real anymore.

Do I even know who he is?

What else has he kept from me? What other secrets does he have?

Unbidden, the words he said before come back, a whisper in the back of my head that sinks like a lead weight in my stomach: *I knew you were connected to Keto. I was supposed to defeat her on this trip, to fulfill my family's destiny. I followed you to Her on purpose.*

Has our whole relationship—the dating, the engagement, the *baby*, all of it—been a sham?

A sudden pain in my palm takes my focus for a second, and I look up to see my hands are clenched tight, making my knuckles even paler than the rest of me. I gasp in a breath, and it cracks through my gills like a gunshot. I wrench open my fingers, and a thin line of tiny red nail-marks dots the inside of my hands. My chest heaves, gulps of water rushing into my throat as I wrestle with the fact that it's all been a lie.

I'm about to have his child. Our child. When it's possible he never even wanted *me*.

I need to calm down.

I slow my breath, counting until the currents running up and down my neck across my gills even out. Dean's staring at me, his eyes wide and pleading, as Keto plays with him. Her razor-sharp nails trace across his hip bones, and he grits his teeth, bucking into Her waiting palm. She juggles him, rings clinking in the deep as I watch the two of them play, his eyes close as he lets out a breath...

The two of them, cutting me out...

Leaving me alone, again. Like everyone always does.

Only this time, the consequences are worse than I could have ever imagined.

I miss Lillian.

My breath goes shaky again as tiny sobs begin to wrack their way up my chest. She's my best friend, the only one who ever loved me for me. And I abandoned her.

Not just on this trip. But before.

"Ever since you and Dean moved in together, we hardly hang out just the two of us. And once you got engaged, I feel like I never see you anymore!"

It hurts to think of that fight. I was so scared, so worried about Keto coming and snatching my baby away. So afraid of ruining my chance at happiness. I was so caught up thinking that I'd lose both Dean *and* Lillian if they got too close, that I didn't even think about Lillian's feelings for *me*. Everytime Dean wanted to include her in our plans, I'd get jealous: worried that if the two best, kindest people in my life ever got too close, they'd clearly want each other over me.

But I was wrong. Dean wasn't using me to get to Lillian. He was using me to get to Keto.

I brought Dean on vacation because he begged me to let

him go, and because I was afraid of my deal with Keto. Afraid to be alone with her.

Which was so stupid, because I *wasn't* alone—I had Lillian with me the whole time.

But I couldn't even see it through my selfishness, my fear, my insecurity. The closer I got to Dean, the more I pushed her away... to the point that it didn't even feel like we were together when we hung out.

In my head, I tried to rationalize it. Dean was the most serious boyfriend I'd ever had. He looked at me like I was his everything, and it was intoxicating. When I got pregnant, he was so protective of me, of our little perfect family.

And I loved it.

All I wanted was to be important to someone. Someone who loved me. *Really* loved me.

Enough to make me family.

Sure, Lillian and I were like sisters. But Denise, Syl, and I had been like sisters, too. Until we tried to be something more, and I lost them forever.

Being bi and dating in college, that was always how it worked. You start dating someone, you fall for them, they bring you back to their *real* partner and then you're alone again. Or you have a serious relationship with someone, they suggest bringing in a third for fun, and then they end up leaving you for them.

How many women picked me up in bars, gave me their numbers, only to introduce me to their partner on a second date? How many boyfriends suggested opening up the relationship because they'd gotten bored with me? Only for me to go along with it, to try to make it work, and end up alone in the end?

It's a tale as old as time.

But I didn't want to lose Dean. He was different. Sweet.

Caring. A total nerd, and someone I couldn't imagine losing.

Sure, he'd suggested a threesome that one time, but when I said no, he accepted it. And I loved him even more for it. But I saw the way he looked at the two of us when we all hung out. And it made me paranoid. I didn't want to lose another relationship, and I couldn't bear the thought of losing them *both*.

The problem was, that crush I'd developed on Lillian in college never really went away. It ate at me, so much I could hardly stand to look at her sometimes because I felt so guilty about it. But I couldn't let her go, either. Not after all we'd been through together.

I held Lillian at arm's length, so I wouldn't lose her.

It still wasn't enough. I couldn't keep up the farce. Couldn't keep hanging in the balance, always afraid that I'd lose one or both of them.

And because I felt guilty keeping my attraction to her a secret from Dean, I ended up pushing her away completely. I said such terrible things to her...

"Maybe I'm just done with this phase of my life, okay? Partying with the girls. Maybe I'm about to get married and have a kid and it's time for me to move on from all of that."

God, I'm such a bitch. How could I say that to her?

It doesn't matter that I was trying to protect myself. Doesn't matter that I was trying to save us from Keto, either —when the fear and guilt and shame all bubbled up, I just ended up hurting her. Brought us all into this mess that's worse than anything I could have predicted.

Lillian's in some cave somewhere just like me, except whereas I'm getting endless orgasms everyday, she's been forced to face the consequences for *my* mistakes.

And all for what?

A lie. A complete and total lie.

Dean never loved me. He only wanted me to get to *Her.* Not Lillian—Keto.

What have I done?

A violent sob bursts through my chest, and the sound catches Keto's attention. The water waves with Her presence as She attempts to feed me another boiled cube of tasteless meat, but I turn my head away.

I'm not hungry.

Tiff, Dean calls, concern lacing his thoughts. *You have to eat something. The baby–*

Oh, of course. You care about the baby.

I snap my head up, glaring at him, and his face pales.

What are you talking about, of course I care! I love you, you're the most important–

Stop lying to me!

I've never been the most important. Why would that change now?

Beside me, Keto clicks Her tongue.

"Oh my, Son of Perseus. You've really done it now, haven't you?"

She strokes her sharp fingers up and down my arm in a facsimile of a comforting gesture. But the touch makes me shiver. I can't forget what those fingers have done to me over the past weeks, touching me and playing with my body without my consent.

We are so far from the initial constraints of our deal at this point that I don't even know what to do. Lillian is in her consort's custody. Dean and I are trapped here until the monsters are born, and I–

I don't even know if I'm going to survive this. I certainly won't if I don't keep my strength up.

And even if I do, what will I be returning to? What do I have left?

Keto, hearing my thoughts even though I'm not attempting to speak to Her, holds up another bit of food, and this time I let Her push it past my lips. I don't even taste it, just chew and swallow, an automatic biological response.

I'm too tired to do anything else.

Atta girl, Tiff.

Frustration flares at Dean's encouragement, but I can't even be bothered to respond.

"Perhaps I should leave the lovers to talk." The goddess shoves one more morsel into my mouth before pressing a kiss to my cheek.

They will always leave you, Tiffany. For as long as you live. No matter how much you give them. They always leave in the end. You can only count on yourself, and your children.

She turns my head, kissing me again. This time, She's passionate, swirling Her tongue into my mouth and pressing me into Her, snaking Her long arm around my back.

I feel Her pour Her power into me, before Her other hand presses a small, sharpened shell into my hand.

A knife. She just gave me a knife.

And the strength to do something with it.

She pulls away, caresses my face, then gives me a knowing look.

"Don't hold anything back."

CHAPTER 8
KETO

The lakebed is calm, silent as I swim across the wide expanse, leaving Tiffany with the tools to murder her former beloved. I had hoped that I would be able to suck the final breath from Dean's lungs when the time came, but I know better than to antagonize a child of Zeus.

One time was enough to learn that lesson. Too much, perhaps.

My little minnow has no such qualms. Humans kill each other every day; the Olympians never concern themselves with the fate of mere mortals. Soon, I will have everything I've waited for. My children, far from any god or goddess or hero who might wish them ill. Revenge against the blood of Perseus. Perhaps even the human Tiffany and her pliant, eager body by my side.

The kilometers pass quickly beneath my tails as I propel myself to the home that not even Phorkys knows about. My sanctuary.

My Atlantis.

I see the granite and basalt towers looming in the

distance, even in the faint moonlight that barely filters through Superior's depths. How many centuries have I been building, occupying my lonely nights, to recreate my throne? The tithes which I was owed those millennia ago yet never given. A kingdom fit for the most powerful of the remaining oceanids. The gods of gods.

At last, I arrive. Carved and sculpted like a basin into the rocky firmament, the ionic columns stretch high enough to accommodate even my grandest form. Agate sculptures crown each simple scroll, likenesses of my father, Pontus, and my mother, Gaia.

If I close my eyes, can I still hear them? Nereus, playing with the dolphins? Thaumas, weaving light shows with his deep-sea children? The banquets we would throw when Aunt Eurybia came to visit from her kingdom in the west?

But, no. Even with my perfect recreation of the grand hall of Atlantis—or, I should say, the *original* hall, before all traces of the titans were erased after the uprising—it has been too long. Even for me. I'm not sure I could even recognize their faces if I were to see them in a tapestry.

My mother was not present on the day of my engagement.

Oh, mother. Your legacy is a complicated one, isn't it?

The shadow of Gaia hung heavy over us all in the Titanomachy. She was the nurse of the usurper, Zeus, and kept him safe from the cruel Kronos until he was strong enough to defeat his father.

What made her choose one son over another, I wonder? Her body grew both Zeus and Kronos, along with my siblings and I. Yet Zeus was her favorite, and she hid him from Kronos—her son and lover—so the monster could murder the rest of Zeus's siblings.

And thus, the Olympians were freed from the mighty Ouranos. Including my beloved.

In those days, the hierarchy of the seas was chaotic. Father, as usual, stayed out of the infighting, refusing to offer any sort of guidance in the matter. So my siblings, nieces, and nephews fought constantly. Save one: Zeus's playful brother, always tending to his horses and enjoying the rays of the sun on his skin as he played in the waves.

Poseidon.

Gods, but he was beautiful. All of the Olympians were, of course, but where Hades was broody and Zeus was cocky, Poseidon always had a smile tucked in his cheek. I'd spy it in his dimples as I curled within the rocky feet of the Cretan shores, watching him. He'd race the tides on his chariots, taunting Artemis and Nereus and Thaumas all the way. No one hated Poseidon. And who could?

Certainly not I.

It was his sister Hera's idea. "You should marry one of the elder goddesses," I overheard her say to him on the beach. "Zeus is to name you king of the seas. You are in need of a queen."

"Then I shall have the most beautiful in all the ocean." His eyes sparkled like sapphires in the sun as I spied them, and my heart soared to watch him. "And you shall bless the union."

It was Hera's domain to bless all marriages. Aphrodite and Haphaestus, Dionysis and Ariadne—any number of cousins, granted eternal bliss with her influence.

Shame she couldn't seem to bless her own.

I remember the night he chose me like it was yesterday. The galas of Atlantis were envied the world over for their opulence. The way the coral sparkled in the towers—not yet ancient—the music of the waves hypnotizing everyone into an uncanny euphoria. All the gods were giddy with it.

The war was over, Olympus had won. And now, Poseidon was free to claim his prize.

I'd fashioned my jewels from the volcanoes of Thera myself. They sparkled in the moonlight that filtered through to the shallows of the sea floor. Emeralds, rubies, opals—anything to catch his joyful gaze upon my skin. But even brighter than the gemstones shone the scales of my tails, my hips glittering and shifting like alexandrite. And of course, the golden eyes of my serpentine mane, piercing the depths of the sea.

My siblings and I lined the edge of the hall, displayed before him. A hush fell over the crowd.

The assessment was brief.

There was never a time when I was not the most beautiful of the deities. Only Aphrodite herself could challenge me, and I would drown her if she tried.

He bade me step forward. Gods, will I ever forget the way I felt gliding toward him, the way the music swelled? How he took my hand and laid the gentlest of kisses upon my knuckles as he spoke my name?

"Keto," he whispered, like a prayer. Like I was not merely *a* goddess, but *his*.

"Nephew." I curtseyed, lowering my eyes. Heat sprung from the place his fingers brushed mine, and my heart was filled with longing. "My liege."

"My queen."

And with that, we danced until Helios crested the horizon.

That is the memory I replay, over and over in my head, as I dance across the granite floor of my sanctuary: knowing that everything I've worked for, all of my dreams, are coming together at last.

CHAPTER 9

DEAN

When Keto leaves us alone in the cave, Tiffany's bindings disappear.

What the...

I pull at my own cuffs, still woefully tied despite me barely loosening the knots under Keto's nose. For some reason, She only let Tiffany free to have this conversation.

What exactly does She intend for her to do?

It's dark, but I can just barely make out Tiffany floating slowly off the cave wall. She looks like she's in shock, her movements stilted and unfamiliar after the weeks of captivity. The blur of her outline stretches its neck, and her arms are undefined, like she's holding them in front of her body.

Check the opening of the cave! If you're really free, we can get out of here!

Still agonizingly slowly, I see my fiancée's silhouette glide to the cave opening, only to drift back a few seconds later.

She locked us in here somehow.

What does it look like?

I don't know. Some kind of magic barrier.

Something in her voice doesn't sound right. She's distant, almost cold.

Tiff, are you okay–?

Why? The word is a whip, snapping from her mind to mine and cutting me off completely. *Why did you keep it from me?*

The dark blur of her shape doesn't move. I have no context to suss out how she's feeling except for her tone of voice. And it's so quiet and lifeless, I can hardly recognize it.

This is beyond tired. I've never heard her like this.

I'm so sorry, Tiff. I didn't want you to find out like this. I tried to tell you earlier, but you–

But I, what? Loved you? Trusted you?

What was I supposed to say? 'Hey, babe, don't know if you noticed, but you smell like a titan! Didja know I'm descended from Zeus? I think I'm supposed to kill your supernatural stalker!'

Our whole relationship, you knew I'd met Keto. Knew that you could use me to find Her. I didn't know shit about you. There's an edge to her voice now, and I can feel her drifting towards me as she speaks. I dig at the binds at my wrist again, poking my index finger through the opened loop to work it loose. *I just wish you hadn't been so sweet. Making me fall in love, proposing, even knocking me up—when you only intended to use me to fulfill some weird, inherited hero-glory kink!*

My jaw drops. *Is that what you think this is?*

That's the whole reason you wanted to come on this trip, isn't it? To finally kill your titan?

I came to protect you! Because I love you! Because you were scared out of your mind! My thoughts reflect the anger building inside me, half at her for accusing me unfairly and half at myself for everything she's right about. Fuck. I should have told her that very first day.

Her shadow freezes, and for a moment I regret my tone.

But only for a moment. Because she wasn't completely clueless about all of this. She still put herself here. She still made a deal with Keto all those years ago.

What about you, huh? Coming to the lake while pregnant, when you knew Keto was here waiting for you both? Were you going to tell me you were putting our child in danger?

I hadn't seen Her in years, Dean—

But you were scared. Terrified. Enough to try to convince Lillian not to go. Enough to take me with you. To—

STOP IT!

Her intentions crack through my brain a split second before she crashes into me, shoving my back into the rough stone of the cave wall behind me and wedging her forearm across my throat. She blocks a set of gills, and my breathing stutters.

Tiff, I huff, struggling beneath her, while desperately trying to avoid hurting her anywhere near her stomach. *What are you—*

And that's when I see it. A sharp, shining line glinting in the inky dark of the cave, clutched in her fist and inches from my face. The water around me is suddenly ice cold as I search the hidden lines of her face.

She gave you a knife?

She inclines her head in a nod, then says, *I guess She thinks you've been tortured enough. That maybe I should finish the job for her.*

I swallow, and it presses my throat into the solid flesh of her arm. Well, less solid than it was before this trip. She's so thin. I continue to dig my finger into the knot silently, working it back and forth, slowly making progress.

You hate me that much?

She stares at me for a long moment, neither of us speaking. My heart is pounding furiously, and I can only hope the sound of the racket in my chest is covering up the teeny, tiny movements of my hand inching closer and closer to freedom.

She backs off—hardly a foot, but enough to give us both a little space—and I breathe an internal sigh of relief. But her next words stop the air in my lungs.

Did you ever even love me?

What? I gape at her. *How could you ask me that?*

Answer me!

At the exact moment she lunges forward, my finger catches the weight-bearing loop of the knot and tugs it free. I spin, avoiding her outstretched arm by a millimeter before realizing I'm the only thing stopping her body from crashing into the cave wall.

I swerve, ducking my shoulder under hers and coiling my arm around her belly, drawing her back to my front and twisting her away from the wall before she can hurt herself. In response she slashes the knife down, slicing a shallow line down my back.

Gah!

Fuck, Dean!

Pain lances across my skin where she cut me, but I hold her tight, curling around until I've got my arms outstretched to either side of her and her back is to the wall. My one hand is still tied, but the other grabs her wrist as gently as I dare, protecting myself from getting sliced again.

I've loved you from the moment I laid eyes on you, Tiffany. You're the most beautiful woman I've ever seen. You're funny, you're sweet, you're my literal soul mate, and there's no one else I'd rather be the mother of my child.

Her eyes widen in the dimness, and her wrist twitches. But I keep talking, holding her in place and staring into those glassy orbs, praying she hears my next words. That she believes them.

I would have fallen for you even if you'd never met Keto. I'm kicking myself that I let you fear Her for so long, that I was too stupid and afraid to protect you from Her. That I didn't prepare well enough before coming up here with you. That I didn't fucking tell you who I was sooner. The truth is, you made me question everything I thought I knew about myself. But one thing I'll never question, is that I love you, Tiffany. With all my heart. I want to escape this place with you and Lillian and our baby and live happily ever after.

Even now? She asks, tugging at my grip on her wrist. *Even when I just tried to kill you?*

You weren't trying to kill me.

She tilts her head. *How do you know? I'm really, really angry you kept this from me, Dean!*

I know she means it, but the scary, cold edge to her voice is gone. There's only friendly fire now—honest fire, to be sure. I've no doubt she *is* angry, and rightfully so. But...

You wouldn't kill me. You love me, too.

The reflection of her eyes dims, and I'd bet anything she's got her face all scrunched up like she always does when we have an argument and I end up being right. I lean forward and kiss where I think her nose is—gently, of course. I pull away quickly, not wanting to piss her off anymore than she already is.

I'm sorry I didn't tell you. You're absolutely right. I should have, much earlier than I did. I thought about it at Christmas, but... I was nervous. I thought you'd think I was crazy. I thought...

You thought I'd leave you.

I swallow, unable to form the words, even in my head. *And then, when we found out you were pregnant... I couldn't risk losing you, Tiff. I had no idea that you'd promised Keto your firstborn. How could I? I just knew you'd met Her somehow, I never dreamed that...*

She nods slowly, and I'm grateful I don't have to finish that thought. *Here,* she says, shifting her shoulders a little and tugging at my hold on her wrist. *Let me cut you free.*

I let go, and she crosses the knife between us to reach up to my other wrist cuff. We're half-tilted in the cave—my legs twisted as the bindings at my ankles are still secured to the wall, and we both snort a little as we untangle ourselves.

But I don't even think to question or fear her anymore. *Thank you.*

For cutting the weeds? Of course.

No. For being on my team.

She floats up from slicing the ties at my ankle, and I scoop her into my arms. My whole body rejoices at feeling her close again, her stomach bumping against mine and my hands reaching up and down her back. I nestle my face into her neck, her hair, and if I could inhale through my nose down here I'd be soaking in the scent of her grapefruit shampoo.

God, I've missed you, Tiff.

I've missed you too, Dean.

She returns my embrace, and before I know it our hands are exploring each other. Now that she's here in my arms, I can't get enough of her soft skin. My lips crash into the curve of her shoulder, climbing up to her jawline before finally ghosting across her sweet mouth. I grip the flesh of her ass, digging my fingers into the squishy softness, hoisting her close against my body. I paint a portrait of her through touch, feeling all that I can't see clearly. My tongue dives between her open lips, and we tangle back and forth: grasping, reaching, scratching—

Ah!

Her nails scrape across the cut on my back and I hiss. *Fuck! I forgot–*

Oh my gosh, I'm so sorry! Let me...

Glints of copper from her hair catch the low light as she whips her head around, searching for some way to bandage up my cut. I laugh.

It's okay, babe. We can be gentle. You don't have to fix it.

But instead of comforting her, I see her shoulders tense at my words.

Yes I do. I need to fix everything. This is all my fault.

She drifts down to the floor of the cave, burying her face in her hands. Slowly, I approach her, only to stop just short of putting a hand on her bare shoulder. Instead, I just scratch my fingers through the floating strands of her hair, burying them up to her scalp, trying to ease some of her stress.

In the heat of our fight, and in everything that's been going on the past few weeks, I forgot that all of this is new to her. Sure, she may have *met* Keto three years ago, but for all she knew that could have been a dream. A hallucination.

She didn't enter a deal with a goddess because she had an entire upbringing dedicated to killing them. She just did it to save her friend. And when that friend was finally able to move on from her grief, well—who's to say that was because a goddess answered her prayer? That it wasn't just a natural stage in her grief process?

I know she was scared to come here this year, but if she'd truly believed Keto would take our baby away, if she was convinced that she was inviting this kind of punishment, she never would have agreed to go. No matter how much Lillian or I tried to persuade her.

I wish I could see her face.

It isn't all your fault. None of this is your fault. It's Keto's. She's the reason we're trapped here, the reason Lillian made that deal—Her, and no one else.

What's going to happen to her, Dean? To Lil?

I don't know, I answer honestly, and it stabs my heart like a physical blow. *But I do know that we're going to do everything we can to save her when this is all said and done.*

She looks at me and nods. I pull her into my embrace, and my whole body relaxes when it comes into contact with her. I can't help myself from touching her: stroking my fingers down her arms, her back, her sides...

A little shiver passes through her, and I pause.

Is this okay?

She moves her hands down my torso before responding, grazing the gold ring at the base of my dick for a fraction of a second before answering. *Is it okay for you? You're a little more... compromised than I am.*

Oh fuck, I almost forgot! I have to laugh, and my whole chest aches with relief as I realize I can finally take these fucking things off. *Quick, before I get hard...*

Together, we slowly remove each snug ring from my shaft, barely suppressing chuckles the entire time. When her soft fingers finally slide the last one down to my head, it's like all my blood flow returns at once. I hiss as her fingertips wrap around the skin, the ring still clinging just under the head as she gives me a tentative pump.

Fuck, Tiffany, that feels so good.

You haven't come in weeks. She nuzzles into the crook of my neck, and her hair wraps around my face. Her scent is the faintest suggestion underwater: warm and *alive,* so unlike the cold, mineral sensation of the water we've been trapped in. *Does it hurt?*

Not—anymore, I grit through clenched teeth, *but it is almost unbearable. Fuck, Tiff, I'm already on edge.*

She scratches at the ring still teasing my head, and my hips buck before I can stop them. I bump into her belly, and she jumps back, laughing. *Oh fuck, you* are *sensitive.*

It takes every remaining ounce of self-control I have, my vision almost whiting out at how good it feels to have Tiffany stroking me after weeks of claws and cold rings and merciless teasing, but I place a hand on her shoulder.

We don't have to... you know. Do anything. I know that She's—you've been through so much...

I'm worried that if we continue, it will only hurt her more. That my touches, my cock inside her, will only remind her of the horror she's endured this month. Thinking of her trapped beneath Keto's body, Her tongue and fingers and tails and hair playing Tiff's body like an instrument—

My cock swells, and I hiss out another breath, bubbles bursting between my teeth. That one ring digs into the end of my shaft, holding me just on the brink. *Fuck,* I'm hard. I would have exploded already if it weren't for that last ring.

I don't want to come again, she says, shaking her head. *Not yet. But I do want you. I need you, Dean. I need you to erase everything she did.*

I blink at her, unsure what she's asking. *You want me to...?*

She lowers herself down my body, settling so her face is level with my stomach, hands braced against my hips.

I want your cock.

Fuck. *It's yours.*

She pauses, and I can just make out the shadow of a

swallow traveling down her throat. *You mean that? Even after everything, you still...want me?*

Oh, Tiff. I grab under her arms and haul her up my body until we're face-to-face. My cock traces a line from her sternum to the apex of her thighs as I pull her higher, until it nestles in the fluff of her pubic hair under her rounded belly. She's got wiry hair covering her armpits now, circles under her eyes, and her skin is so much paler than it was when she was reading on the beach less than a month ago.

And still, I think she's the most beautiful woman I've ever seen.

I'll never stop wanting you. I kiss her without abandon, pressing my lips to hers and stroking them with my tongue until she opens for me. The kiss grows deeper as we explore each other like we're starved for it, and *fuck*—isn't that exactly what we are? I haven't touched this girl in weeks, and it feels like it's been a lifetime.

We don't stop, locked at the lips and reveling in every place our bodies touch. I pump as slowly as I dare against the seam of her lips. The whole time, I whisper into her mind: *I love you. I'll always love you.*

She reaches down between us, pushing our bodies the slightest bit apart. Her hand grips my shaft and I moan into her mouth. I feel the corner of her lips quirk up at that, and before I know it I'm bending lower, fastening my mouth around her nipple.

Ah! Dean!

I need you, Tiffany. Please.

You've got me.

May I–?

Yes, she gushes, and I suck greedily at the tender bud of her breast. She moans again, and I reach up to tweak her other nipple. They're bigger now than they were before she got pregnant, and the curve of it fills my whole hand as I squeeze. I back off, licking up and down and sideways as quickly as I can with the lake water providing resistance, but either way she seems to like it. *Yes, please, Dean—your cock, I want you cock.*

Are you ready?

A giggle sounds in my head at the question, and she spreads her legs. *Feel for yourself?*

I reach down, pumping my shaft a few times before stroking the swollen head against her entrance. There's no way I'm getting the ring off now, and I only hope it won't keep me from coming entirely.

As it is, I feel like I'm seconds from blowing my load.

My eyes close in a groan as my cockhead swipes at her dripping entrance, her natural lubrication more slippery than the wetness all around us. When I notch into her tight channel and slide home, it's almost more than I can take.

Fuck, Tiff—you feel so good.

Fuck is right, she breathes into my mind, practically caressing me from the inside out with her words. *I can feel the ring stroking me, babe...*

It's good?

So good! Her fingers clutch at my shoulders, and she uses the leverage to sink herself all the way down to my base. I twitch inside her, barely holding on as she moans. Are her eyes rolling back in her head? All I can see is her head tilted back, and the glassy reflection of the rising sunlight filtering through the depths in her eyes. *It's so good, Dean!*

*I'm not gonna last—*I grunt, feeling my balls tighten with weeks worth of built-up cum. *Fuck, you feel... I'm gonna–*

Fill me up, Dean! Please! Please!

Please, please, please... it echoes like a mantra, following each stroke as I pump again, and again, frantically, swelling until I can feel the ring cutting off my circulation—

Tiff!

At last, I explode, stars bursting behind my eyes as the bite of pain beneath the head of my cock anchors the orgasm slicing through me like lightning. I lose all sense of time as I unload inside her, twitching with each jet of my release. It's like it won't stop: I clutch my arms around her back, crashing my lips to hers, as we come together for what feels like eons.

At last, having spent the last of my cum inside her, I slide out of Tiff's pussy. The last brass ring pops off my dick as I do, floating slowly to the cave floor with the pearly wisps of our release.

Ha! Tiffany laughs, sounding tired even in our heads. *I guess that takes care of that, then.*

Thank the gods, I laugh back, squeezing her again and pressing a kiss to her forehead. She sighs, her whole body feeling languid and warm in my arms.

Call me sentimental, but with her all to myself, I can't help but want her to feel as loved as she can in this moment. I travel down her body, pressing sweet kisses to her temple, the curve of her jaw, her shoulder, elbow, wrist, until I press a final smooch to her knuckles. As I pull her hand away, her engagement ring sparkles in a slender beam of light.

It catches my eye. The main stone of her ring isn't a diamond, as would be tradition. It's an omphalos stone. A little chunk of polished marble, something my family has passed down for generations because it symbolizes our connection with...

Tiffany! I'm gazing at her ring with new eyes, squeezing her hand so tight, she pulls on my fingers. I drop it, moving instead to clutch her waist, spinning her around in triumph. I can't believe it! That's it!

What, Dean, what?

Your ring!

What about it?

My cheeks stretch wide, the muscles burning at the unfamiliar movement, but I can't help grinning.

This is it. This is it!

It's our way out of here!

CHAPTER 10

TIFFANY

Long ago, there was a princess of Greece, Danaë. She was an only child, and her father, the King, was disappointed that his one heir was a woman. So he went to the Oracle of Delphi to seek answers.

The Oracle foretold that the mighty King would be killed by his own grandson, so he locked his daughter away. But Danaë was beautiful, and lonely, and Zeus—in his glory and mercy—offered her companionship. Their union brought about a child: Perseus.

When the King discovered the child, he cast both Perseus and his mother into the sea in a locked chest. But Poseidon blessed them, delivered them safely to shore on the island of Seriphos.

The troubles were not over for their family, though. Poor Danaë became the object for the Island King's lust, and Perseus knew he had to protect her. But the King sent him away on an impossible quest to get rid of him: bring back the head of Medusa.

The gods saw the injustice, and blessed Perseus with all the tools he needed to defeat the evil Gorgon, and using his wits and the gifts of the gods he was able to succeed.

He was a hero of innocent women, a slayer of monsters, and earned the favor of the gods with his many trials. It's his lineage from which my family descends: Perseus.

I blink at Dean, my pussy still twinging every now and then in a pleasant reminder of the fantastic sex we just had. And maybe it's that—how sweet he was to me, how gentle and perceptive as we made love—that keeps me from rolling my eyes at his over-the-top backstory.

Oooookay, I think slowly, munching on the meat scraps that Keto left behind. Now that I'm free from my ties and have a burst of goddess-given energy, I'm famished. *But what does that have to do with my ring?*

The stone, the marble-looking one in the middle of the sapphires, is an omphalos *stone, Tiff. It's from the Temple of Delphi, carved for the Oracle herself. A gift, from the Oracle to Danaë and Perseus, that's been in my family for millennia. It's a connection between humans and the gods.*

And that's... good?

Good? Tiffany, it's great! It literally channels the power of the Gods. I bet I can use this to break through the barrier of the cave opening!

His face splits in a grin that spreads from ear-to-ear. It's slightly brighter in the cave now, whether from the light of the day filtering through the clear lake depths or the rising moon is impossible to tell. But I have to say, the view is working in Dean's favor.

He's lucky he's so damn cute. Because it takes everything in me not to slap him upside the head with his not-so-coherent explanation.

Granted, I should be used to this, as this is *Dean* we're talking about. My computer science major, certified geek fiancé. It's like he's trying to explain Python or C++ to me all over again. Assuming I can put together pieces that I have only ten percent of the context for.

How, Dean? Give me specifics.

Well, uh... he pauses, scratching his ear. *Just give me the ring. Let me show you.*

I wiggle the thin band of gold off my ring finger and place it in his palm. I remember when he first gave it to me. At the time, I wasn't all that impressed. It's a simple, round stone: an off-white marble, polished into a perfect sphere, perched in a four-point setting and offset by two teardrop-shaped sapphires. It didn't look *anything* like the ones I'd not-so-subtly hinted at whenever we happened upon a jewelry store together. I knew he could see my disappointment in my face when I opened the tiny velvet box, because he placed a hand over mine when I opened it.

"It's not what you were expecting, I know," he said, that sheepish little smile of his tucked into his cheek. "But it's a family heirloom. And when I see you, Tiff, I see family. My family. *Our* family. The future we have before us." That was when he plucked the tiny band of gold from the soft, velvet lining and slid it on my finger.

It fit perfectly. "Will you marry me?"

I was already pregnant when he proposed to me, and despite the honest affection I could hear in his words, even then I didn't feel like I could trust it. But now, after all we've been through, after being driven half crazy by Keto and almost killing him, it's clear that he meant every word: then, and now.

It's that promise that rings in my head now as I hand over the symbol of our love. I may not have truly believed it then, but I believe it now. Dean loves me. He did when we were captured by the monster of Lake Superior, he did when he proposed, and he does now, while we're fighting for our lives.

He folds his fingers around the thin, gold band, giving my fingers a quick squeeze before he turns and swims toward the opening of our prison.

Bear with me. I've only seen it glow once before...

I follow him over to the barrier, visible only in the faint silver shimmer that catches the light refracting off the waves every so often. It's the same one I pushed against when Keto left us earlier, when my bonds fell away and she pressed that knife to my hand.

I shiver, thinking just how wrong that all could have gone. I was so angry about the secrets Dean kept from me, convinced he never loved me... I could have killed him.

Was that what Keto wanted? For me to murder my own fiancé?

I shake the thought from my head while Dean inspects the film of magic separating us from the rest of the lake.

Don't stand too close... I float back as he closes his eyes, holding the ring pinched in both thumbs and index fingers. His lips mouth words I can't quite make out and, for a moment, nothing happens.

That is, until the grey-streaked stone in the center starts to glow.

Gods of Olympus, please, answer my prayer...

Eyes still closed, he raises the ring above his head with both hands, and slams it stone-first into the barrier.

White lines splinter like lightning across the entrance of the cave, a veritable matrix of light so bright I have to turn away from the glare. But Dean pushes through, squinting, and I hear him grunt with the effort of it.

Help me!

I grab his shoulders, kicking with all my might behind

him as I flatten my upper half against his torso and push his body into the wall of magic. The exertion makes my head light, and I can feel the currents at my neck as my heart pounds for more and more oxygen, gills and heart working hard to pump fresh blood through my tired veins as we both force the ring against the wall with all our might.

The cracks in the invisible barrier spread and widen, light filling in the spaces of the splintered matrix before us, until the entire plane glows solid white. Then, all at once, the resistance vanishes.

We tumble into the open water, gills fluttering furiously as we gain our breath. Out here, the light of the moon is practically blinding, shining straight through to the lake floor through the crystal-clear waters.

Holy shit! Holy shit! I flap my hands excitedly, jolting about the water that feels as open and free as I remember it from my very first swim in these waters. I spin with joy, kicking my little feet and relishing the light on my skin. *Dean, you did it! We're free!*

For now, he says ominously, face serious, feet treading steadily beneath him. *I don't think that will work a second time.*

Why not?

He holds up the ring; surprise and sadness cut through my chest like an axe. Down the center of the marble stone is a giant crack, its white color scarred and blackened as if it was burned.

Well, damn. I'd just come around to liking that ring. And now it's broken.

But we are free. And that's much more important than the sentimental attachment I might have to a piece of rock and metal.

I don't need a symbol to convince me that Dean's devotion is real. Not anymore.

Do you—do you think it's magic is gone?

Dean nods, frowning. *I guess I'll need to get you a diamond after all.*

I shake my head, diving under his bent head and pressing my lips to his. *Babe, if we get out of here alive, I'd settle for a fucking Ring Pop out of a gumball machine. Now let's get out of here and find Lil before it's too late.*

He nods, slipping the broken ring back onto my finger. It's weirdly heavier now, an actual weight on my fourth digit instead of the familiar sensation I'd grown used to. I tug it off and hand it back to him.

No, keep it for now, I think, folding his fingers around the cracked stone. *You might need it again.*

His lips thin, but he takes it, slipping it onto his pinky and motioning us forward. As we're paddling away, I remember something, and dart back to the cave.

Dean calls after me, worry in his voice. *Where are you going?*

I almost forgot! I call back, diving into the cave and searching blindly, until my hand closes upon the thin blade I'm hunting for. I emerge from the cave, holding it aloft. The mother-of-pearl edge shimmers in the moonlight. *If we're going to be swimming in open water, I'd feel safer being armed.*

That's my girl. Dean pulls me to his side and squeezes an arm around my waist, pressing a kiss to my temple. *Now let's get out of here.*

CHAPTER II
LILLIAN

I am a hot air balloon.

Not exactly something I'd ever thought I'd feel like, especially not while 20,000 leagues under the sea, but there's little else I can compare myself to. Everytime I look down at my body, Erik's voice rings out in my head, warning me to stop bad-talking myself.

Your body is performing a miracle, and I will not stand for you insulting it.

Erik...

My kraken-shifter Viking boyfriend might have a point—what I'm doing *is* a miracle. But that miracle has also expanded my belly to the point I can't see my legs. If the circumstances around this entire situation weren't already cosmic horror levels, it would be the most terrifying thing I'd ever experienced.

And yet, Erik looks at me like I'm a supermodel. Affection shines in his eyes every second he dotes on me—both he *and* Phorkys, the monstrous titan that shares his body, hover around like helicopter parents.

101

Which, I guess, in a way they are.

My treasure. What do you need?

And isn't that the question of the century?

Since the... *incident,* shall we say, I've been nestled in this underwater cave and pampered every minute of every day. Phorkys squirreled us away in here, having prepared it for his young in the hopes that He and His mate would someday find a human willing to incubate their demigod children. While my whirlwind courtship with Erik involved Phorkys more as a foreboding force than a third partner, that dynamic has shifted considerably in the three-plus weeks we've been sequestered here. I've seen far more of the full kraken monster than I ever thought I would when I fell in love with the long-haired, muscular warrior cursed to share a body with Him.

But that's what happens when you agree to grow a titan's children in your uterus, I guess. The family dynamics change. Both Phorkys and Erik have been extremely supportive throughout this entire pregnancy, albeit in different ways.

The hormones raging through my system are no joke. They keep me bouncing from ravenous to miserable to horny as if each emotion were a different color in a strobe light. Because of that, the energy of our nest is a little... frenetic.

My lover changes forms constantly, the titan taking over whenever He senses movement or distress from any one of the monsters growing within me. He leaves to gather food while I'm sleeping, although mysterious packages will arrive every so often while Erik and I make love, which makes me think that perhaps Keto is also providing for Her young behind the scenes, too.

I haven't seen Her since She took Dean and Tiffany away. And in the few moments between mood swings and orgasms, I can't think of anything but how terrified they must be.

I need to know she's okay.

Your friend?

Yes.

Erik's brow furrows above his glowing eyes, his gaze never far from that godly cyan since the incident. That's how I know that Phorkys is listening: His eyes overshadow Erik's crystal grey ones, two beings looking out through a single face. He's both boyfriend *and* dad now, and the protective instincts are running on overdrive.

I cannot leave you. Not while you are awake. And He will not let me stray while we gather food—

I know. But you asked.

The worry in his expression tugs at my heartstrings, and the feeling grounds me somehow. *He* grounds me. I'm doing this for him, in part. For us. Having Keto's and Phorkys's babies will allow Phorkys to leave Erik's body once and for all. Will save him from this monstrous fate. Will allow us to have a future together where we can have a family of our own.

Whenever we lock eyes, I'm filled with the comforting knowledge that the two of us are still *human* inside, despite his tentacle legs and my...

Well. My whole situation.

You are doing it again.

Erik, I'm pretty sure body dysmorphia just comes with the territory when I'm growing a thousand plus sea monsters in my uterus, okay? It's really not something I can control.

Despite my bratty tone, he smiles. He's getting used to

my sense of humor now—even learning a few fun modern phrases that he's been trying out for himself—and I can't help but feel a swell of gratitude for the big lug.

I'd ask what I ever did to deserve him, but the evidence of the sacrifice I made to break his curse is kinda the elephant in the room these days.

Or rather, *I'm* the elephant in the room these days.

Erik presses his lips to my forehead. *You contain multitudes, my treasure. Physically and spiritually. We will endure this.*

Damn these pregnancy hormones. I swear I'm never more than a couple words away from crying. It's almost enough to make me grateful we're surrounded by water. No obvious tears is one less sign of just how hot a mess I am these days.

I know. But knowing doesn't stop me from blubbering.

He reaches for my hand and squeezes it. I feel a stirring in my stomach, something akin to a kick, and it causes another stirring below.

Erik's eyes glow brighter, and I feel a tentacle graze the swell of my belly beneath my line of sight.

This way of growing children...it is a magical experience.

Maybe for you, Phorkie. You get to experience it vicariously. Everytime one of those suckers kicks I have to pee like a racehorse.

I do not mind.

More tentacles stroke up and down my legs as He takes over Erik's body and floats out of view.

I sigh. While Erik has been getting better at picking up on my punchlines, Phorkys is still ignorant as ever. He never laughs at my jokes. Bit of a buzzkill, to be honest.

But I can't deny that when the titan does adopt his true form, it's clear He doesn't mean me any harm. His emotions don't relay as clearly to me as my viking's, of course, as He isn't human, but when I do catch glimpses, they're... surprising.

He's grateful. Awed.

And fuck me if He doesn't seem excited to be a father.

His "excitement" never stays innocent for long, though. Sure, His touchy-feely moments always start out innocent enough: suctioning an arm around my belly and enjoying the movements of the monster babies inside me, but eventually He gets other ideas in those prehensile brains of His.

The *downstairs* brains.

He's starting to do it again now, pairs of arms stroking and flicking between my legs, drawing a rise out of me, when a massive boom cuts its way into our safe little bubble. The cave walls shake with the fury of it, sending little clots of dust and rocks raining slowly down upon our private nest.

Keto!

Tiffany! My brain instantly goes to my best friend and her fiancé, trapped with a goddess of unknown power. What *was* that? An explosion? Did she kill them?!

Phorkys resurfaces, having fully taken over, His dinner plate-sized eyes flashing as I reach my arms out for him, but for once, He isn't looking at me. He glances, panicked, to the opening of the cave as if He wants to bolt out of there.

Somehow—don't ask me how—I manage to snatch onto one of His tentacles, and I dig my nails in. He flinches.

You need to check on her, I plead.

I expect Him to brush me off, but to my surprise, He

remains trapped in my grip. At first I wonder if it's because He's about to comfort me, but then I notice a new paleness to the monster's skin. Angry purple marks appear on His tentacle where my fingertips squeeze.

His bulbous eyes grow wide, and He shakes His giant head.

Keto can take care of Herself. You are the one–

Not Keto, Tiffany! I shout, anger and panic rising within me.

But the voice that rings through all our heads doesn't sound like mine. It's tone is also different from the internal conversation I've grown used to, sounding guttural and raw. Gritty. It echoes back from the cavernous walls in a way that—quite frankly—scares me a little bit. The titan tugs on my grip, but I hold fast, and when I look down to see how I'm able to match His strength, I see claws where my nails used to be.

The shock of it snaps me out of the moment, and by the time I snatch my hand back, it's fully human. Almost like I imagined it.

You can and you WILL, I add, and His face shines purple. I blink, and the odd coloring disappears, but the fear in His eyes remains. I take a deep breath, calming myself, and continue. *The deal is off if she is unsafe. Do you trust your goddess not to harm her?!*

I...

The hesitation in His voice scares me more than the noise itself. Hot anger floods my chest as I stare Him down, and I witness the god literally shrink before me.

She is not the mother of your brood anymore, Phorkys. I am. And if you care for the health of your progeny, you will bring my friend to me. ***Now!***

He hesitates for only a moment before Erik's face and

torso reappear before me. My mate nods in assent, mouth set in a firm line, before the two of them propel out of the cave like a rocket.

Hang tight, Tiff, I think—as strongly and with as much gusto as I possibly can—in the hopes that somehow my intention might reach her. *We're coming for you.*

CHAPTER 12

TIFFANY

When the two of us speed out of the cave, it becomes immediately apparent that we're as deep into the waters of Lake Superior as I've ever been. Luckily, moonlight still manages to filter through the clear waters above us, but even so—when you're over 1000 feet underwater, it's going to be dim.

But I can actually see the lines in his face now as he scans our surroundings, no longer blocked by the shadows of Keto's cave. Giant pillars like stalagmites shoot up from the ground surrounding the eerie boulders of the lair she's been keeping us in, colored by long, stringy patches of weeds and floaty plants. And of course, fish swim to and fro around us, hardly even acknowledging the two unnatural humans paddling in their midst.

It's spooky as hell, and the vibes are not made any better by the clock ticking away over our heads, counting down to the mystery moment when Keto will return to exact her revenge.

Where do we go?

Dean bites his lip, feet drifting back under his body as

we both stop our forward momentum long enough to take in our surroundings.

I'm not sure what I was expecting. A beacon of light to follow? A bright green road sign with an exit arrow reading, **Supernaturally Pregnant Bestie, 1 ½ mi ahead**? I guess part of me thought I'd just *know*, that the power of my guilt and affection would guide me towards her like instinct.

But of course, that isn't the case. Dean and I are just floating here, in the middle of the lake, clutching our ring and knife respectively, as if these two little trinkets of the monsters we're trapped with will provide us with some sort of direction.

I need to pray, Dean answers at last, and I snort. He shoots me an annoyed look, and I shrug in response.

Sorry, sorry. Force of habit. Even after meeting Keto, I've been agnostic for the majority of my adulthood. Before this whole ordeal, I'd chalked up the whole experience of my deal with the goddess and Lillian's change of heart to a dehydrated fever dream. *You have to admit, prayer as a plan doesn't exactly inspire confidence.*

He fiddles with the ring.

Yeah, no, you're right. It's a pretty desperate place to be.

His frown prickles in my chest, and I wish I could take it back. After all, his magic ring got us out of the cave. His faith might be the only thing that *can* save us now.

I drift closer to him, resting my hand on his shoulder. *What can I do to help?*

I'm not sure. We need to eat. You need to get somewhere safe, and I–

Uh, I think you mean we *need to get somewhere safe?*

There's no way I'm leaving his side, not after the fresh hell we just escaped.

No, Tiff. You *do.* He wraps his arm around my back,

pulling me into him, and swallows my protest with a deep and searching kiss.

And don't get me wrong, Dean's a good fucking kisser. But this is different from what I'm used to from him. There's power in this kiss. Strength and love and desperation.

I melt into him, his tongue sweeping past my lips and tangling with mine so intensely it feels like something more than just a show of affection.

It feels like a goodbye.

He breaks it off, and the bubbles around our necks tickle me with how much faster our hearts are beating. He stares into my eyes, and once again I'm struck dumb by *seeing* him again. I haven't gotten a good look at my fiancé for weeks, and what I see is...

Heartbreaking.

His eyes are lined with worry and exhaustion, sunken and hollow in skin paled by weeks without sunlight. Purple bruises line his neck and even his gills, suggesting that he's been strangled at some point while I was passed out in Keto's cave. Cuts scar his slim, muscular chest—far more than the one knick from the knife I gave him an hour ago.

Dean...

I reach a hand up to his cheek, one of the few places where he doesn't have some kind of mark, and he reaches up to squeeze my fingers.

I need to know you're okay, he communicates to me, eyes hard and searching. *I won't be able to focus on what I need to do if I'm worried about you. If She gets near you again, I can't promise that I won't lose my mind. You're the most important person in the world to me, Tiff, you and—*

His other hand slides from my lower back to my stomach, the slight squeeze of his fingers saying more than words ever could. Tears choke the back of my throat.

Let me help you, Dean, please. I don't know where to go on my own, what to do...

I'm looking at him as my mind drifts into hopelessness, pleading with my eyes. *Don't leave me,* I want to say, but my heart is too torn to fully form the thought.

He descends on my lips again, and this time I don't hold back. I return the kiss fiercely, giving as hard as I'm getting. Before I know it, my arms are wrapped around his neck, my legs around his waist, and he's cradling me as best he can, surrounding me with his strong, scarred body, as we practically devour each other.

I'm sorry I never told you about my childhood, he whispers into my mind as he explores my body, grasping at my shoulders, back, thighs. *Never explained how my dad trained me for this. For the small chance that, someday, I might encounter one of the enemies my ancestors left behind. But I don't know how to face them any other way than alone.*

The last thing I want to think about right now is his parents, but some part of my brain recognizes that this is important to him. I just don't know how to convince him that it's more important to me that we stick together.

You don't have to be alone, Dean. I don't want you to be alone. I don't want to be alone—

Then find Lillian, he says desperately, tearing his lips from mine as he locks eyes with me imploringly. His gaze is desperate, almost crazed as he practically screams in my mind. *Find her, and protect each other!*

My heart is pounding so fast my chest aches. I know, in his mind, he thinks he's just asking me to be strong. To find my friend so we can break free from these monsters. But he doesn't know what he's actually asking of me when he tells me to leave him for her. He can't.

He isn't the only one who hasn't been completely honest about their past. His childhood certainly doesn't sound like a cakewalk, but my young adulthood wasn't either.

Both of our pasts might have left us with invisible scars, but they still hurt.

I force a swallow past my throat, my guilt a physical block that my muscles work to overcome. I close my eyes, unable to hold his stare for another second.

Dean... I need to confess something.

You love her.

He says it simply, as if it's the most obvious and unsurprising thing in the world. Like it's something we've talked about a million times—not the soul-deep secret I've locked within the stone walls of my heart. The conversational equivalent of a shrug. "No big deal," his tone says. "You're just in love with someone else."

My eyes pop open, mouth gaping enough that water fills my it. I swallow again, shaking my head.

It's not like that. I don't think of her just as a friend, Dean, I–I've got a crush on her. I have for years. And I've been afraid, that...

But once again, the words just won't shape themselves in my head. Keto got so good at parsing out my deepest fears without me having to consciously think them through, that I stopped feeling the need to define them inside my head. To actually communicate them.

But I know one thing: I can't keep it from Dean any longer. It isn't fair to him, or to Lillian. My indecisiveness has been hurting them for too long.

That I wouldn't understand?

Not that, I hedge, shaking my head. *But I know I can't have you both, and I love you so much that I didn't want to invite anything into my life that might ruin that. Ruin us.*

A wrinkle forms above his nose as he looks at me, trying to understand. And this is the thing I was afraid of: the love of my life, looking at me like I'm an abomination. A pervert. Someone that's just trying to have their cake and eat it, too.

Why would you loving your best friend ruin us? I love her too, Tiffany. She makes you so happy.

I blink. *What?*

A beautiful sound fills my head, and it takes me a second to realize it's laughter. Dean's laughter. His arms squeeze around me in a hug, and I feel him shake his head into my hair as his thoughts start to trickle into me, soothing an ache in my heart that I didn't know *could* be soothed.

You don't have to choose for me, babe. You need to tell Lillian, of course, because she'd have to be cool with it too, but I never wanted you to feel like you had to choose between us. I tried to tell you in the beginning, when I saw how you looked at her. If it's cool with her, it's cool with me. I think you both are the prettiest, funniest, and all-around coolest women I've ever met. I'd love to get to know Lillian better. I'd love for our child to have two amazing women to look up to.

I'm still gaping at him, the joy in his voice not computing with the years of guilt that have been weighing down my heart. Is he serious right now?

I thought there was something wrong with me. All my years of dating, of being attracted to multiple people, and no one ever once told me it was okay to want to be with more than one partner. It was a stigma that even my queer friends judged others for.

He must see my disbelief written on my face, because he grips my shoulders tight and locks his gaze to mine.

We don't have to go through life like our parents did, Tiff. Maybe for us, love looks different. And maybe that's okay. Maybe that's how I want it. Maybe that's actually how you want it, too.

Pressure builds in my eyes, and before I know it, I'm sniffling into Dean's chest. I don't know how to cry underwater, and my throat and mouth and chest are all fighting for control as my salty tears melt instantly into the freshwater around us.

Dean pats my back, cutting himself off as he starts to panic a bit, worrying whether or not I can breathe.

Then it's my turn to laugh, as he pushes me to arms' length so he can check me for injuries. I shake my head, and eventually the two of us calm down enough that I can breathe like normal—or, as normal as filtering O2 from lakewater through my gills can be, I suppose.

You... you're actually okay with us having a—an open relationship?

He's thoughtful for a moment, and for a second I think maybe I misunderstood completely. Luckily, he answers me before I can fully enter panic-mode.

Not with just anyone, he says at last. *But I know how much you care for Lillian. I always have. And I would never want you to deny yourself something so important to you as your feelings for her. You two belong together. As much as you and I do.*

I kiss him then, gently and fully, pouring all the love I can possibly siphon into it. He kisses me back, and then we both hear something almost like a cough.

We break apart, our hands sliding to more appropriate places, and turn to face the intruder.

I... hope I'm not interrupting?

CHAPTER 13

ERIK

The monster is in full control of our limbs when we bolt through the deep waters to fulfill Lillian's errand. For the entire duration of her pregnancy thus far, Phorkys has kept the location of Keto's lair hidden from me. Somehow, despite us being closer than ever, our emotions mixing and conflating as we care for my mate while she grows His brood, He is still able to hide His secrets.

But I have also become better at hiding my intentions.

In two weeks' time, my treasure will give birth to thousands of god-monsters, creatures of the deep I cannot begin to imagine. And while she recovers, I will need to ferry us to safety. I do not know if she will be capable of fending for herself, how or if her body will return to its human state after such trauma. I believe Phorkys does not know the extent of Keto's magics or Her plans for my mate, either.

Even He was surprised just now, when my treasure's eyes burned violet, illuminating the cave with their supernatural glow.

It is not just her body that is changing.

With each passing day, as the moon waxes, her influence over my monster has grown.

I have always struggled with bringing Phorkys to heel when He overtakes my body. The amount of control it takes is immense. Even after hundreds of years, I still am not always able to maintain my humanity. But now that Lillian bears His brood...

He is more powerful than ever. And yet, *she* is the one with the power.

She is not fully human anymore, He rumbles in my mind, and I start.

Like me?

No. Not... not like you.

An unidentifiable grumble is the only other context He leaves me with. I am beginning to believe that He is just as confused with Lillian's transformation as I am. Is she becoming a goddess in her own right? A titan? The mother of monsters?

She was always going to need to change to withstand her body's transformation. But I thought...

No. I will not let this be about me. She is safe, she is alive, and she is healthy. That is all that matters.

I can scent Her.

Tiffany?

Keto. This is Her lair.

We gaze up at the wall of red-laced rock that towers over the lake floor. Iron. The lands here are rich with deposits of the strong metal, and Phorkys grazes his tentacles along the seams of red and brown buried within the dark rock.

It is why I couldn't sense Her before. The iron. It keeps Her magic from leaving the cave.

But why would She–?

She was angry with me. It's... Perhaps it was better I did not know She was so close.

I wonder at that, at the secrets His lover kept from Him all these years.

He loves Her, I know. The courtship of Phorkys and Keto goes back millennia, since the time before Olympians, before my people sailed the northern seas. A twinge—not guilt, exactly, but something uncomfortable—nudges my conscience when I remember my people's part in the centuries-long fight between the titans. Our ship crashing into their eggs, destroying their young. Phorkys taking over my body in a moment of weakness to save himself from perishing in the ensuing battle. Keto, unable to recognize Her lover, unable to breed again with our mingled bodies, and Her flight into the depths of the lake.

We creep along the lake bed, searching for an opening in the massive wall of rock. Somewhere in there, Tiffany and Dean are being kept against their wills, locked up as collateral until Lillian gives birth.

I know that Lillian is worried for her friends, as am I. They are important to her, and thus, important to me.

But I do worry that Keto may change our circumstances for the worse if we kidnap Her toys.

Here.

A mouth, large and imposing, opens in the side of the rock, and the edges shimmer with a silver glow that Phorkys studies when He takes over my form. The lake around me morphs into odd, blurry shapes of vibrant color as His eyes blossom on the sides of my head.

The shattered forcefield of the opening's edges is even brighter in comparison to the stone and sand around us.

Magic? I question. He has not made an attempt to touch the flickering barrier, and yet the glow emanating from it makes me wonder if perhaps it is best not to try. Keto is not above laying traps, I know, and Phorkys seems to be thinking the same thing.

Perhaps. But it has been broken.

Broken? By whom?

He ponders this while I take back control of our body and swim about the borders of the giant rocks. All about the outcropping, little divots and breaks in the formation sparkle with the same silver light of the broken magic barrier, and it all raises more questions than it answers.

And then I see them. I am almost convinced it is a trick of the moonlight, too convenient to be real.

This is the first I have seen Lillian's friends in the open, not bound and tied at the mercy of Keto. Tiffany and Dean.

And they are... quite engaged with one another.

I...hope I'm not interrupting?

They break apart, and a refreshing burst of color tints Tiffany's cheeks. Unfortunately, that looks to be one of the only healthy things about her.

Hair floating limply about her bony shoulders, skin stretched across gaunt cheeks, this woman doesn't contain any of the healthy plumpness that Lillian does. Except for her stomach and breasts, which are round because of her expected child, she appears to be dangerously thin.

As a warrior, I have seen the effects of prolonged hunger. What it does to a body. I saw it wreak havoc upon my own limbs when I was at my most hopeless in my years of solitude.

Lillian was right to send us here, I parlay to Phorkys. *Your lover has not been taking Her stewardship of these humans seriously.*

The monster does not respond. Perhaps I imagine it, but my concern for Lillian's friends seems flavored by a whisper of guilt. I wonder if He, too, realizes just how close to death these two were.

Once I take inventory of Tiffany, enough to verify that she is well enough to make the swim back to the nest (while taking care to be respectful of her nakedness), my focus shifts to her lover. Dean.

He is in no better shape—perhaps worse, if his bruises and scars are any indication. His arms and torso maintain the definition of muscle mass; a physique I recognize as one deceptively powerful for its size.

In my days fighting for my village, our warriors varied in height and width. Some, like me, were muscular and broad across their shoulders with trim waists. Others held their muscle in their centers: barrel-chested with thick thighs, perfect for hauling the extra supplies needed to withstand weeks on the battlefields. Others yet never seemed to develop a brawny physique, and yet they were more than capable of bursts of strength in moments of crises.

My assessment concludes with taking in this young warrior's face. Confusion etches lines into his forehead when he notices me staring at him. His hips shift, turning into his lover even as he tilts them to obscure their private parts.

I feel my face heat, and I shake my head in apology. *Lillian sent me to retrieve you. We heard a–*

How to describe the sound from earlier? My mind flashes back to the shards of magic clinging to the cave walls.

Was that the source of the noise? Did these two shatter Keto's barrier?

Impossible, Phorkys whispers in response to my

thoughts. ***These two are not powerful enough to escape her.***

I hum in agreement while replacing the mental barriers I have been fortifying against his inner voice over the past lunar cycle. I test them as I always do, by imagining Lillian's perfect breasts to elicit His lusty instincts.

When I don't feel the supernatural tug in my loins, I know they are intact.

I swim forward, closing the gap of space between Tiffany and Dean and me. Other than a slight tightening of his arms around her, they don't cower from my approach.

Lillian needs you, I think aloud, firmly enough that Phorkys can also hear it. But beneath the cover of my mental walls, I add, *how did you escape Her?*

Tiffany looks as though she's about to answer, when Dean glances at her meaningfully. His fingers squeeze again before he answers, *my ancestors provided me tools to fight against Her kind.*

I raise an eyebrow. *And this is the first time you have used them?*

Something like a snort echoes in our heads, and the shadow of a smirk crosses Tiffany's lips. *Long story. You know where Lillian is?*

Yes.

Is she okay?

Her eyes are wide as she inquires about her friend. I nod, and her body almost wilts in response. She sinks a bit, and I cannot help but wonder if anxiety alone was keeping her afloat.

Dean shifts his hold on her, supporting her tiny frame. How can a body that frail even grow a life within it? Her belly is quite large—easily approaching her last third of her pregnancy. How will she even be able to carry such a weight on land?

He seems to be worried about the same thing. His eyes dart from the woman in his arms to me, and I know what he is about to ask me before he meets my gaze with determination.

Can you take her there? To Lillian? I need to—there is something I must try. He lifts his head to the water's surface, and his countenance glows with the moonlight. In the corner of my eye, I see a flicker of light spark from a ring around his pinky, but it fades quickly enough that I wonder if it was a trick of the waves.

I hold out my arms, nodding. *I can.*

Wait! The exhaustion in her voice is enough to inspire my protective instincts. This poor woman has suffered much—both of them have. But there is something in her lover's face that I feel a kinship with. This man is not without strength.

It seems like he has a plan, but I respect him for not voicing it aloud in Phorkys's presence. Not for the first time, I wish that my curse were lifted. Interacting with humans other than Lillian only serves as a reminder of my separation from them.

I am not like them. Nor can I be trusted in their presence until I am free of my titanic curse.

Go with him, babe. I need to do this.

In a blink, one of my tentacles shoots out and curls around his leg. Shocked, I struggle to release him, only to find I am not in control of my lower body.

No, stop—not now—

"You seek to harm my mate?"

The growl of the monster inside me freezes all of us, and

my face twists with my struggle to lock him back inside the walls, to keep him from Lillian's friends.

Who are you?! At once, Dean's face morphs into suspicion, and he clutches Tiffany closer, twisting his body to maneuver her away from Phorkys's grasp climbing up his thigh.

Stop...it... I growl, gritting my teeth. *Let him go...!*

The rumble in my chest is louder than the engines of the shipping vessels that cross these waters. It pushes out everything in my mind, enough that I think I might shift, might lose myself once more to the titan's will.

Lillian commanded you!

The growl stops, and the fear in Dean's eyes relaxes just a bit. I feel the monster rescind His control over my limbs, and I withdraw the grip on the human's leg.

"It is of no use, regardless," He snarls, voice still echoing around us despite it retreating from my mind. **"Fighting Her is futile. You will only accelerate your own demise."**

Tiffany grips her lover's back so tightly her knuckles go white. And yet, Dean still places her into my arms. They kiss one last time, and I am certain they are exchanging goodbyes that I am not privy to. He pries her arms from their circle about his shoulders, and with one last nod to me, swims up and away, leaving us hovering above the lake floor.

The woman in my arms seems to shatter in slow motion, curling into a ball inside my arms and burrowing her head into her arms.

I know my words will be of little comfort to her, monster that I am. Even now, I can feel Phorkys fuming beneath the surface, torn between His love for His mate and the demands of His brood mother.

I will take you to Lillian.

For a brief moment, a flicker of relief and gratitude sweeps over her face, and the fire in her eyes alludes to the beauty lying dormant beneath her sallow skin.

In that moment, I see a hint of the woman who has earned my treasure's friendship. Her mate's respect.

This is a strong woman—a beautiful woman—but she has suffered greatly.

It is time to right that injustice.

CHAPTER 14

DEAN

I gasp for air as I finally surface from the lake, lungs burning from the strain as my body rejects it at first. Coughing, water spewing from inside as my body figures out it's on land again, I crawl onto the beach.

We're out. We're safe. *Free.*

No, I remind myself, the image of Tiffany being swept away in that muscly Viking's arms burning in my brain and sending my anxiety skyrocketing, even though I know she'll be safer with Lillian than she'll be with me.

Because I'm in the middle of fucking nowhere.

A glance around this sparsely wooded island is enough to see that I'm far from the cabin that Tiffany and Lillian timeshare. Judging by the skyline around me, I'm still surrounded by Lake Superior, miles from the Upper Peninsula where all of my supplies hide in the bed of my pickup.

Dammit.

I should have known better than to keep all of my hunting gear in one place. While it's true I didn't have any more *omphalos* stones hiding in there, I did have a couple of old treasures I'd brought for extra safety. A vest sewn from an old lion skin. A hunting knife forged from the remnants of steel passed down from the first generation of our family to immigrate to the U.S., which may have contained some blessed iron.

Dad always said not to put all your eggs in one basket. And here I am, kicking myself for thinking that stupid gas-guzzler was a safe enough bet to pack all of my precious, life-saving eggs in for the trip.

Well. What would Dad do now?

His voice comes ringing back to me like an old friend: *"You aren't always going to have your weapons on hand, son, which means you'll need to be resourceful. If there's one thing these monsters love, it's using their environment. You're going to have to learn how to beat them at their own game."*

I already did that once, with the ring. It pulls on my pinky, almost as if it had been made light by the thread of magic connecting it to the gods, but now that it's severed, weighs heavier than the densest stone.

I wish I had pants. A pocket would be a boon right now.

But I don't have any clothes. I'm buck naked, save for a couple sapphires and a broken marble on my pinky ring. Right. So, what's available to me right now on this island?

A rustling a few yards away draws my attention to the treeline—and a bird flits between low branches.

Okay, so we have trees. That's wood. Wood can turn into anything: a shiv, a handle. That's...something.

A quick scan across the narrow strip of sand bordering the water doesn't inspire any other brain blasts.

Fuck. Am I about to have to fight a titan with a whittled shiv?

Above me, the waxing gibbous moon lights up the clear navy sky, sprinkled with glowing stars and gaseous swirls.

But it's almost sunk to the treeline, meaning dawn isn't far away.

I stare at the giant orb, calculating its mass and mentally dividing the missing crescent into slivers. How many days do we have until Lillian gives birth? Three? Four?

Is it enough?

The branches rustle, and a solitary tweet sounds in the quiet forest. *Probably that same weird nocturnal bird.*

Well, Dean, you got three days to figure out how to kill a Titan. Best get to work.

I TOSS ASIDE another splintery branch, cursing my lack of tools. I scratch my upper arm, momentarily relieving the cry of one of many mosquito bites I've sustained since sunrise. Thankfully, the midmorning blaze seems to have deterred the swarm I encountered just before dawn, leaving me with a million itchy welts that I'm trying—and failing —to ignore.

I'm irritable. Hungry. Itchy. Sore. Exhausted. And none of the twigs I've found that are soft enough to be carved by the couple of sharp pebbles lining the beach are strong enough to shape into shivs. Furious, I drop my rocks into the sand and throw my last few sticks back out into the treeline.

An annoyed peep rings out, making me jump. The little bluebird that's been following me since I landed on shore hops angrily toward me, scolding me with its song.

"Sorry," I tell it, before shaking my head. *Am I seriously apologizing to a bird?* "Usually I'm better equipped than this. I'm frustrated."

Yep. I'm talking to a bird. It gives a sympathetic tweet and rests its little feathered head on my shin as I hang my head in my hands.

I've *always* been prepared. I've trained for just about every emergency survival situation one *can* train for. But learning to survive is not the same as learning to wage a one-man war on a magical underwater sex goddess.

By the time I came to in Keto's cave, I'd already been stripped of all my clothing and possessions. Tiffany and I were tied up, rendered helpless by our captor. I wouldn't be surprised if the hunting knife I'd been wearing on my belt was drifting somewhere along the lake floor on the coast of Canada by now, along with my paracord anklet and multi-tool keyring.

And trying to find stones that are sharp enough to whittle these sticks is next to impossible. I'm not whittling, I'm peeling bark with friction. Despite their volcanic origin, these stones just aren't hard enough to do what I'm asking of them. Millennia of freshwater tides have worn down Superior's rocky beaches to soft agate pebbles and sand.

Even if I could carve something decent shape-wise, the woods around here are mostly soft: pinewood, ash, birch, and saplings—maybe springy enough to make a decent arrow or two, but nothing nearly so hearty as I'd want for a stabbing weapon.

What else even is there around here? Bone? Please. The wildlife on this tiny ass island is severely lacking. Other than my little winged stalker who's too stupid to know it's time to fly south for winter already, I've seen approximately three rodents and a shitton of bugs. There aren't even deer here—we're too far from shore, and there isn't enough greenery around on this tiny little strip of land to sustain them.

My feet ache from wandering around this wasteland, my skin itchy, cold, and clammy from the damp autumn air. Even my butt is numb from perching on this rotting log on the beach while I work, freezing the backs of my thighs while I sniffle helplessly into nightfall.

I'd give just about anything for a cellphone. A knife. *Even a cheeseburger...* my stomach grumbles as I eye the orange glare of the sun hanging low in the sky. How long has it been since I've eaten a good meal? And how long, before that, since I had enough calories to sustain me?

I eye Tweety out of the corner of my eye, oblivious to my hungry thoughts. Hopping around my graveyard of sticks, pecking at the pebbles in between.

Enough wallowing. I made it out, and now I need a plan. Tiffany is counting on me. Lillian is, too. Assuming her Viking shifter can't get her out of this, which is probably safe, considering she agreed to play surrogate to Keto in the first place.

What's the story *there*, I wonder?

Lillian's been single for as long as I've known her; that's part of why I'm so surprised it took Tiff this long to admit her feelings for her. I wonder how serious she and that guy are. If he's anything like me and Tiff, open to multiple partners.

My stomach flips a little at imagining not just Tiffany and Lillian, but also a fully human version of *him* lounging in bed with the three of us. Turning Lil into putty with his fingers while she and Tiff make out. And me, crawling toward the three of them, stroking myself as I line the head of my cock up with his...

I jolt at a tug in my lower belly, and I shake the vision from my head. I'm probably just hungry. I ought to hunt some dinner.

Provided I can find a weapon better than a wet stick.

"Aurgh!" I cry, when yet another attempt at carving a spear ends in a pile of splinters and a cramped hand, startling the everpresent bird away from my lap again. "What am I supposed to do? I need to save them!"

Wrapping my fingers around the sides of the flat rock I'd been using as a thumb knife, I fling it far out into the tide. It skips two, three, four times before stuttering into the horizon. The last vestiges of sun burn my retinas as I stare after it.

"Guide me, Zeus," I pray, finally turning to my last resort. "Help me as you once did my ancestors."

Tiffany's dismissal of my faith still rings in my head, a reminder that we are well and truly fucked if I can't find a way to get us all out of here. I stare out into the inland sea, feeling more scared and hopeless than I ever have in my life.

Then there's a sharp peck at my foot.

"Ow!" I whip around to see Tweety once again, looking at me with those vacant, black-button eyes. Only now, it's tilting its head at me curiously. Like it wants to talk or something.

Delirious. I'm clearly delirious with hunger. "What? What do you want?"

To my surprise, the bird actually opens its beak and sings out a few notes.

I must be hallucinating. Because the song coming out of it doesn't sound like birdsong to me. No, the notes actually string together something like a melody—something almost *jazzy*—and I'm about to kick it away when I start to hear actual *words*.

"Your prayer is important to us. Please remain on the line as our menu options have changed."

My jaw falls open so wide, I'm surprised I don't taste

sand. I hear it *pop* as my mouth falls slack, disbelief the only plausible reaction to what I just saw. "Wait a minute. Are you—?"

But I shut it just as quickly as the words continue.

"Thank you for praying to the King of Olympus. If this is a mortal emergency, hang up and use a landline or mobile phone to dial human emergency services. If you are planning a sacrifice, say "sacrificial inquiry." If you are scheduling a physical tournament in honor of an ouranic or cthonic deity, say "Olympic games." If you are a descendant of Zeus, say "Child support services.""

I blink, completely frozen as I stare at the open beak of the bluebird. Is this—am I actually listening to an automated answering service *for the gods?!*

"If you would like to arrange a meeting with the Oracle—"

I scramble to answer before it plays on past my option. "Child support services!"

"Connecting you to child support services. Your call will be forwarded in the order it was received."

More jazzy music, and then, "we're experiencing an above-average volume of calls. Please remain on the line until we can connect you to an available acolyte."

The bird's beak freezes open as an enthusiastic trumpet solo takes over, and I guess that means I'm back on hold.

I have so many questions.

But the one at the forefront of my mind is, *why did Dad never tell me about this?*

I've been training for decades, all in service of the gods —hell, my family has been training for *millennia*—and the whole time, the *whole fucking time,* there was a frickin' Olympian call center?!

A click, and the music and bird pause. Then, a new

voice, this one *not* pre-recorded, speaks. As it does, Tweety clicks his beak and adopts mannerisms as if *it's* the one talking. ITs head tilts as it shrugs its wings and holds them bent in front of its body, splaying its feathers out like it's about to get a manicure.

It's terrifying.

"Thank you for waiting. Before we begin, can you name the demigod from which your line descends?"

"Uh... Perseus?" I sound out the name one syllable at a time, still gaping in disbelief, as the bird awaits my answer with those creepy, unblinking black eyes.

"Perseus...Perseus..." the sounds of key clicks accompany little twitches from the feathers on the bird's wings. "We'll need you to provide a blood sample for a paternity test. Please present your finger to the messenger mascot so we can process the validity of your request."

"Wha–?" Before I can answer, Tweety hops up and delivers a hard peck to my thumb. "Ow!"

A tiny tongue darts out, licking up the bead of blood that wells from my finger, and the wound instantly starts to seal back up. My mouth gapes again, and I begin to wonder if the gills Keto gave me actually made me part fish.

"Please hold while we process your sample."

Again, Tweety freezes with his mouth open and the jazz picks back up. I'm still staring at the shiny pink welt on my thumb, in shock.

What the actual fuck is going on right now?

"Congratulations! You have been confirmed as a descendent of Perseus." A little pre-recorded fanfare sounds and Tweety flaps his wings. "You contain approximately 0.00081 percent Olympian blood. What is the nature of your call?"

Well that was quick.

It takes me a second to get my thoughts together before I can answer the acolyte. Truth be told, part of my delay comes from the disbelief that I'd need to prove my bloodline *at all* to these people. How many descendants of the literal gods could there possibly be? And how many humans in today's day and age would be trying to fake their Olympian heritage to get child support from Zeus?

We're experiencing an above-average volume of calls, they'd said.

How many calls do they *normally* receive?

"Sorry, I'm a little new to this...uh, first time caller and all that. But my pregnant fiancée and her best friend have been kidnapped by a titan, and I need to save them."

"Which titan are you experiencing issues with?"

"Uh. Keto."

"Can you spell that for me, please?"

I roll my eyes. *How the fuck am I supposed to know how to spell it?* I grit my teeth, holding back a groan. "My ancient Greek is a little rusty."

"The anglicized alphabet is fine, son of Perseus."

I breathe out through my nose. "K-E-T-O."

"Hmm. Nothing's coming up in the titanic database for that name."

I feel a muscle in my cheek tick. "Try C-E-T-O?"

More key clicks, more finger-like feather twitches like Tweedy's typing at a keyboard, and then: "Ah, here we go. Ceto, daughter of Pontus and Gaia. Mother of the Gorgons, Echidna, Ladon, and the Graeae. I see the reason for your confusion. What you're dealing with is a primordial sea goddess, not a titan. Easy to mix those two up. Is that the only primordial deity you're in conflict with?"

"No, uh, her consort Phorkys is also here."

"Spell that for me?"

I massage my temples. "Look, ma'am, I don't have time for this. Maybe you missed the part where a *titan kidnapped my fiancee–*"

"Primordial sea goddess."

I'm about to strangle the little bird and its creepy anthropomorphic face, when the acolyte on the line sighs.

"Alright, Son of Perseus, understood. As a descendant whose bloodline retains a purity of under 100 generations, per the settlement of Jackson et al v. Olympus, you are entitled to receive one weapon blessed by the gods. You can choose from the following list, or if you prefer a holy shield, I can have a courier deliver it to you within three to five business days.

"Your options are–"

"Three to five business days??" I shout, causing the bird to hop back a little on the rotting log. "I'm in danger *now*; I need a weapon ASAP! They're about to release a whole hoard of monsters on the midwest!"

"I'm sorry, did you say hoard?"

I let out a huff of relief. "Yes, Ceto's brood. My fiancee's friend has been impregnated with her entire clutch."

"Impregnated."

"*Yes.*"

"With a titanic clutch?"

"I've been told the correct term is *primordial sea goddess,*" I sneer.

"Please hold."

Sensing my simmering anger, Tweety hops up to the nearest branch that's out of my reach as the jazz music kicks back up. My hands are shaking, and I pace for what seems like hours on the sandy beach as the over-compressed saxophone crackles through the cool air of the forest. I swear I've heard the same lick about a hundred times now, and my stomach is cramping with hunger.

By the time the acolyte hops back on the line, the sun has set beyond the horizon, and I can just barely make out the glint in Tweety's eye reflecting in the dusk.

It flutters back down to the beach. "Are you still there, Son of Perseus?"

"Yes," I grind out.

"Thank you for holding. Due to the nature of your request, we've escalated the urgency of your child support claim. Your delivery of **The Golden Sword**–" a pre-recorded, siren-like voice delivers the name of the weapon, before returning to that of the support acolyte, "has been upgraded to Hermes Plus. Expect a courier in the morning with your heirloom weapon. Is there anything else I can assist you with today?"

"Wait, that's it?" My frustration from earlier boils back up into rage as I gape at the silhouette of the bird. "You've got humans out here, battling literal armies of primordial god monsters on earth in the name of Zeus, and your solution is to send me *one* sword via overnight Fedex?"

"If you're dissatisfied with your service, I can direct you to a survey–"

I snatch the bird from the log and punt it back into the forest, the voice of the acolyte cutting off with a distressed squawk.

This is bullshit. Bull. Shit.

Since I was old enough to talk, I've been learning the names of the gods. The importance of Zeus's legacy. My role, as an Olympian descendant, to protect humanity and destroy the enemies of our ancestors.

And despite all my doubts, despite the years—decades —of resentment, when I found out that it actually was all real, that I actually was descended from a line of heroes and there were actual monsters out there that were a threat to humans everywhere, I believed that I was needed. That my training, that my legacy... I thought that maybe it made me, I don't know. *Special.*

Sure, the world was full of terrifying monsters that threatened humankind, but *gods* existed. They've instructed their lineage to be ready to battle. And when the time comes, they'll bless us with the tools we need to overcome evil. To fight the good fight.

But as I sit in the dark, on the same crumbling driftwood log without even Tweety to keep me company, the emotions I pushed down during the phone call crawl back up to haunt me. The implications of what just happened begin to sink in.

If you're a descendant of Zeus, say "child support services."

How many of us are out there? Fighting the gods' battles? Wrestling with beings a million times stronger than ourselves? With blood watered down by almost a hundred generations of humans weakening our power?

There in the dark, another feeling presses in on me. One I've been fighting since Tiffany first came running back to me on the beach, tears streaming down her face.

"She's gone, Dean! Lillian, she's—she's been taken!"

Fear.

Paralyzing fear. The kind of all-consuming, body-freezing fear that makes it impossible to do anything, even when a giant sea monster rises from the tides of Lake Superior and snatches you and your fiancée right off the beach.

What if I'm not enough to save them? What if all of this training, all of my life, has been for nothing?

If my hero's journey is so mundane that its call to

adventure is handled by a literal *call center,* what hope do I actually have of success?

Dad didn't prepare me for this. He couldn't have. Nothing could have prepared me for the pure dread coursing through my veins.

A cry, deep and tortured and inhuman, rends itself from the water beyond, startling me out of my spiral.

Tiffany!

Hermes himself couldn't fly me that sword quick enough.

CHAPTER 15
TIFFANY

I can't swim nearly as quickly as Erik. I unwound myself from his arms soon after Dean swam out of sight, not yet comfortable with this strange man's hands on my body. I'm not so sure I want any strangers with tentacles touching me after all that I've been through.

Trapped in Keto's cave for weeks, barely eating enough to stay alive, I didn't realize how much strength I'd lost.

But of course, my body isn't just trying to keep me alive anymore. It's also trying to grow an entirely *new* life.

I can hardly remember the last day I felt like I had energy. Lying in the sun, on the beach, drinking seltzers and reading romance novels with Lillian beside me. God, I will never take sunshine for granted again. Being trapped underwater like this, in the dark...

The longer we swim—slowly, of course, because Erik is keeping pace with me—I begin to inventory my body. Almost welcoming each new ache as it alerts me to a part I'd forgotten about, being strung up in Keto's weightless prison. My arms start to burn from paddling my way through the water, my ankles tweaking a bit as I kick, trying to command them to perform with strength I don't have anymore.

I've been suspended from a wall. The only muscles that have seen any kind of work have been the ones between my legs while Keto tries to get me to beg and scream her name.

Swimming like this... it hurts, it burns, but it also reminds me that I'm alive. That I'm more than just a victim.

Dean and Lillian aren't the only ones that can fight for our freedom. I don't have to be useless. I can help to get us out of here, too.

I don't know if it's out of solidarity or pity, but Erik's gotten rid of the octopus limbs and is instead just a burly, giant man cutting his way through the water with practiced strokes and kicks, almost lazily drifting like this is just a casual swim. Granted, I doubt I could keep up if he was making any real effort, even if I wasn't half-starved, what with him and all his rippling pectorals.

I've yet to really talk to the guy. I have some vague, fuzzy memories of seeing him in the showdown between Keto, Lillian, and I, when she swapped the terms on our deal. When Lillian sacrificed her body for me.

The whole time, he looked positively tortured. Eyes only for my best friend as she agreed to have the monsters' babies.

So... you and Lillian.

His shoulders stiffen, smooth strokes stuttering for the first time since he took me from Dean. He turns his head back to look at me, eyes sparkling a pretty grey as he considers my question. The first thing either of us has said to another on this little swim.

Yes. My treasure. A smile ghosts his lips briefly as he waits for me to catch up to him. *We met on one of the small islands in the middle of the lake. She is a magnificent woman.*

When her leg cramped as she attempted to swim back to camp, I...

In spite of myself, my heart warms to hear the way he talks about her. "My treasure," he said. A pang of jealousy works its way through my stomach as I think about the two of them together.

Not that I have any right to claim her as mine. Even with Dean's blessing, I can't expect Lillian to treat me with anything other than caution. I can't even say she's my best friend anymore, after the way I treated her.

I look over at Erik, the pained look on his face.

You saved her.

It isn't a question. I *know* if it weren't for him, she'd have drowned after our fight.

He meets my eyes.

As did you, once.

I've caught up now, and we resume an easy pace across the lake floor. Occasionally, I kick at a boulder beneath us to get an extra boost of speed. My arms are practically worthless down here, and my gills are working overtime to get enough oxygen to my straining lungs. This is *not* a short trip. Keto really had us isolated from everyone else.

I can hardly say so anymore. My deal didn't help her. It just numbed her for a while. And now, because of me, she...

Tears burn at the back of my throat, and I can't think about it anymore. This whole mess is my fault, and mine alone. I deserve every ounce of suffering for what I've done.

Lillian confessed to me her pain. I have seen how it can consume her. Grief like that... even a small respite from it is a gift. You granted her that. You sacrificed much to do so.

So much for that, I scoff, trying to kick off another stone on the ground and just stubbing my toe instead. *Ow!*

He twists to a stop immediately as I crouch to cradle my

foot. It isn't bleeding, but all this time underwater and the pregnancy have weakened my nails something fierce, and my stubbed toe is mangled. He swims up beneath me, gently taking my ankle and examining me, before carefully raising his gaze to mine.

Somehow, he avoids staring at my bits, despite his face being inches from them.

Damn. A real gentleman.

Perhaps it would be best if I carry you? I can transform—

No!

My response is a little too quick, a little too frightened, my heartrate ratcheting up to a thousand and the thought of having tentacles wrapped around me again. I don't like the other reactions my body has, the pulse between my legs and the Pavlovian spike of arousal that seems to happen whenever I think about those suckers getting anywhere near me...

Erik senses my hesitation, but I don't miss his pupils widening, almost overtaking the grey in his eyes. Fuck. Can he *smell* me? Are his senses as heightened as Keto's are?

Why does that thought make me even *wetter?*

God, I'm fucked up.

Erik straightens, floating up until we're eye-to-eye. He places a meaty hand on my shoulder, sending a shiver down my spine as he meets my gaze.

Tiffany. I would never hurt you. I wouldn't touch you with them. I can keep my human arms for carrying you. But you are clearly weakened, and now injured. This would get you to Lillian's side faster.

Right! Lillian.

This is Lillian's boyfriend. She's his... treasure.

And my fiancé is gods-knows-where, trying to find a

way to defeat a monster when he's just as weak and naked and vulnerable as I am.

While *I* get turned on from thinking about my best friend's boyfriend's tentacles.

Yep. Completely and totally fucked-up.

Dean's and my conversation about confessing my feelings for Lillian feels like it happened years ago. After talking with her boyfriend, and seeing how much stronger and better he is for her than I could ever be...

Lillian deserves someone like *this*. Someone who only has eyes for her, who cherishes her the way she ought to be cherished. Who is fighting tooth and nail to protect her, even when he's half-possessed by a monster.

Fuck, how did I get myself in this mess?

I'm too flustered and tired to respond, so Erik gathers me in his arms—as gently and non-sexually as possible—and before I know it, we're rocketing through the water at easily four times the speed we were before. I don't even notice his lack of human limbs beneath me, aside from the teensiest hint of muscles I can feel, just barely, flexing underneath me as his tentacles propel us to Lillian.

Hopefully, once I see her safe and sound in her little pregnancy nest, my brain will be able to process this better. My body will recognize that she's happier without me, and then I'll finally be content with the love that I have.

I'll be able to think and get stronger. I won't be dead weight anymore.

Assuming Keto doesn't find us first.

CHAPTER 16

KETO

My heart is light as I hunt for Tiffany's sustenance in my territory's waters.

The revelation of her lovers' origins was something of a surprise, I will admit. Zeus's bloodline is powerful, and I have been unable to harm them directly since I was cast out from the Olympians' graces thousands of years ago.

But my minnow does not suffer from that weakness. And I have granted her all the tools she needs to remove that complication for me.

And soon, I shall have my brood, my consort, and my birthright after all these years. My domain. My *kingdom*.

As always is the case when my mind wanders, I arrive at the site of my palace. The home of my future children. A mere two days until the dream that was so cruelly taken from me comes to fruition at last.

I can picture it. Even more beautiful than Atlantis, my Kingdom shall be.

I place my hand on one of the columns, imagining the

palace filled with my beautiful progeny and their children. Generations of perfect beings, in my image.

And at the head of it all, their matriarch, their queen. I will at last be shown the love and worship that I deserve...

WHEN IT WAS ANNOUNCED that I was to be Poseidon's wife, it was declared that I would be wed upon the confirmation of my fertility. The King of the Seas was to sire a new generation of gods and goddesses, a loyal lineage that could bring about a new era of prosperity for the sister Kingdom of Olympus. As the daughter of Gaia and Mother Earth herself, I assured the gods that I would be the perfect mother for this blessed generation.

So, we waited.

While it is true that my cycles are fertile, they are rare. Hera wanted us to wait until I was most likely to conceive a brood. Yet I was sure it would not be long: my maturity was apparent in my body. My blood was more ancient, more pure than that of the fickle Olympians, and as such, it took time for my eggs to develop. I was determined to bear only the best children for my king.

So as my body ripened, we prepared for the wedding of the millennium.

The day of our union approached in a haze of bliss. Hera, prurient bitch that she was, refused to honor our marriage unless I remained chaste: a slap in the face to our mother before us, who had birthed half the Olympians and previous gods to various sires. Zeus's queen insisted I practice abstinence until our wedding night to retain the purity of Poseidon's line. And I, foolish and humbled by her presence, obeyed.

But while we never fully consummated our union, we did enjoy practicing.

Night after night, I would sneak into bed by Poseidon's side. Learning his preferences. Teasing him in his royal chambers. My betrothed was a magnificent lover, and he yearned to fill me with his royal seed. But I wouldn't break my promise to Hera.

Ours was to be a mighty kingdom, greater than all the chthonic realms. I wouldn't let one premature night of passion ruin our vision of the future.

Every night, he'd whisper in my ear as he licked and kissed and teased my body again and again:

Mother of my children,

Bride by my side,

Queen of my kingdom,

The most beautiful in all the seven seas.

He was not the only one who grew impatient with our engagement. I craved it: his spawn. I wanted nothing more than to propagate the seas with Poseidon's perfect children, our Olympian horde, to dominate Atlantis and Olympus as one. My mother Gaia was fertility Herself, and I was more than ready to bear his blessed young.

So why, in all the worlds, was it taking so long to bloom into fertility?

The months before our nuptials stretched on and on, drawing him to his breaking point. He became irritable, frustrated. At times, he even sought to throw me from his chambers because the temptation was too great.

"I assure you, my King, I will bear you multitudes in time! Our union will be everything you desire and more. Such heirs as you cannot imagine!"

"I hear your promises, but I cannot bear the torture of you beside me another moment. Until your womb is

ready for my seed, until we can become one as blessed by Olympus, I cast you from my chambers. Leave me, my love. If you will not bed me properly, then I will not tolerate your torturous presence in my chambers."

Weeks passed, days that stretched like years without my love by my side. I appealed to Hera that we might wed sooner, but she was steadfast in her decision.

My eggs could not mature quickly enough.

When I felt it, the tell-tale yearning in my loins that spelled the waxing of my womb, I informed Hera immediately. She announced the wedding would commence in three days' time.

At last, I would be one with my perfect mate.

Atlantis was abuzz with activity, gods and goddesses scrambling about in preparations for the most magnificent ceremony since the union of Zeus and Hera herself. I did not see my betrothed for the entirety, and by the eve of the celebration, I longed for him terribly.

As we prepared my ceremonial garments, I caught a glimpse of my Poseidon in the hall. So eager to wrap him in my arms, to share our excitement together, I raced out of my dressing chambers to catch him.

I cut through the water like a swordfish, ignoring the pleas of my seamstresses to mind the pieces of my bridal gown. Despite their warnings, I couldn't care less about the senseless adornments. I could feel the stitches stretch to the point of tearing as I raced to follow him, turning down hall after hall in my search, but I didn't care.

All I wanted was to feel that light in my heart again, to meet his sparkling sapphire gaze with my own and glory in the ecstasy of his full attention.

I couldn't wait another moment.

"My king! My king!" I crashed into his chambers, voice

alight with love and joy. I longed to see it written on his face, his pleasure buried in the dimples of his cheeks, when at last we were reunited. "It is—"

There are no words to describe the feeling when I saw her in his bed. *My* bed.

Aside from the death of my children, I have known no greater pain.

Little more than a *nymph*. Lounging naked, her light blue legs spread wide for his enjoyment. And my betrothed, my perfect mate, standing before her, thrusting into her and wasting his divine seed on her whore cunt.

"Get out!" I shrieked, ivory gown ripping to shreds about my body. I grew rapidly, my head and shoulders cracking the marble ceiling as I embraced my titanic form. *"Out!"*

Amphitrite could no more than shake and shudder beneath my rage. As she should. I was not merely the most beautiful of the primordial goddesses. I was the most fearsome. The most powerful.

She did not stand a chance against my might. And *he*—

He shielded her.

Protected her.

"Calm yourself, Ceto!" His voice, that beautiful voice, which once showered me with praise and poetry, cut into my heart like a dagger. I gaped at him, the anger twisting his features, not one dimple hinting at the humor in his heart.

Anger, and something else. Something even more cutting.

Pity.

But why? *Why?* I was to be his bride. I was the most perfect, the most beautiful, selected by his own hand.

"Get away from her!"

"She is my lover."

He said it so calmly, so plainly—as if it wasn't a declaration of my inferiority.

"You cannot expect me to *share* you, my king?" Surely this was a misunderstanding. She would leave his chambers—*our* chambers—this instant, never to return. **"You are mine. As I am yours."**

And then that look again. More cruel than the hottest rage.

Pity.

"I am King, Ceto. I belong to no one but the sea."

I scoffed. My father *was* the sea, and I was as much the inheritor of his legacy as anyone. For Poseidon to claim that he was somehow above me, above the titans who bore him...

Even after the titanomachy, I would not treat this slight as anything other than the betrayal it was.

I felt my claws rupture from my fingertips as I flexed my many limbs. **"I will kill any woman who seeks to know you as I am promised to know you."** I stalked across the room, pointing at the nymph.

Such a waifish little thing. As easy to slice as a filet of flounder. I would make an example of her.

But he was in my way. Blocking my path.

Cruelty shined in his eyes as he scowled at me. His voice, commanding and calm, crackled out like thunder. **"You are not to harm my consort."**

"*I* am your consort!" I bellowed. My tentacles tore through the room, upending bed and vanity alike, reaching around and across, over and under, but unable to break past him to reach their intended prey.

Only Poseidon was strong enough to hold me back. And that's exactly what he did.

How could he do this? How could he shield that whore? That *abomination*? On the eve of our wedding?

My King. My husband.

Cheater.

"You are my *subject!*" He leveled his trident and in a flash of molten heat, cast me from the room. The force of it blew me back, striking my heart like a wrecking ball. I crumpled, helpless to the strength of the anointed King of the Seas and the holy powers of Olympus granted him by the Usurper. **"And you will learn your place!"**

But I would not kowtow. For I was the Queen of the Oceans, whether or not I wore his ring upon my claw.

Yet I could not stand. Crawling towards him, curses scraped past my throat.

"I am no one's subject!"

"Then let your words be your sentence."

Another flourish from his three-pronged scepter, and I was cast from Atlantis forever. My body shot through the walls of his chambers, scattering debris about the entire castle. I did not, could not, slow until I'd been blown past the edges of the sacred Kingdom.

For days, I threw myself at the wards. Again and again, until my body ached. Until my wedding gown was merely threads clinging to my shoulders. Until my womb grew heavy and full with my unfertilized brood, I pounded against the gates of Atlantis.

Again and again and again.

Only my brother, Phorkys, took pity on me. Comforted me. He followed me into exile, out into the open ocean, far from the blessings of our brethren.

When I could no longer stand to carry the weight of my unwanted progeny, it was Phorkys who bed me. He sired our young, who forged their own path back into the Olympians' domain.

Beloved, he called me. **Treasured.**

And I was so broken, so alone. So vulnerable. I let him comfort me, his sweet words a balm on an unmendable wound.

Let us leave here, and find the seas where you may rule unchallenged. My goddess...

For many years, I fought it. My brother's call to leave the Aegean sea for good. Our home. Our birthright.

For years, I grimaced through rumors of each and every affair of our great King.

But when I heard rumors of Poseidon bedding my daughter, Medusa, sprouted from the very brood that should have been his, and me unable to lift even a finger against it... I finally broke.

My own daughter. Chosen over me, the goddess of the seas.

And what was her reward?

Death, at the hands of Poseidon's own nephew. Family killing family. Humans overpowering gods, *with their blessing*.

It wasn't until my womb grew heavy once again that I succumbed to Phorkys' pleading. **Please,** he begged. **We can raise these children outside of Olympus' influence. Far away. We shall find our own kingdom. Our sanctuary. Where no young god, demigod, or human will ever tread upon us again.**

Until now.

Godspeed, sweet minnow, I whisper to the waves, letting my intentions for Tiffany seep into the waters, blessing the knife I left in her capable hands. ***May you get your revenge on your Olympian, if I cannot get mine.***

I smile upon my domain, my own Atlantis, knowing that soon it will be filled with children that will never have to live under the thumb of those miserable gods.

CHAPTER 17

LILLIAN

ying alone in my makeshift nest gives me some time to think.

It's the first time I've been by myself in weeks. Or at least, the first time I've been alone and conscious. Usually, Erik and Phorkys don't leave me to hunt until they've tired me out with at least four or five orgasms.

Don't get me wrong: it's been pretty great, all things considered. The endless pleasure is enough to distract me from the discomfort of my expanding body, the squirming sensation of the monsters slowly developing in my womb. The aches and pains of my body straining to cope with the demands of not just one little life growing inside me, but *thousands*.

Not to mention the mental strain of it all.

All in all, I'd say I've done a pretty good job of not losing my fucking marbles over this entire situation. And yes, the orgasms help. But my two-in-one boyfriends have been right not to leave me alone to dwell on it all.

I can feel a spiral coming on, so I try to focus on them instead: Erik. Phorkys. Weirdly enough, the tentacled titan has started to grow on me a little. He's not just a monster. He's got a sentimental streak in that big-eyed, gelatinous head of His. I can feel His thoughts passing through to me while Erik sleeps within their body: dreams of meeting His children, hopes for their future, aspirations that He can be a better father to them than He was to His last brood.

That last bit tugs at my heartstrings every time. The guilt He feels for letting Keto's eggs get crushed in the storm that wrecked Erik's ship threads through every one of his thoughts. I'm amazed I never sensed it before.

He sings lullabies to the babies in my womb, when He thinks I'm asleep. Rocking my enormous belly in his long arms, picturing a future where He doesn't have to fear for their lives. One in which Keto loves him back.

I think that's the part that hurts me most of all. Despite sharing Erik's body for centuries, Phorkys has been alone that entire time. His own mate disowned Him, disgusted by His human form, His "weakness".

I was already wary of Keto, and obviously afraid of Her, but I can't help but feel a bit of anger for the way She just abandoned Her mate like that. I've known Erik for less than a month—tried once to leave him for my own safety—but I'd never intentionally give him the silent treatment for years on end for a decision he needed to make to stay alive.

Can She even say She loves Him, if that's how She treats Him?

When I think of Erik, my entire chest warms. My ever-attentive Viking boyfriend. He's been incredible through this whole ordeal. Still looks at me with nothing but love and heat in his eyes, even after the pregnancy has made my body all but unrecognizable.

It isn't just his muscles, strong jaw, and incredible dick:

Erik is hands-down the most caring and supportive man I've ever met. I don't know what I ever did to deserve him.

Stupid. You're carrying a litter of titan spawn to break his curse.

Am I foolish to believe that he'd be just as incredible even if we met under entirely normal circumstances? Even if he hadn't needed me to break his curse?

After all, he'd been willing to let me go before Keto brought us under. Would have given up his freedom entirely for me. More than anything else, that proves that our love for each other is more than just fate or destiny or prophecy.

It's real. And I'm so fucking lucky to have it.

So... why isn't it enough?

Tiffany...

My breath catches in my lungs every time I think of my best friend strung up in Keto's prison, waiting on me to finish this crazy ritual.

I can't help but suspect that something's changed with the female titan that rules Lake Superior. I'm not sure what it is, but the longer I'm pregnant with Her brood, the stronger vibes I get into Her psyche. It's like there's some kind of connection between us: similar to the connection I have with Erik and Phorkys, but void of love or lust.

This is different.

It's almost like sometimes... I can *see* what She sees. Feel Her power coursing through my veins. And at night, when I dream, I get... visions. Scenes that feel like memories from a past life.

Only, I don't think it's *my* past life I've been getting glimpses of.

It's *Hers.*

There's more to Her story that She hasn't told us. Not

me, not Tiffany, maybe not even Phorkys. She wasn't lying when She spoke of the pain of losing Her children, but there's more to Her history. Betrayal beyond whatever pain the humans have caused Her.

No, this was something from Her own people. Long ago.

But whenever I try to remember the dreams, no matter how vivid they felt while I was asleep, the faster the details slip through my fingers.

A new scent spikes on the current, and my heart leaps. *Erik!*

Erik, Phorkys, and...

Tiffany!

We're coming, my treasure. Both of us.

Is she okay?

She is alive. Weak, but safe now.

Now? Anger flares low in my belly, and as if the monsters inside me can sense the change in their home, little muscle spasms ricochet through my core. *What happened?*

I do not know the full story. We will need to ask her. But my treasure, be... gentle. She is not as strong as you.

By my sides, my fingers flex involuntarily.

Keto broke her promise.

She has not been keeping Tiffany safe.

And that is unforgivable.

CHAPTER 18

TIFFANY

When we enter the cave, three things strike me that I could have never prepared for.

First, Lillian is *huge*. And I'm not trying to be a bitch: I know she's always been a curvy type, but that's not at all what I'm talking about here. She's more than pregnant—she's *grown*. Whereas two weeks ago, she was my 5'7" best friend with wide hips, a magnificent rack, and a bit of a tummy, now she's...

Well, she's giant.

Probably eight or nine feet from head-to-toe now, she's half-reclined in a nest of lake plants. If it weren't for her head being propped up by a pillow of weeds at her head, I doubt I'd be able to see her face over her massive body.

It's never been clearer to me the sacrifice Lillian made to save me and Dean. She looks about a thousand months pregnant despite the mere three weeks she's been trapped here. Her stomach is huge, of course, and the rest of her has grown to match. Her boobs, which were always on the bigger side, are now ginormous, as if they're preparing for the task of breastfeeding her entire clutch of titan children.

Yet, somehow... it isn't a bad look.

Which brings me to the second thing: there's a magnetism about her, an undeniable tug in my core as I take her in. I know they say that pregnant women have something of a "glow" about them—to be honest, *as* a pregnant woman, I've assumed that's a load of bullshit. The only thing I see when I look in the mirror is a big stomach, swollen joints, and big ol' IKEA bags under my eyes.

But Lillian... she's nothing short of *stunning*.

Her form reminds me of those ancient fertility sculptures archeologists dig up from ancient civilizations. And while I've always found my best friend attractive, with her golden hair, deep blue eyes, and curves for days, *this* version of her holds an appeal that is altogether *instinctual*. Any doubts about my feelings for her jump out the window faster than I can even remember them.

I love this woman. I always have. And seeing her like this, this goddess-like being she's become... I can't even put words to it.

But there's one more shock to my system, and this one is perhaps even more shocking than everything else. It has nothing to do with my feelings, or her supernatural pregnancy.

Lillian is not just glowing from her impending motherhood.

She's *literally glowing*.

Her eyes shine a vibrant purple brighter than a neon sign. Way brighter than the moonlight that illuminated our journey here. It almost hurts to look at her, the color piercing through the inky water and forcing my hand up to block some of the brightness. Her hands are also glowing with a smoky purple haze, her fingers squeezed into fists and her brow drawn down into a furious, terrifying scowl.

What did She do to you?

The power in her voice makes my heart stop beating in my chest, and I quickly drop out of Erik's arms. He, too, is taken aback by her appearance, which gives me the impression that the purple lazer eyes and smoking hands are a new development.

What's happening to my best friend?

It's then that I realize she's shaking as she waits for an answer, and I force myself to take a breath through my gills.

No-nothing, Lil, she just–

This isn't nothing. The wrinkles in her forehead furrow deeper as she looks me over. As my eyes adjust to the light from her eyes, I realize her expression isn't just angry. She's worried.

Worried about me.

Tiffany, come here. Please. I need to know you're okay. Concern threads her words, and my chest squeezes for a whole different set of reasons.

All at once, it's like the last three years never even happened. The curse, the fight, the gills, none of it. Suddenly we aren't two women trapped in a breeding battle of the gods. We aren't two confused adults who can't parse out their relationship.

We're just best friends, who haven't seen each other in too long.

And I need her more than oxygen.

Lillian...

I rush to her side, and her arm wraps around me, pulling me into her soft, comforting body. I can barely wrap around her in this new giant form, but I do my best to squeeze an arm around her back and one lightly across her stomach. The sound of muffled sniffling reverberates at the crown of my head, and I feel her lips kiss my hair.

Her voice is more gentle, more human when she speaks into my mind again.

I've missed you so much!

I've missed you, too!

I press my arms tighter around her, and she hugs me harder in return. Then, she's lifting me in front of her, until I'm floating above her body and in front of her face. Her eyes, a more manageable shade of indigo now—something between the glowing purple and their natural blue—are shiny with unshed tears.

My belly bumps hers as I bob in her grip, and a giggle pops out of my mouth, sending a tiny stream of bubbles into her face.

She laughs at that, and pretty soon we're both cracking up, dozens of bubbles obscuring our view of each other. I feel him before I see Erik swim up to Lillian's side, stroking her halo of golden hair from her face and tucking it behind her ear. A gesture that's wholly affectionate, seeing as it just floats right back to where it was.

You're here, she whispers, and I know it's only to me. I nod.

You saved me. I gesture to Erik, and he smiles at us both. *Again.*

I haven't saved anyone yet. We're still at Keto's mercy until the full moon. Her voice hardens, and the scowl is back. She tilts her head. *Where's Dean?*

I take another breath, the brief moment of levity completely wiped away. *Gone. Off to find some way to kill Her.*

He cannot kill her!

Erik's eyes glow blue as a new voice enters the chat. I wince.

Yeah, Tiff. Great fuckin' idea. Alert the other *Titan in the room that your boyfriend is off to kill His mate.*

Granted, I'd kinda forgotten that Erik was sharing his body with Keto's consort. I even momentarily forgot about his creepy tentacles. Being in her presence again, laughing with her, I could almost convince myself that we're just two besties again hanging out with her new merman boyfriend —not that there's a powerful monster living inside of him making him that way.

I've had other things on my mind.

I share a look with Lillian, trying to fill her in on everything that's happened without words. But of course, that's impossible. Even *with* words, how could I possibly explain to her that Dean's apparently descended from the ancient Greek hero, Perseus, and oh—by the way, the Greek gods we learned about in English class are real, and my boyfriend can talk to them when he prays—and he went off to the surface to try to commune with Zeus?

And if I *were* to try to say it via mind-speak, something tells me Erik's pet titan wouldn't take too kindly to that.

I can't forget that, even if I'm safe from Keto for the moment, none of us are completely safe as long as Phorkys is still in our presence.

Erik's face twists, and the monster's voice rumbles through our heads again. **No human could possibly defeat Her. She is far too powerful. Your mate is a fool.**

Yeah, I sigh, taking His dismissal as a gift. Hopefully, if He isn't threatened by Dean, He won't try too hard to get him out of the picture. *You can say that again.*

Lillian's eyeing me, but I avoid meeting her gaze. Instead, I wind up staring at her chest. It's not a better option, certainly not a polite one, but there isn't exactly anywhere I can stare right now that *is*. And if I let her look into my eyes, I know she'll see the angst hiding there. The confusion. The anger. The fear.

I may not agree with everything Dean's doing right now. I may not fully understand what he was trying to tell me about being descended from Perseus or having gods' blood or whatever. But I can't deny that that ring with the god stone in it *did* break Keto's barrier. Just like I can't deny that I love him.

I wouldn't have almost given up my friendship with Lillian if I didn't.

But now, here, lying in her arms and remembering all the reasons I love her in the first place, I'm so glad that I don't have to give her up after all. We still have a lot to talk about, obviously—she's in a relationship now, and that means that I may never get to express my true feelings for her.

But I don't have to push her away. I don't have to lie to Dean about it. And that's something.

It might even be enough.

Fingers thread into my hair, stroking at my scalp and sending a shiver down my spine. She's comforting me, and I can't express how grateful I am for it. My eyes close instantly, savoring the easy, gentle touch after too many days and nights of contact that's been less than loving.

I nuzzle into her embrace, suddenly so, *so* tired that I can hardly keep my eyes open anymore.

Erik? Phorkys? She says, still tickling my hair with gentle scratches. *I'm hungry. And Tiffany looks like she could use about twelve dinners tonight.*

Erik nods, blinking away the last traces of his titan self before pressing his lips to hers and swimming away.

She waits a moment, eyes distant as she stares off after his retreat until she's sure they've left the cave. Then she tucks her fingers under my chin, lifts my face, and levels her gaze on me.

Alright. Now that they're gone, spill. What the fuck do you mean Dean went off to kill Keto?

CHAPTER 19
DEAN

After the most freezing, fitful night of sleep I've ever had, plagued by restless nightmares of Tiffany and Lillian getting eaten by faceless squid-like monsters, the sun rises. And I, shivering and hungry, watch its glacial ascent over the frigid waters of Lake Superior.

The moon was fuller tonight. It's not completely round yet, but I estimate two days before the incubation is complete, and Lillian gives birth to Keto's children.

And what then? What could I—what could *any* of us—do to stop it?

It feels like it's been over a year since I left Chicago in the rearview, following the girls' car along I-43 north to their cabin on Michigan's upper peninsula. But looking around the shore now, none of the beaches look familiar. There's a chill in the air I can't shake, and I wonder if it's the locale or the season that's throwing me off so much.

Or if it's just the fact that my whole existence has been a lie.

"Survival 101, Dean. How to build a fire."

I look at the waterlogged pile of charred driftwood and

pine needles I tried to ignite on the beach last night. I managed to get some kind of a flame, enough to keep me alive, but the smoke from the wet logs woke me up almost as much as my nightmares. I'm surprised no one further inland saw my smoke signal and attempted a rescue operation.

Then again, it's past the end of summer. No one's vacationing on the shores of Lake Superior anymore. We're in the weird no-man's period between Labor Day and the beginning of hunting season, when it will be even more dangerous to be stumbling alone and naked through the woods bordering Lake Superior.

Dad's voice keeps ringing in my head: his tips and tricks and teachings from over two decades of training for this exact moment, all of it seeming like a load of crap now that I find myself vulnerable and stranded. Waiting for a literal gift from the Gods to fall from the fucking sky.

I feel like a little kid again, abandoned on one of Dad's "survivalist weekends," where he'd drop me off in the middle of a state park with a flint and a knife and tell me to find my way back home. Even then, I didn't doubt him. It wasn't until years later, in college, that I finally recognized his obsession with our lineage for what it was: insanity.

But as a ten year-old kid? I thought it was so cool that I was descended from the gods and was training to be a hero. Terrifying, sure. An awful way to spend a weekend? Absolutely.

But it made the regular school days filled with dodging bullies and enduring endless teasing almost worth it. Knowing that there was something special about me nobody knew. That on the weekends, this nerdy little gamer boy would hunt for his own dinner, string up his own hammock in the middle of a forest, make a bonfire and *survive*. Would someday save humanity.

I imagined it would be different when I got my hero's moment. My great test. My sacred duty. I'd swing onto the battlefield from my paracord harness, my trusty knife armed at the ready, eyes shining with the blessing of Zeus's own blood pumping through my veins.

Funny. In my fantasies, I was also always, conveniently, *wearing fucking pants.*

Amazing how much your confidence falls apart when you're covered in mosquito bites, nursing sandburn on your ass cheeks, and your dick is permanently shrunk from the cold.

If my math is correct, it's been almost six weeks since Lillian was taken. Which means it's well into October now.

I'm running out of time to keep these monsters from storming the Great Lakes.

I gather some scraps from my kindling pile, which thankfully dried out a bit overnight. Some splintered rotting branches serve as a decent enough wick for friction as I twist a cracked twig frantically between my hands, and soon my pile of leaves begins to smoke.

A spark, a catch, and I breathe the tiny embers into something resembling life.

Alright, now get some fallen branches from the forest, stoke this up, maybe catch a fish or two for breakfast...

My eyes dart to the incoming tide. A shiver runs down my spine that has nothing to do with the cold, and my chest cramps.

Tiffany's still in there.

While I wait for a sword to drop from the sky.

Fuck. She didn't want to come here this year. I wish I'd never told Dad about her meeting Keto. I wish I'd never let him convince me to follow them here, to tell Tiff it would all be okay.

Then Keto and Phorkys would have never stolen Lillian to be their broodmare, and neither she nor Tiffany would be in this mess.

Rrrrrring! Rrrrrring!

I whip my head around back to the treeline, where a trill that sounds like something between a bird call and an old-fashioned telephone reverberates from the branches. I scan the canopy above, plastered in the vibrant yellows and reds of autumn, and it takes me a second to spot him.

Tweety, back to play ball.

"Come down!"

The bird shakes his head, still trilling the obnoxious ringtone. Around me, the forest goes quiet, the morning chorus of birdsong and scurrying rodents suddenly obvious in its absence.

"Come on, I promise I won't kick you again!"

It gives me a disbelieving look that is far too expressive for a bird, looking almost as cartoonish as its nick-name-sake in my head.

"I swear. I'm sorry, I was hungry. No one's nice when they're hungry. Truce?"

It hops along the branch nearest my head, before trilling once more and flitting down onto a boulder not too far from my campfire. Then it opens its beak.

"Delivery imminent for *Dean Apostolos,*" a recorded voice plays out—my name coming out in my own voice, as if it were an outgoing voicemail greeting I'd recorded.

Instantly, my heart rate picks up, my self-pitying mood sizzling away with the distraction of hope.

"Really? Where? When will it be here?"

The bird lifts its wings slightly in a facsimile of a shrug, before fluttering away in a blur of blue.

"Thanks for nothing!" I shout, only to be answered by a bark of birdsong that sounds remarkably similar to the words, "fuck you."

Huh.

With a shrug, I return to stoking the fire and rubbing the numb chill out of my fingers. My stomach is growling like a motherfucker, and I'm about to abandon the fire and go hunting for a squirrel or something when the sky flashes in my peripheral vision.

It takes a solid minute of squinting at it like a dumbass before I realize what it is.

A parachute.

No—a sword, *hanging* from a fucking parachute, floating down into the tide line. Like something out of *The Hunger Games.*

A gust of wind catches it and it veers off course, heading further down the beach.

"Hey—wait!" I chase after it, ignoring the complaints from my stiff, exhausted legs, practically collapsing in the shifting pebbles beneath my feet. "Fucking Zeus on a goose, that's *mine!*"

By the time I intercept it, I'm another quarter mile down the beach, winded, and pretty sure I damn near twisted my ankle when I dove to catch the fucking thing. But I *did* get it.

A wide blade, wrapped in a worn strip of leather and a length of hemp cord; some characters in Greek stamped along its hilt.

"Chrysaor...?" I sound out as I examine the familiar letters. My Greek is a little rusty, but I know enough to be able to read and write at a passing level. Something about that name rings a bell...

Slowly, I make my way to a boulder where I can unwrap the gift and examine it further. This is my boon from the gods, after all. I ought to make the most of it.

As I carefully unwrap the cord—coiling and knotting it into a wrist wrap so I can save it for later—and unfold the leather, I realize this isn't a normal sword. First off, its blade is *gold,* or at least a golden color. Bronze, maybe? I suppose that would make sense, if it was in fact a weapon of the gods of ancient Greece.

Solid metal makes up the handle, which is significantly thinner than the base of its blade, but rounded, textured with geometric swirls, and easy enough to grip. The blade itself is as wide as my hand at the C-shaped base of the guard, before narrowing into a sharp point at its tip about sixteen inches away. Short and stout, but surprisingly light, likely because of the wide fullers forged down its entire length, spreading from a single point, like rays, from its tip.

Chrysaor...Chrysaor... I scour my brain for the name, digging through files and files of ancient history my old man crammed into my head between combat training. It sounds familiar, but distant. Almost like it was a footnote in all the history books and scrolls my dad made me read back in the day.

Is that the name of the type of sword? Or is it the name of the god who wielded it? A lesser god, maybe, one that might be some kind of key to defeating Keto...?

I dig around the leather wrapper for a letter or something, any kind of hint as to the sword's origins, or even just a "thanks for calling the Olympian hotline for Zeus's abandoned kids" note.

Nothing.

Huffing, I examine the scrap of leather. Only slightly larger than a hand-towel, it won't be good for much, but I could maybe use the sword to fashion some kind of sheath with it.

But first, I need to use this thing to catch some breakfast. I'm weak and woozy with hunger, and I won't last a second in a battle against Keto if I don't get something to eat first.

I PAT MY FULL STOMACH, grateful to be eating something other than boiled fish, for once. I've already downed two squirrels and a rabbit, and I have a couple more rodents roasting on a spit for leftovers.

Gods, if—*no, when*—I get us out of this mess, the first thing I'm going to do is get all of us—Lillian, Tiffany, me, and even Erik—donuts.

Seriously, my kingdom for a *HoHo*.

All the same, it's amazing how much easier it was to hunt and survive once I had some string and a blade. I caught two squirrels in half an hour, rigging up a simple trap with some twigs and the little bit of twine from the delivery.

While it roasted, I braided the hemp cord into a thin belt and punched holes into the leather wrap to fold together a makeshift sheath I can wear at my side. It's rough, obviously, but it will do. Something that will keep the couple of tools I have close while leaving my hands free.

And it might be silly, but the reminder that I'm not completely helpless—that, when I have the right tools, I can actually fend for myself and get things done—*does* help me feel like I might be able to get us out of this mess. If I can just figure out what the trick to this weapon is, I'm more confident that I have what I need to at least get me and the girls to safety.

I study the inscription on the blade.

Why does that name sound so familiar? It isn't anyone in the greater pantheon. Is it a muse, maybe? Or the site of a famous battle from the Trojan war? Who, or what, is Chrysaor?

Do they have a connection to me?

Chrysaor...Chrysaor...

And then from rote, the story of Perseus comes back to me like a boomerang: memorized at this point from the years and years of being told the same bedtime story every night for years.

"And then, the mighty Perseus, using the reflection in Athena's shield to see, aimed Hermes's Harpe sword into the neck of the gorgon Medusa. From her neck sprang forth the children of Poseidon: Pegasus, the mighty winged steed, and the giant Chrysaor, whose name means sword of gold..."

"That's it!"

I leap to my feet, sand scattering into the campfire as I hold the sword aloft, eyeing it in the glow of the autumn sun. Chrysaor the giant, whose name means sword of gold...

Huh. Not sure if "giant" is the term I'd use for the rather stubby cinquedea clutched in my hand, but it *is* gold, and it is most certainly a sword.

Is it... him? Is this some kind of–

"'Bout time you figure it out!"

"Gah!!!"

The handle flies from my hand. I hop back in shock, tripping over the driftwood log I was using as a seat, falling flat on my naked ass and getting sand wedged so far up my buttcrack I'll be shitting it for weeks.

I'm hallucinating. I have to be. Weeks of surviving on fish scraps have left me delirious with hunger; that's the only possible explanation. Because there is no way—*no fucking way*—that that *sword* just spoke to me.

"Ow–OW! Hot! Hot, hot, get me out you idiot, my melting point–!"

The sword that must have flown into the fire when I flung it away from me like...

Like a *talking sword*.

"Jesus!" I scramble over to the fire, thankfully having enough of my brain online to remember to use the leather wrap to grab the now *flaming* sword out of the cooking fire so I don't burn myself. It's still shouting expletives at me as I juggle it like a hot, pointy potato between my hands and carry it over to the icy cold water of the lake, where I immediately submerge it.

Bubbles float from his... mouth?... as I hold him down in the surf, until the slight orangey glow of the blade settles back into a more reasonable tarnished brown.

I lift it back to the air, still being careful to use the leather as a potholder to protect my fingers from any lingering heat.

"Sweet Hephaestus, ya couldn't've introduced yourself like a normal mortal? Talk about trial by fire."

I gape at the blade, wide-eyed, as the C-shaped guard of the sword separates from the blade, flapping open and closed like a mouth as it—*somehow*—talks to me.

Stamp-marks from forging glitter like eyes in the fullers of the blade as it waits for a response, before making a grating, scraping metallic noise that I can only assume is a cough.

"Who–what–are you?!"

"Is my name not carved on my butt anymore? I thought they stamped it on there back in the Bronze age..."

The flat-sided instrument twists in my grip, as if trying to examine its own handle. I squeeze, gripping it tighter to keep it from flying out of my hand again.

"*You're* Chrysaor?"

"Call me Chris. The whole name is a bit of a mouthful. Speaking of, you got any extra o' them kebabs? They smell positively *divine,* and I haven't eaten in centuries."

I'm still trying to get over the surprise of a weapon having a mouth and talking like a Brooklyn gangster.

"Eaten?" I shake my head, making my way back to the campfire on shaky legs. "You're a sword."

"I'm a *god,* kid. Or, son of a god. Haven't seen Dad in a minute, but he knows where to find me. Otherwise, he wouldn't have sent me here to help you! So give me the scoop, sonny, who we fightin'? Cyclopses? Dragons? Gorgons? You know, my mother was a Gorgon. But I'll try not to let it affect my performance in the heat of battle."

"*We're* not fighting anyone. This is *my* battle."

"Yeah, and from what I hear, you've been whining about it like a little bitch to Zeus's Child Support Hotline. Hence me flyin' here to bail you out. Now catch me up, kid, what's the battle plan?"

Bail me out? Is that what Olympus thinks this is? I ask them to help me clean up their mess and they send me a fucking metal Muppet to give me a pep-talk?

I collapse onto the log back by the fire, spinning the spit of extra squirrel meat and wincing at the char on the underside. Yeah, these are probably done.

I remove them from the fire and stick the spit upright in

the ground to cool a bit before responding. "I'm still... figuring that out."

The blade bends forward in a facsimile of a nod, and "Chris" makes an affirmative noise. "Right, right, okay, well we can work with that. Let's go over the specifics and come up with a strategy. Where's the enemy?"

I tilt my head to the lake, and the sword twists to follow my gaze.

"Ah, water arena. Alright, not exactly my strong suit, but hey, my dad ain't the King of the Sea for nothin'! How about you, what do you got? You a shape-shifter? What are them marks on your neck, you got gills? Gills is good, gills is very good for an underwater battle! Who's our adversary? Is it Amphitrite, that whore? Never had a good relationship with my step-mom, to be honest, she never truly accepted me and I won't hesitate to take her out if we have to–"

"It's Ceto. A primordial sea goddess."

"Ceto...Ceto... not ringin' a bell. She uh... she from before my time?"

"I think so. Might have even left the Mediterranean by the time you were born."

"What's her deal?"

I frown, balancing what I know from our weeks in captivity against the Greek history rattling in my brain to find whatever might be of use to me and Chris. Would he be able to fill in any blanks in my knowledge? Point out any weaknesses?

There has to be a reason Zeus sent me Chrysaor, as opposed to Harpe or the shield of Athena. Right?

I parse through my mental family trees to try to place Keto in the line of Olympian succession. She's the mother of the Gorgons, that's something. And if Chrysaor came out of

Medusa... "Technically, I think she's your grandmother. On your mother's side."

"Medusa? She was one bad bitch. Her sons are a sword and a flying horse, you gotta be a helluva dame to get through that labor, lemme tell you! Not that I remember it."

Obviously not, considering it'd been a C-section of the neck. According to the myth, Chrysaor and Pegasus burst out of Medusa's body after Perseus—my ancestor—cut off her head.

He continues, "So She's a primordial sea goddess, Medusa's mama. She got snakes for hair? Those can be tricky."

"She does, but as far as I can tell they aren't the kind that turn you to stone."

His face lights up at that, the hammer-mark eyes squinting at the corners as his guard-mouth curls into an even curvier grin. "Alright, alright, see that's good information! What else ya got?"

"What else...?" I start to wrack my brain for any more history lessons that might come back to the forefront of my mind, when the pure insanity of this moment catches up to me.

I'm talking. To a *sword*.

A sword who's somehow *related* to me... on my hundred-something-greats grandfather's side.

My mind goes blank as it all sinks in. A wave of nausea crashes into my stomach, and panic crawls up my throat. I set Chris down and put my face between my legs, breathing slowly and steadily, trying not to throw up.

"Just... just gimme a minute," I wheeze. "This is a lot for me to take in."

He doesn't give me a minute.

"What? Ceto? Is this your first time battlin' a primordial

sea goddess, kid? Ah, jeez, see this is the problem with education these days. First they defund the libraries, and then before ya know it they're banning the classics and all the kids are going to monotheistic charter schools and losin' touch with their roots..."

Chris is still talking, but I tune him out. I have to. Breathing in and out, until the world stops spinning.

While he goes on yammering, I grab the cooling spit and take a bite of squirrel meat. This situation would send anyone's mind reeling, but my current lightheadedness certainly isn't *helped* by the weeks of malnourishment. I need my strength.

First, food. Then I can focus on the rest of this.

I prop Chris up against a stack of driftwood while I eat more of my breakfast. But there are two charred kebabs here, and I feel rude keeping them all to myself, so I stick the other one in the sand next to Chris's face for his breakfast. Because, apparently, he also eats.

Luckily, with his mouth full, he isn't able to talk as much. So I get a moment of peace to stare into the fire and think.

When the worst of my panic has receded and I can't eat anymore, I can still see Chris's face in the hammer marks lining his blade. The mouth of his guard, gnawing away at the bones of his breakfast. And I realize I can't deny it any longer.

Zeus sent me a talking short sword to kill Ceto. One who doesn't know any better than me how to save my fiancée.

Fuck.

CHAPTER 20

LILLIAN

After listening to Tiffany tell me the truth about Dean, I'm a little... numb.

Let me get this straight. Dean is a descendent of Zeus?

Her face hides behind her hair while she shrugs. *I guess, technically, yeah. I mean, he's so far removed at this point that there's hardly a drop of God in him, but–*

Girl, have you seen Hercules? A drop saved him from Hades! Sometimes a drop is all it takes!

I hear the tell-tale chuff-snort that lets me know Tiffany is trying not to laugh at my Disney reference. Even when we can't physically speak, our language is still the same. I reach over to sweep her hair out of her face so I can see her better, and her eyes catch mine. My chest tightens.

There's so much more we have to discuss.

When Keto captured me, she said that Tiffany had been in love with me for years. That her feelings were the reason she sold her first-born to knock me out of my depression in the first place. Since then, my mind's been wrestling with the implications of that. Of the years we spent together as roommates, besties.

How long was she holding back?

I've always assumed that I wasn't interested in women, because I'd only ever dated men. And frankly, I never even had much success in *that* department until Erik.

But since embracing my libido so... *thoroughly* during this vacation (if you can still call it that), it's like all the mental barriers around my sexual identity have just collapsed.

The truth is, I love Tiffany. I always have. The idea of being separated from her again is physically painful. Hell, my fear of losing her is what got me into this mess in the first place.

Even now, holding her in my arms while she tells me what she's been through, curling my fingers through her hair, it all feels... *right*. Safe. Natural.

When I think of pulling her closer, kissing her... sure, it's a little scary. There's always that fear of rejection when you lay your soul bare to somebody. It was scary to talk to Erik about my feelings for Tiffany, too.

But that's the thing about fear: everything's always scarier in your head than it is in real life. Especially when it comes to feelings.

Look where *not* facing our fears got us. Who's to say, if Tiffany hadn't let me know earlier how she felt, if she and Dean hadn't come clean to me before, that we'd even be in this mess at all? Sure, I wouldn't have met Erik, and that would be awful. But we also wouldn't be prisoner to a couple of crazy titans in Lake Superior right now.

I'm tired of my fears causing problems. I'm tired of not speaking my feelings because I'm worried that I might get rejected. If being with Erik has taught me anything, it's that life is too messy and the stakes are too high to avoid hard conversations.

It doesn't mean I'm not still scared. But it *does* mean that I'm not going to let that fear hold me back anymore.

My heart is beating about a thousand beats a minute as I hold Tiffany's gaze, my fingers trailing from the shell of her ear down to the soft pale curve of her neck, the delicate bone structure of her shoulder.

She's so thin. This stint underwater hasn't done her any favors, and she's also growing a life inside her. I move my hand to her back and draw her into a hug, rearranging us so the front of her body is flush against me. It's bumpy and awkward—we're both bigger and rounder than we're used to—but when her surprise subsides and I feel her body curl around mine and her arms snake around my sides and squeeze back, the awkwardness fades.

I dip my chin to kiss her forehead, and her shoulders shake with sobs. I stop immediately.

Hon, what's wrong?

I'm so sorry, Lillian. This is all my fault.

What? I pull away a bit, removing a hand to tilt her chin up so I can try to read her face. *What do you mean? None of this is your fault.*

All of it is! She whips her head back, attempts to swim away from me, but I pull her closer. And this time, she doesn't fight me.

My chest squeezes when I feel that she's too *weak* to fight.

We can't control the gods, Tiff, I say, stroking her hair.

Erik can't get back with dinner fast enough. She needs food, needs to get her strength back.

But as true as that is, I'm grateful that we have this little bit of time, just the two of us, to have this conversation.

Clearly, we've lost something over the years if neither of us is able to be honest with the other. And if she's been holding onto this much guilt...

She stifles another sob before she looks away, hiding her face in the crook of my shoulder.

I'm so selfish. I don't know why you put up with me.

What? What do you mean?

I wish she'd look at me, but it's almost as if she can't bear to. I know she's exhausted—I've caught her almost falling asleep a few times already during our conversation —but this is important. I can't have her holding onto this guilt anymore.

I didn't agree to give birth to a bunch of titan babies to save her, only for her to feel like she still can't be honest with me.

I don't want to drive a wedge between you and Erik. I've already ruined your life with my stupid deal. I was so useless against Keto, Dean had to leave me behind to try to get us out of this mess. And you...

She tilts her head back up, studying my face in a way that has me feeling even more naked than I am. Looking into her eyes, seeing how sunken her face is, how deep her regrets go... it's painful.

Jeez, Lil. You're like a titan in your own right. The second you left me, you found the love of your life and literally got powers. And now you're stuck in this cave because of me. I've been holding you back, haven't I?

Powers? The rest of what she says is a stab in the heart, but I don't understand where it's coming from well enough to argue with it. So instead, I start pulling apart her logic with the one barb that is clearly the most ridiculous. *I don't have powers, Tiff. I'm human, just like you.*

Girl, have you looked *at yourself?*

I tilt my head at her. What is she talking about?

Before I realize what she's doing, Tiff takes advantage of my confusion to disentangle herself from my arms. She scans me from head-to-toe—something I'll admit I haven't been able to do since leaving our cabin almost a month ago—before her eyes dart back up to mine, holding my gaze.

She gestures with her finger, up and down. *Well, first of all, you've grown about three feet taller.*

What? I tilt my head down, but I only see the swell of my stomach. *Where?*

Everywhere, Lil. You're literally a giant.

My hands move to my stomach, and she shakes her head.

Shut up. That's not what I'm talking about, you goober. I mean, obviously you're pregnant, and clearly with more than one kid. But your stomach doesn't seem all that extreme when looking at all of you. It's weirdly...proportional with the rest of your body. She moves closer again, fingering a lock of my hair between her fingers. *Your hair's longer, too. At least a good nine, ten inches. Maybe more, since it's down to the small of your back.*

It's that long?!

I twist a little in my nest, grabbing a chunk of my hair to try to measure it. But it's like my perspective is off. My hair was longer anyway, almost down to my elbows, when we left for vacation. But if I've physically gotten bigger since agreeing to carry Keto's young, then I guess...

No. There's no way I've grown three feet in a couple of weeks. That's ridiculous. Thinking about it makes my head spin.

But Tiff has drifted closer to me while I've been think-ing, and before I know it her hands are cradling my face.

Or… trying to. With her palm resting on my jaw, her fingers can barely reach my ear.

That's when I realize that she isn't just frail. She's *small.* That's why she seems so much more fragile than she used to. Because she's so tiny now.

Or… I'm big.

She stares into my eyes, tilting my head side-to-side between her hands as she examines me. I stay silent as everything she's telling me sinks in.

But the biggest change is your eyes. They're purple now. And glowing.

I swallow, a kick in my gut sending my pulse racing again. Glowing eyes?

The memory of Erik's and my first time, where I couldn't look away from his crystalline grey eyes because he needed me to keep watch for the monster. The heightened emotions of that night crash back into me. Heat flushes my face, the passion of the memory so intense it bleeds into the present.

And then the significance of it strikes. What "glowing eyes" means—for me, and for Tiffany.

Get away!

I push her off of me, heart pounding, fear clutching my insides like a clawed hand. A monster's hand.

Keto's hand.

What's wrong? What did I—

I shake my head, heart pounding.

It isn't you. It's me. If my eyes are glowing that means… that must mean Keto's inside me somehow. That I—that you aren't safe here. Tiffany, I could hurt you! I could—

Stop. Calm down, deep breaths—just hold up a second, girl, you're having a panic attack.

Am I? Eddies are swirling around my neck as water

pulses in and out of my gills, and my chest is squeezing around my lungs, but I'm not worried about catching my next breath. Like everything down here, it's like the true depth of my sense of touch is dulled by the water. I can't feel the pressure on my lungs like I normally would during a panic attack.

But even that has my mind spinning. Why *aren't* I having a panic attack, with a realization like this? Has Keto finally infiltrated my mind, my being, to that degree already? Is She so deep inside me that my weak, human emotions can't hurt Her or Her young anymore? Have I lost control of my body, my vessel, to the gods' whims once again?

That's it, slower now. Count with me.

Tiffany's words are barely a blip on my radar as I try to take inventory within myself. Where is She? Her voice—that's the first sign. That's how it begins. Has She been talking in my head this whole time without me realizing?

Lillian?

No, that's not Her. Her voice is deep, seductive. Her tone is like Her hair, like a snake, slithering up and down my spine and drawing out my darkest, most hidden thoughts and desires...

Lillian.

Am I even me anymore? Has this all been part of an even bigger, more elaborate plan, to make my body Hers through this crazy breeding ritual? Does Phorkys—

Lillian!

A slap against my face somehow cuts through the thought spiral, and I come to, only to see Tiffany staring at me. Her hands grip the sides of my head, her fingers pressing into the muscles of my cheeks.

There you are.

She needs to get away from me.

She's inside me, Tiff. You're not safe–

I don't think She is.

What do you mean? Despite my doubts, the calmness of her voice instantly seeps into my shoulders, and I relax a fraction of an inch. *How do you know?*

Your eyes. She says it so simply, so easily. Like it explains everything.

But that doesn't make any sense. My eyes are the problem. If they're changing color, then that has to mean—

You said they were glowing?

Yeah. She shrugs. *But they're purple.*

What about this isn't she getting? Why isn't she more afraid of me?

When Erik's taken over by Phorkys, his eyes glow blue. So wouldn't that mean that Keto's taking me over? It makes sense! You need to get away! Quickly!

A swallow bobs down Tiff's throat, and I follow the movement before looking back up at her face. Her eyes close for a moment and her lips purse, as if she's shaking away a memory, before she opens them again. But she doesn't move.

When she looks at me, her expression is determined. Even if traces of the abuse she's suffered line her features.

Keto's eyes aren't purple, Lil. They're silver. And when She uses Her power, they...

Her face darkens for a moment, and an unfamiliar growl starts to bubble in my belly.

What did She do to you?

She starts to shake her head, but I grab her wrist, pulling her closer.

Did She hurt you?

And that's when I see it. Her whole face is illuminated, like a violet spotlight is shining on her.

Me. I'm the spotlight. I can see the reflection of my light in her eyes.

I blink, and as quickly as the glow appeared, it's gone.

I squeeze her arm, and we both take a breath.

You can tell me, I say.

I know. She pauses. God, she looks even more fragile than when Erik first brought her here. My best friend, broken by a titan.

Or is it that I'm stronger? Maybe she hasn't actually been weakened by any of this. Maybe my point of reference has just been thrown off by all the changes I've been through.

She steels herself, and it seems to confirm my new hypothesis.

That's right. She isn't weak. She's strong, too. After all, she's been through hell this month. And surviving it couldn't have been easy.

Whatever "it" was.

I will tell you everything eventually. I promise. But I'm not ready yet. Let's... let's get through this first, and then... then I'll tell you everything.

I nod. *Okay.*

It's not okay.

It's not even a little bit okay.

The hurt in her eyes, the thinness of her body, the strain that these weeks have put on her, on Dean, on their baby...

I know she's stronger than I thought. But that doesn't mean that she hasn't suffered more than any person ever should.

Don't worry, Tiff. You're safe now. I squeeze her arm

again, and draw her closer into a hug. I draw my nails up and down her back gently until she relaxes into my hold.

Feeling her sink into my arms feels right. Feels *good.*

Before I know it, she's actually fallen asleep against me.

Good. She needs to rest. And I need her body against mine, to reassure myself that she's here, and she's safe.

You don't have to worry about Her ever hurting you again, I whisper to her sleeping form, pressing a kiss to her hair. *Because if Dean doesn't kill Her...*

I will.

CHAPTER 21
PHORKYS

y mind is still reeling from the actions of these humans.

Escaped. Tiffany, Dean...those two non-magical beings managed to break my Ceto's barrier.

How? It is impossible. She is the most powerful of all the gods and goddesses, so powerful even that only Poseidon could banish her from Atlantis, from his kingdom, from the seas. So powerful that she was no longer permitted amongst our family.

So mighty that we had to flee to give her children—*our* children—a better life. Somewhere where the others couldn't reach. Where no one would seek to challenge her power ever again.

And yet these four humans somehow think that they have what it takes to defeat her?

It is laughable. Despicable. Practically perverse.

I let Erik control our body as we hunt for enough fish to fuel both Tiffany's and Lillian's growing bodies. Lillian alone requires more food to sustain than even I, and it is tiring to constantly be at her beck and call.

And yet...

I know she is there, conscious, while Erik sleeps within me and I listen to her belly. When I sing to my children. She allows me those moments with my young. She allows me to feel like a father.

Whereas Ceto–

Do not touch me!

My treasure, I begged, pleaded, as she lay in our new-found home, swollen with our brood. *Please, I only wish to–*

I care not what you wish. It is too emotional for me to have you swarming while I am feeding our young. Perhaps it is best if I lay them somewhere safe, somewhere you are not.

Ceto, my love, I am not Him. Please believe me when I say I would never hurt you, or our children.

You could not protect our children when it mattered most!

Her need for sustenance was also great in those days. Just like Lillian, she required so much fuel for her growing body, and caring for them outside herself—hiding them from me—drained her body's resources even more.

How was I to know, when I went to capture the Viking ship full of fresh meat for her, that I was drawing the boat so close to her hiding place?

To our children?

PHORKYS!

I can still hear the anguish in her cry. A scream so guttural it physically hurt to listen to it. Not only because it tore the flesh from my body, weakening me even further against my battle with the mortals, but also because it reflected the pain within my own heart.

I didn't know if I'd ever feel the joy of becoming a father.

Until her...

ERIK

PHORKYS IS EERILY quiet as we gather food for the women. I worry that his silence is a cover for him plotting against our bids at freedom. At Dean's desperate attempt to rally his gods to our side.

I have long since abandoned praying to Odin. Faith is a difficult thing to cling to when stranded without hope for hundreds of years. It is both the only thing one has, and the sole reminder of how hopeless one's situation can truly be.

For it is madness to pray to a god that does not listen.

And yet, *something* sent Lillian to my island. A being such as her: can I truly believe it was coincidence that she found me in the middle of the inland sea? Perhaps I had been praying to the wrong gods all along—perhaps it is Dean's mighty pantheon that holds the key to our salvation.

Even as its members also spell our imprisonment.

I behead and descale a dozen or so large fish before heading back to my treasure's side. It takes a considerable length of time, as even the underwater wildlife seems to sense the power growing in our nest and nursery. They steer clear of our quadrant of the lake.

The time of Lillian's labor approaches.

Yes, human, Phorkys speaks at last. **The full moon is upon us on the morrow.**

Tomorrow? I freeze in the water, hear pounding. *So soon?*

The routine of our days and nights: hunting for sustenance, making love in the hours between, caring for my mate, led me to lose track of time. *Has it been a month already?*

One cycle of the moon. I can hear them, the voices of my children. They are ready to be born.

My chest aches thinking of it. In the weeks of our internment, I've become intimately acquainted with every fold of Lillian's body. Her sex, especially, I've mapped with my tentacles and fingers and tongue a thousand times by now. Yet, I fear witnessing her open to release the monster's children from between her legs. I do not know how she will survive.

I know she has grown considerably during her pregnancy. Seeing her beside her friend revealed them in stark contrast; it is not just her stomach which has expanded.

And I cannot help but wonder if other changes are taking place inside her as well. There is a power in her voice that was not there before. A glowing in her eyes.

According to Phorkys, it is not Keto's power.

At least, not as He would describe it to be.

We return to the cave to find Tiffany and Lillian both asleep in each other's arms. It is an endearing sight, with the smaller woman's head cushioned upon my lover's breast, tangled in each other. I wonder for a moment if their love for each other goes deeper than that of friendship.

I shake the thought from my head. That is neither here nor there. For now, our women require food. I will wake them gently, and take care of them.

For we must prepare for what is to come.

CHAPTER 22
DEAN

"I thought you said you could sense magic?"

"Yeah, *sense* it. What, you think I got fuckin' titan GPS in my hilt? Doesn't work like that, kid. Hero work requires patience. Now stop distracting me."

I close my eyes and pinch my nose with my free hand, holding back a noise of frustration. My other hand is wrapped around Chris, who's currently humming a singular tone like a robot and squinting in concentration while he scans the lake horizon.

I assumed he could somehow find Her, sense where She's hiding, so we at least have some idea that we're heading in the right direction when we go to take Her out. If we swim across the entire lake before we find Her, I'll likely be too weak to win the battle.

My stomach twists. Despite having had a full breakfast and a magical sword from the gods dropped in my lap, I'm still not too jazzed about my odds of defeating Ceto. On the one hand, I have some reassurance that Zeus and the other Olympians are at least rooting for me in some capacity, but on the other...

I can't forget how helpless we were down there. Bound and tortured for weeks on end.

And Tiffany's still down there.

"You went quiet on me, kid. What's on your mind?" Chris's blade is twisted back on itself as he squints at me now. "I don't trust you when you go radio silent."

"You literally just told me to stop distracting you."

"Yeah, stop with the distractions, not the pleasant chit-chat. I don't got the highest self-esteem, ya know, being one of the lesser pantheon. If you ignore me I'm gonna think you're angry at me."

"You know, for someone with as many supposed limitations and insecurities, you sure don't seem to have a problem with expressing yourself."

"Centuries of therapy, kid. You *wish* you had as good a handle on your issues."

It's on the tip of my tongue to shoot out a snarky response, but then his words sink in. And well, fuck.

He isn't wrong. I don't think I've ever had a handle on my issues. And after this? We could *all* use some therapy.

"Ooo, hit a little close to home there, huh? You can talk to me. What's goin' on in that melon? Got a little hero's angst in there?"

I snort. *Hero.* Yeah, right. Is that what you'd call me? "Not sure I'm much of a hero."

"What makes ya say that?"

He tilts his weight to gesture over to a big boulder by the shore, and I plop down on it, staring at the sentient sword in my grip. But with him staring at me, supernatural and weird, the words get stuck in my throat.

My breathing goes shallow, too, and the shock of everything that's happened over the last month weighs heavy on my shoulders. Not just Ceto, either.

I swallow, breaking eye contact to stare out into the water. "What if I can't save them?"

"Who?"

"Tiffany. My fiancé. Lillian. All of them."

"Woah, woah, slow down kid. You're engaged?"

I groan, setting him down against another rock while I run my fingers through my hair. It's grown out a little longer than the typical crew-cut I keep it at, another sign of how long we've been stranded here. I can almost tug at it with my fingers if I try.

The full moon is *tonight*. I don't have time for this.

"Yeah, I am. And my fiancé and her best friend are still trapped out there. Which is why we need to hurry up and kill that tentacled psychopath!"

He jumps a little in my hand, and I almost drop him. "Two damsels? Why didn't you tell me there were damsels to save? We gotta get out there!"

I readjust my grip, harder now as he turns and swivels impatiently. "Yeah, I'm aware! Hence why you're supposed to be finding the goddess we're hunting!"

"Right, right, I know, I know... uh, where'd you last see Her? The goddess, not the dame."

I stare at him, disbelievingly. "Chris..."

He coughs a little, looking uncomfortable.

You know, for a sentient sword.

"Yeah?"

"You have no idea how to find Ceto, do you?"

"Well, uh, I–"

"Gods *dammit!*" I curse, stomping to my feet and propping him back on the rocks so I can think without feeling him stare at me. "Are you even magic? Can we even beat Her? Or did I just put the love of my life and her best friend and our baby in mortal peril for a fucking shot in the dark?"

I can't fucking belive this. All of it. Three years ago, I'd been completely cured of these hero-delusions, ready to live a normal life as a software engineer.

Then I met Tiffany, and my whole reality crashed down around me.

"Hey now, don't blame me, this is as much my chance to prove myself as it is yours! Zeus might be a horny bastard who doesn't care about his kids, but he wouldn't have sent me if he thought you were truly hopeless. The Olympians help their heroes, kid. They always have."

"Sure, right," I snort. "Sending me a short sword and a talking bird."

"There's a bird?"

I sigh, and it sinks in just how little Chris knows about me or my situation.

Why did I ever think praying was the way to get out of this mess? All of this has only been a waste of time. "It doesn't matter."

"It *does*, kid. Please. I know I'm not exactly the boon you were hoping for, but I'm being honest when I say the gods do what they do for a reason. Especially when mortals are involved. Problems like yours don't come along every day, and not every descendant gets sent a weapon from the minor pantheon.

"But I can't help ya unless I know the whole story."

I look at him, tilted precariously against the rocks, and sigh. As frustrated as I am, the sword has a point. It isn't his fault that he was the one sent to help me. And how can I trust him to help me out if he doesn't know everything that's at stake?

"Alright," I start, adjusting both of us into a more comfortable position. "I'll start from the beginning..."

The sun is high in the sky by the time I've filled Chris in on my childhood, meeting Tiffany, her friendship with Lillian and the deals they both made with Ceto, and the pickle we're all in now because of it. When I finish, Chris's guard is hanging slack, and he's staring at me in disbelief.

"Holy Hera, kid, that's a tough hand you've been dealt. And now you've got a kid on the way and your baby mama's trapped in the ocean?"

"Lake, technically."

He lets out a whistle. "Damn. I wouldn't wish your fate on my worst enemy. But I can't help but think..."

"What?" I ask, staring at him.

"Look, neither of us know where Ceto is, that much is clear. But it seems to me, the real stakes here aren't whether or not we defeat Ceto—it's whether or not we save your damsels."

It's like getting struck with a bolt of lightning.

He's right. What's any of this worth, if not saving the people most important to me?

I feel so stupid, once again getting swept up in the madness of my upbringing and my hero's journey. Thinking that because the gods answered my prayer, the objective has somehow changed.

But this isn't about killing Ceto.

This is about saving Lillian and Tiffany.

Rehashing my history made one thing clear: whether I asked for this or not, my girls are in trouble, and I'm the only hero they've got.

"You're right, Chris." I'm not going to stand by and moan about Ceto while the mother of my child is out there struggling. I don't need to find *Her*. I need to find *them,* and get them out of here.

I take a deep breath, shoring up my nerves for what I'm about to do. Despite it all: the gods, Chrysaor, my training —I'm still afraid to step back into the water. Still afraid of the monsters lurking there.

But I have to. I have to dive back in there.

I have to save Lillian and Tiffany.

With Chrysaor in one hand, the other clenched in a fist, I prepare to submerge into the waves. But something holds me back. I squeeze his handle, hoping it will give me strength.

The thin metal band of Tiffany's engagement ring cuts into my pinky.

Tiffany... I'm sorry.

And then a horrible scream rends the air.

It's all consuming—shaking me to my very core. The world around me freezes, and at once I'm back underwater, watching as a beautiful monster attacks my fiancée and commands her to scream Her name.

Ceto. Ceto knows we escaped. And She won't stop until She finds us.

No, not us. Tiffany. Lillian. The two women who She's been obsessed with from the very beginning.

It's time to stop wallowing on the beach. It's time to stop pretending I have some kind of epic plan. I don't. But that doesn't mean I should let Tiffany and Lillian suffer while I try to come up with one.

"I hope you're ready, Chris. Because you and I are about to protect the women I love."

"*Now* you're talkin'!"

With one last look at the sun in the sky above us, I slip Chris's blade into the sheath at my side, tighten the cord about my hips, and step out into the surf. Then I take a deep breath and dive straight into the water, paddling west—the direction I'm fairly certain Erik headed with Tiffany back when we split up.

It's time to put my training to the test.

Time to kill a goddess.

CHAPTER 23
KETO

Where did they go?!

I drop the armful of boiled meat the second I see the remnants of my barrier sparkling at the edges of the cave. Something shattered it—*destroyed* it—and took my prisoners from me.

I was beginning to see such promise in Tiffany. My sweet minnow, filled with a despair and rage so similar to my own. She, too, knows the pain of ultimate betrayal. She knows what it means to love with all her heart and still be found wanting by the very people who claim to love her.

The water around me grows choppier and choppier as I circle the perimeter of my territory, scouring the lake for the other human.

Dean. Son of Perseus. The clan of Zeus's bastards who couldn't stop looking for trouble, even after five thousand years. I know this is his fault.

How, when I planted the seeds in Tiffany's brain, when I read her shame and anger swirling in her subconscious, how could she resist slitting his precious throat when he was strung up at her mercy? How could she, after all the suffering she's faced at the hands of her many lovers, *free* him from his cage?

From *my* cage?!

How dare they break through my barrier, taunting me once again with their foolish games!

He is no better than his ancestors. Is it Lillian they seek? Has he convinced Tiffany to disavow her friend in hopes of murdering my young once more? Or even worse, stealing my children only to poison them against me, like that bastard Poseidon?

Seeking their worthless glory by conquering *my* children, my beautiful, powerful children! So perfect that even the King of the Seas–

No. No, do not think about that.

Do not think about him with *her*.

Medusa. The eldest of my first brood: small in number, yet mighty. My gorgons, my greys, the outcast Ladon, and the youngest Echidna.

Perseus brought the demise of all but two.

And even I do not know how he managed such a feat, except by the favor of the Olympians. For anyone but I to look upon the visage of my eldest three would face an instant death, turned to stone.

Such perfect offspring! My three most beautiful daughters, with living manes of serpents and power to make men tremble to look upon them! Snakes that need not even strike at their opponents to render them powerless!

My only wish, as I grew them within me was that any daughter I had would be the true owner of their beauty. For what good is it, to be the fairest of the sea, for it only to be tossed aside by men in power?

I granted them just that. For no one could gaze upon their beauty without giving their very lives for the privilege.

A power I wish I shared. Without it, I was only ever a victim of the gods' insatiable lust, to be used then cast away when they grew tired of me.

But Poseidon never stopped wanting me, did he? Or else he wouldn't have given Medusa children.

Betrayal swarms hot in my chest once more, as fresh as the day I laid eyes upon her swollen stomach, the day I came to warn her of the hero who sought her head. The one blessed with the shield of Athena and the Sword of Hermes: Perseus.

Only to find her fat with a child of Poseidon. My former lover.

Men! It's all the fault of men!!

Tiffany will learn, as all women learn, just how little she can trust the man she thinks she loves. Even in my clutches, he warded his mind against me, against her, so he could hide his true intentions. As all men do.

I cry out again, the great lake in its entirety shuddering with the force of my anger. And this boy, this *pathetic* boy, whose blood is so watered down by generations of mortals. This corn-fed, freckle-faced, skinny—

A shock runs through my entire body, zinging from my crown to the tips of my tails like a pulse. My barriers. Someone broke through my barriers.

What is the meaning of this?

I shout my cry out into the saltless waters, seeking my consort. Phorkys is keeping an eye on the humans. He is ensuring they do not escape.

Answer me, Phorkys!

The male has escaped to the surface. I have the female.

And you allowed this to happen?!

Oh, ho, ho—this is rich.

These humans. These half-starved, pathetic *humans*

think they can use my own consort to escape me? *Me?!* I am the goddess of the sea! Granted my powers by my mother the Earth before me, I am the all-powerful! I am the mother of—

A flicker of a scene appears before me of the human Lillian floating in her nest of weeds, my tentacles flicking up her legs in greeting, full with children... *my* children... and her glowing, purple eyes.

She grows strong, my love. I cannot disobey her. Her eyes... She reminds me of you.

Phorkys's voice is faint as he calls to me, the visions flickering with distance. Even now, he is running from me. He cannot sustain a call across this inland ocean.

His betrayal burns hot in my breast. My last loyal consort. And in the end, he was swayed by no more than a human female.

But I hear the warning in his message.

Lillian grows stronger. Strong enough to command him to steal my Tiffany away. Strong enough to worry him. Not unlike the human he lent his powers to, who—over time—was able to suppress my lover's body and desires.

It was a mistake to engage these humans in the affairs of gods. A mistake to bring them into our lives.

I should have abandoned Phorkys long ago, should have known that I could not depend on him. The signs were there, back when our eggs were first destroyed in our new home. There are four other lakes I could have retreated to—countless other beings I could have chosen to sire my children.

And yet, I was sentimental. Phorkys is different, I told myself. He was loyal to me when the rest of my family turned away.

I was a fool.

Why do I give my loyalty to men, when men have never granted it to me? Not once?

Poseidon was a cheater and a pedophile.

Phorkys was too weak to save our children, is still too weak to resist a pretty face.

And any human man I've known to walk this earth is just one disappointment after another. Even the warriors eventually fall to their mortality and lust.

Perhaps it's time I give these men a taste of their own torture, and take from them that which they believe they can take from all of womankind.

Our futures.

Our dreams.

Our passions.

Forget Dean. He is a worthless child of a bastard. There is another who is more deserving of my attention, who I might still win over to my side. She comes apart so beautifully in my arms, after all.

She could be my toy. Until I grow tired of her.

And finishing her would end the line of Perseus once and for all.

"Sweet minnow, where are you....?"

CHAPTER 24
TIFFANY

*S**weet minnow...*

I awake with a start, a plush pillow beneath my head, warm arms wrapped about my back, and golden hair fluttering in my face. It takes me a moment to realize where I am; the light is dim, save for a navy haze about me and a suspicious lavender glow coming from whatever I'm laying on.

I grope around, grabbing with my hands across the firm cushion under my ribs, and when I reach up to my pillow, a soft moan sounds in my head. Followed by a pulse of the purple light.

Lillian!

My comfortable bed jerks awake, and a flurry of tentacles follows, searching and suctioning up and around the two of us. The sight is so similar to the visions in my nightmare that I jerk up, only to be crushed back down to Lillian's breast when she doubles over.

It's not how I imagined, being smothered by my best friend's tits. My cheeks smush together, and despite the fact that my nose is free, my neck is not, and I scramble for oxygen as her boobs cut off my gills.

I can't breathe, Lil!

Sorry! The word is accompanied by another groan, and her body hardly shifts to allow me enough leverage to break free, but her arms loosen their death grip around my torso. *Fuck, it hurts!*

What is it, mate?

I—I–

Another, more desperate moan screeches through my mind, and I realize it's not all in my head. Somehow, Lillian's pain seems to be able to overcome the barriers of underwater speech, and her cries rumble through her.

A long, thick tentacle wraps around my hips and lifts me off of her body. Instinctually, I start to fight it, but the terror for my own safety is quickly doused when I open my eyes and see where the purple light is coming from.

It's Lillian's stomach.

But it isn't a steady glow. Blobs of light are swirling beneath her skin like a lava lamp, and their shapes form bulges in her stomach from her bustline down to the swell above her hips.

Oh fuck. Oh fuck. Are you going into labor right now?

The grip around my hips falters as Phorkys shifts into His half-human form. No, not His form, *Erik's* form.

It's absolute chaos around me, and my skin is still clammy from my nightmare. As Erik pushes me aside to rush to Lillian, I float to the edges of the cave. It feels so much smaller than it did yesterday. What's going on? What has changed? Something important woke me up, but what was it?

Breathe, my love, slowly: in through your gills, out through your mouth. I will count with you. We need to breathe through the contractions so we can prepare your body.

That's good advice. He's a good boyfriend. Lillian scored herself a winner, there, for sure.

So she's taken care of, which means I need to take care of myself now.

Okay, Tiff. Breathe. In through your gills, out through your mouth.

The steady stream of bubbles every few seconds tickles my nose, giving me a focus point while my brain sorts itself into something less like spaghetti. With Erik's voice steadily speaking like a mantra below me, I open my eyes and take in my surroundings from this higher vantage point.

I'm in Lillian's nest with her and Erik. And Phorkys, I guess. We're all here, and we fell asleep after eating last night.

I pat my stomach, amazed at how full I still feel. After weeks of being constantly hungry, it's nice to know that I actually was able to eat enough last night. Between the boys, Lillian, and me, we easily knocked back a dozen fish. And I'm not talking lake trout, here, these were big honkers —the kind you see in guys' tinder profiles.

Okay. So I'm fed. I'm rested. The three of us humans snuggled up last night: Erik cradling Lillian on one side while she held onto me like an emotional support stuffie on her other side. According to Erik, it was the middle of the night when they got back with food, which means it's likely daytime now.

Still no word from Dean.

My heart squeezes as that sinks in, and with it a crushing loneliness that I haven't felt since Keto first captured me when I went searching for Lillian. After Dean and I returned to the beach and she hadn't come back to the cabin, I'd run into the surf, shouting for her.

And then I went under.

The line of bubbles streaming from my mouth hitches as the fear from that moment comes crashing back and my lungs catch. I power through, breathing in from my gills for a four-count, before trying to exhale in a steady stream again.

In, out.

Focus, Tiffany. What was it that woke you?

Minnow...

Keto!

The steady whine of pain that's been echoing through the cave fades, and my attention is stolen, once again, by Lillian. She's panting, face red with exertion, and Erik has one arm rubbing her upper back and another squeezing her hand. As I watch them, I realize why the cave seems so much smaller than it did yesterday.

Lillian's gotten bigger.

Much bigger.

Too big for him to really hold her, even with all of his tentacles doing their best to support her back.

Her legs relax, stretching out to the cave entrance, and even she looks about with confusion, as if she's just now realizing how cramped the nest feels all of the sudden. The purple glow of her stomach ebbs a bit, and the darkness closes in on us together. Erik leans his forehead to hers, his face about half the size of his mate's now, and he presses a kiss to the point of her nose.

I hate to interrupt your moment, I think to them as I lower myself back into the fray and glance about the cave. *But I think we have another problem.*

What do you—

"Tiffany..."

Erik's eyes go wide as this time, we all hear Keto's voice as she calls to us from outside the cave. It's impossible to know how close or how far she is, as her voice can cut clear across Lake Superior if she wants it to, but the intention is obvious.

I can't put you in danger. I need to go. I'll find Dean, and I–

No, Tiffany! Dean entrusted your safety to us!

The Viking warrior's face is wild as he looks between me and Lillian: the love of his life and a woman he barely knows, and I'm amazed to see there's an actual struggle there. He truly wants to protect us both, and doesn't know how to do it.

You are speaking nonsense. Phorkys's voice rings out into the cave as His human's eyes shine blue, and I finally understand what Lillian meant when she talked about watching out for glowing eyes. This is what it looks like when the monster is driving the body, as opposed to the man. **Ceto knows that the time of her progeny's birth draws near. She approaches to meet her children.**

Then why is She calling for me?

Cyan and grey flicker back and forth as the titan fights to come up with an answer.

I'd be lying if I didn't say that I was terrified at the idea of Keto coming after me again, especially when I don't know Her intentions. My experiences with the goddess have been limited to striking deals and being strung up at Her mercy, and every conversation we've had has only left me more confused than the last.

But I do know one thing in my mind, and that is: I don't want Her anywhere *near* Lillian. Especially once she's done fulfilling Keto's purpose.

She may have granted me one favor three years ago, but I don't trust Her to keep Her word.

Listen, Lil, She hasn't said one word about Her children in the entire month She's had me hostage, I blurt, ignoring the way Erik's eyes keep flickering between grey and blue. I may barely know the guy, but I trust him to keep his monster contained while I confide in my friend. *You may be keeping your end of the bargain, but I don't know if it matters to Her anymore. I don't know what She's really after, but She tried to turn me against Dean.*

Concern, and then understanding lights in her eyes as I plead with her.

She gets what I'm trying to say. Keto knows about Dean, and his connection to Her past has thrown everything out the window.

I have to leave. Who knows what She'll do to you or Erik if She finds out you've been hiding me?

If it is you *She seeks, then your only hope of survival is staying with us!* The Viking is fully back, and he grasps my wrist as if physically holding me will keep me from leaving.

I adjust in his grip, twisting until I can place both his hand and mine just above Lillian's heart. She lifts her own to squeeze our fingers, and I squeeze back.

I can't risk anything happening to you, Lil. I love you.

Purple light fills the nest again as her eyes begin to glow. She glances down at our hands, blinks once, and then meets my gaze head on. *No,* she practically growls, shaking with anger. *She can't have you. Not if I'm fulfilling my end of the bargain.*

I'm not too sure She cares about the bargain anymore, I admit, thinking about the way She handed me the knife when She left me and Dean alone together in Her lair. *She's fucking crazy, Lillian.*

She is not crazy. She simply yearns for her children!

Lil squints at the force in the monster's voice, but her face remains twisted even after the shout fades away. An awkward silence stretches between the three of us, the only movement that of our hands as Lillian's grip pulses over mine and Erik's hands.

And then another groan escapes her.

Suddenly, his fingers disappear. When I look down, tentacles are stretching possessively around Lillian's stomach, fastening to her skin with their suckers. I try to jump back, startled, but Lillian holds my hand fast to her breast as she groans softly.

Slowly, the prehensile limbs circle lower, and my face heats.

Uh...

I'm sorry, Tiff, Lillian gasps, reaching out to grab my other arm with her unnaturally large hand. *It's another contraction, and I–fuck! It hurts. My body isn't meant for this. It's too much. This is the only Tylenol I have.*

What are you saying?

Her eyelids flutter as Erik disappears, the monster form engulfing him and vanishing below her stomach. There's a pulse between my own legs as I see her cheeks flush beneath the glow of her eyes, and her lips part on a soundless gasp.

Holy shit, I mutter to myself as I realize what Phorkys is doing. What Lillian needs.

She coughs a laugh, bubbles spraying from her plush lips. *Yeah. They take care of me–argh!*

The light in her stomach grows brighter, and her eyes fly wide as another contraction overtakes her.

Tiffany! Her voice is a whip in my mind as she pulls me closer, her legs bending beneath her as she struggles with the pain. She curls her arm around my waist and brings me into her embrace. It's uncomfortably tight.

Her breathing halts as she grits through the creatures swirling in her stomach, preparing for their exit.

Please breathe with her, Erik pleads to me, his voice strained and distant without his body to anchor it. *I cannot hold her head and attend to her pleasure at the same time!*

Lil! I slap a hand to her face, turning her head until she locks eyes with me. Her lips are pursed and twisted from the contractions, and the sight cuts me like a knife as I wrestle with our current situation.

I didn't think about the logistics of her giving birth to a hoard of monsters. It seemed unreal, distant—like a problem far, far in the future when Dean and I were struggling with our own real and present monster. But now, looking into her eyes as she pleads with me to stay with her, I realize I can't leave.

I need you, Tiff, she chokes out, tears swimming and blurring the line of her lashes before dissolving into the lake around us. *Not just to keep you safe. For me. I can't—I can't do this alone!*

Her fingers squeeze, and I squeeze back, leaning into her and remembering how Erik talked her through her breathing. *Okay, Lil, okay. I'll stay. As long as you breathe with me, okay?*

O—argh! Okay, she struggles, chest jumping with each clench of her muscles, each intake of breath.

In through your gills, okay? In, two, three, four...

Just like before. Just like the day that started it all.

It hurts!

I know, I know it does. But you're strong. So strong. Breathe with me, Lil. Out through your mouth...

Her forehead smooths, just the teensiest bit, as her next inhale hitches with a twitch of her legs.

Yes, my treasure. You are strong.

Her eyes half-hooded, she turns her glazed expression towards me, and I take in her face.

No, this isn't just like before. This is different. Back then, it was only pain. Only secrets. The two of us separated by a canyon of grief and unspoken feelings, unable to see the truth of one another.

Tiffany...

My lips connect with hers before I even realize our faces are touching, my tongue tasting her moans away with every stroke. My hand drifts to her full breasts, kneading and plucking in time with the noisy swipes of her other lover's tentacles on her sex. Together, we massage Lillian's pain away, one orgasm at a time.

Loving her through it. Until her moans ring out from pleasure, from the ecstacy these monsters can bring, instead of the horror.

I love you, I whisper to her, confessing the full depth of my meaning as I tug her bottom lip between my teeth, nibbling it until the bubbles of her gasp tickle my nose. *I've always loved you.*

I'm not giving you up, Tiff, she says, after the crest of her orgasm carries her through the worst of her next contraction. *Even when we're free. We'll figure it out. I promise. I'm going to get through this, and when I do, we won't have to choose anymore.*

No, I agree, stroking my fingers into her hair and nuzzling her neck. The thought of the three of us and Dean escaping together forms a picture in my mind, and I hear Lillian sigh into my hair.

Just like that, she whispers, before she succumbs to sensation.

CHAPTER 25

DEAN

After two days in the open air, it's strange to feel my body instantly adapt to the water again, almost as if it's where I'm supposed to be. I don't even take a breath before I hop in, instinctually filling my lungs as the water passes over my gills.

I set course for the western shore—which only drives us deeper into the heart of the lake.

What's that? Chris asks, and it takes me a second to figure out what he means.

Over there?

Yeah, it's a different color from the rest of the lake bed. What's that about?

He's right. Far below us and to our right, there's a haze. Not the bright silver of Keto's magical glow, but something warmer. Purple.

Let's check it out.

It gets brighter and more concentrated the longer we swim, until most of the water has a slight lavender tint to it. We paddle deeper into the brightest part of the glow, but before long something else drives me forward.

Screams.

It's those that eventually lead us to the women.

I don't know what to expect when I dive into the cave entrance with Chris held protectively in front of me. I try to gird myself for the worst. I may need to slice Lillian from Phorkys's clutches if her Viking boyfriend finally succumbs to the monster. I might need to abandon both of them to save Tiffany—something I would never *want* to have to do, but still. I prepare myself for the possibility.

She's the mother of my child. I'll protect her no matter what.

Not that I've been doing the best job. I've already been away too long. This has been the most impossible lake vacation of all time, filled with curses and torture and monsters.

But despite all of that, I'm *still* unprepared for the sight that greets me when I slip into Lillian's cave.

Kid...you didn't tell me your girlfriends were into this *kinda shit. Lucky man!*

And then he whistles.

Quiet, I hiss at him, not even bothering to correct him about the tangled knot that is my relationship with Tiffany and Lillian. Partially because I'm still on the lookout for danger, and partially because I can't look away from the scene before us.

Hey, no judgment here, kid. Nice work if you can get it, you know what I mean?

Where even *are* Tiff and Lillian?

A giant kraken is hovering between two enormous legs, which are spread wide as eight massive tentacles massage, tease, flick, and suck along their length. I assume the monster is Phorkys, fully devolved into his monster form. Somewhere beyond him is the source of the supernatural purple light: a bioluminescent glow that fills the cave so brilliantly I could follow its rays all the way here. But that doesn't explain who the giant is.

The sea creature's bulk blocks the view of whatever he's doing at the apex of those massive thighs, but I can guess.

There's really only one thing that leads to *those* kinds of sounds.

Despite smells not really transmitting underwater, the water is heady with the sweet, cloying atmosphere of sex. It mixes with the moans ringing from the woman in the monster's grasp, and it's difficult not to get sucked in.

In fact, it takes me a second to realize that Tiffany *is* involved. I can just barely see a slender foot poking out from behind the writhing bodies, and the slight red chafing on the ankle from Keto's bounds informs me that it has to be her.

Tiff! I call out.

Oh, Erik, yes!

The voice that answers isn't my fiancée's—which is a good thing, considering she and I haven't spoken about involving anyone else into our sex life aside from Lillian—but when I *do* recognize the powerful words echoing throughout the cave, it's just as surprising.

It's Lillian.

Tiffany, answer me!

...Dean?

Slowly, as if waking from a trance, she rises from the mound behind the pair of legs, eyes dazed and lips flushed like she's been biting them. I blink at her expression, lit from below by that purple gleam. And then I take a quick inventory of the rest of her.

She's less pale than when I left her: a sign that she's at least eaten something in the time we've been apart. And the sight of her, safe and healthy and clearly comfortable, makes my chest squeeze with relief.

Tiff!

I kick myself forward, rocketing toward her as fast as I can, until I'm holding her body in my arms. She feels so good: soft and warm, living and breathing and safe. Her body against mine is so *right,* I can't believe I ever convinced myself to leave her side—even if it was to find a way out of this mess.

I ease the arm holding Chrysaor across her lower back —careful not to slice her—and delve my other hand into her hair, cradling the base of her skull as I kiss her long and deep.

I missed you, I whisper to only her, mind-to-mind. A soft moan answers me, and her hands come up to grab me back.

Only... they grab my butt cheeks.

Oh– I stammer, pulling back for a second to check what she's thinking. *Are you–?*

But I don't get a chance to finish the question, because the sword in my wrist is twisting around to ogle the scene.

Hubba-hubba, this is one sexy fertility goddess!

Chris's comment snaps me out of the moment, and I jerk his handle only to see him staring, open-mouthed, down at the source of the light below us.

And that's when I realize that the glowing purple giant-ess? Isn't a giantess at all.

It's Lillian.

Giant, glowing, magically-transformed Lillian, easily twice the size she used to be, and ready to pop with kraken babies.

Which means the monster is...

She'd been crying Erik's name earlier. Both of our

friends have transformed into something completely inhuman, and they're... into it, apparently.

I gape at the transformed woman, then turn back to Tiffany, who looks like she's waking up from a dream. Her eyes are half-hooded in a sleepy, lusty expression and her hands are still groping my behind. The longer she touches me, the more I feel a tingling in my stomach that means a boner isn't far away.

Even Chris, when I look at him, has a glazed-over sheen to his eyes, and I feel like it won't be long before the orgy claims us all.

Tiff, is that–?

Lil, she thinks, tilting her head to her friend, glassy eyes reflecting lavender, *we have company.*

I lose my grip on Chris as she unwraps her arms from my body and takes me by the hand, leading me down to hover over Lillian. The sword companion floats up toward the ceiling, shouting in alarm, but his voice becomes nothing but background noise as I lose myself in my fiancée's eyes. They feel as if they're staring directly into my soul, sending a jolt of electricity down to the base of my spine and making my cock leak with anticipation.

Dean... that deep, sultry voice which seems to command the entire cave murmurs below us, and everything else slips out of focus.

It's just me and Tiffany and Lillian the Goddess, and my only purpose is to be with the two of them for all eternity.

Tiffany places my hand upon the goddess's breast, and my fingers instinctively knead the soft skin. Warmth spreads from my fingertips, up my arm, and down my spine, and I forget how I got here.

It was important, wasn't it?

More important than making these two women come their brains out, though?

Hmm...

Ah! The light dims, and the warmth in my body turns spikey, almost. Like lightning, sharp and electric and tinged with pain.

Suddenly, Lil's arms jerk forward, pushing Tiff and me together against her bosom as her whole body curls in on itself. I wrap my fiancée into my embrace, shielding her from the sudden switch. But in response, she places her hand on my chest, telling me I can step down.

Lillian's eyes close tight as her whole face crumples into a grimace, extinguishing the glow from her eyes and casting us into relative darkness. Only the soft haze of purple from her skin illuminates the space, until her eyes burst open once more, zeroing in right on Tiffany.

You're going to be okay! Breathe, Lil, Breathe!

It hurts!

With me! Breathe!

The fog in my head clears as I watch the two women breathe together: Tiffany counting and coaching while streams of bubbles leak from both of their mouths.

Oh fuck.

Oh, *fuck.*

What's happening, kid? Didja finish too early? I can tap in if you need a minute, happens to the best of us!

Before I can tell the stupid sword to shut the fuck up, the massive monster behind Lillian's stomach peeks above her waist.

It is time.

CHAPTER 26

TIFFANY

Phorkys announces that Lillian's going into labor in earnest, and it's like a bucket of cold water crashes over my head.

Or, it would be, if we weren't already underwater.

My pussy is throbbing something fierce, though, and my breasts are positively aching. Looking down at Lillian, I have a hazy memory of kissing her, and my hands roaming across her body...

My face heats to about a thousand degrees, and then I see *Dean* in front of me.

Dean! When did you get here?

He blinks at me like a deer in headlights, then shakes his head as if he's trying to get water out of his ears. *Doesn't matter. Keto could be here any minute.*

I look from him to Lillian, and I don't even hesitate.

I can't leave her. She needs me.

I know! I would never ask you to abandon her. He grabs my shoulder with one hand, then sets another on Lil's collarbone. She looks down, fear shining in her purple eyes, and I can't tell for sure if she can really see us or not. This whole day has been like a crazy fever dream, and I still don't know if we've really settled the dispute between us.

But right now, none of that matters. *I* know that I love her, whether she's aware of it or not, and that means I need to be with her and see this through.

A large hand covers both mine and Dean's at the same time, and Lillian leans forward to press a kiss on each of our temples. It takes me by surprise, and Dean, too, from the look on his face. But when she pulls away, she's smiling softly at both of us.

We're going to get through this, she assures us telepathically. **I just have to...**

Have a thousand babies, I finish for her, twisting my face into something I hope is a laughing sort of smile. But, let's be real. It's probably a grimace.

I'll protect you both, Dean says, glancing up at the ceiling. I do a double take.

Is that a... sword?

Chris! Dean calls, and Lillian raises an eyebrow at me.

Did he just call the sword "Chris"?

I'm pretty sure that aside was just for me, and a bubble bursts from my nose as I snort.

Don't worry, I'm not taking the slight personally. Seems like you guys have a lot going on. I'll catch the next orgy.

Uh... my eyes go wide as the sword appears to split in half as a weird New York accented voice pops out of nowhere into my head. Seriously. For a second, I thought Danny Devito was in the cave with us.

Dean scowls at the sword, grabbing it by the handle as it knits itself back together. *Did that thing just* talk?!

I'll fill you in later, my fiancé dismisses, swiping a quick kiss across my cheek, and then Lillian's. He puts his non-sword-wielding hand on her shoulder and looks her in the eyes, then says, *You got this, Lil. We're all here for you. For this, and for... well, ever. If you'll have us. But we can talk about all of that later. Erik?*

Yes? Erik/Phorkys rises from his perch between Lillian's legs in full kraken monster form, holding them aloft with more tentacles than seems strictly necessary. His giant, bulbous eyes reflect cyan and purple as he crouches in front of her, filling the rest of the space with his swirling limbs in a pose that reminds me of a baseball catcher.

Then again, he's about to deliver a lot of monster babies into the world, so I guess it's a good thing he has an abundance of hands.

It's almost funny. He's a literal cephalopod monster, and he's posing as a pair of stirrups. He's talking with us like just another person, helping out with an at-home, water birth.

What the hell has our life become?

But Dean takes it all in stride, swimming down and patting the monster on the head.

I'm trusting you with our girls.

The cyan leaves the monster's gaze, as his eyes blink into that human grey that I've learned means Erik is driving. *I will not let you down.*

Uh, guys...? My attention swivels back to Lillian as her face screws up in a familiar grimace. ***Can we—AAAAAAR-RRRGGHHH!!!***

Purple and cyan fill the cave again as Lillian screams and Phorkys takes over once more. Dean says he loves me—us—before diving back to the entrance to keep watch for Keto while I grip one of Lillian's hands with two of mine and encourage her to squeeze with a pump of my fingers.

She does, practically cutting off my circulation as her

supernatural strength overwhelms my weak, human hands.

Breathe!

I AM FUCKING BREATHING!

Then push!

Another scream cuts through the cave, so loud it feels like it's coming from inside my own head. I don't know if it's inside me or around me, but it's anchored right to the hold that Lillian has on my fingers, crushing them in her grip as she pushes through the next contraction.

I glance down at her stomach, and my eyes widen in awe as I see the swirls of light beneath her skin concentrate toward the bottom of her torso. *They're...crowning,* I think to myself, and I can't help but be curious to know what Erik's seeing right now. My throat goes impossibly dry as I realize in less than five months, I'll be going through something similar: splitting my body open to bring new life into the world.

Will Lillian and Erik be there for me? Will the four of us stay together when we find our way out of this? Will we raise this child, my child—no, *our* child—as one big, happy family?

I'm forced to squint as the brightest light yet blasts from under Lillian's stomach, and a new cry breaks through the cave.

A baby... it's a baby's cry!

Ah! Lillian howls as the first tiny monster breaks free, and Phorkys pushes it up Lillian's body with one tentacle. I gaze on in amazement as the tentacle retreats halfway, only to stop to attach one of its suckers to the apex of Lillian's thighs.

Her forehead relaxes slightly and her breathing hitches. The small, almost tadpole-like monster the size of a softball with tiny, webbed tentacle arms that spread from its waist like a badminton birdie wriggles its way up its mother's body before latching onto her nipple.

Another gasp bubbles from her mouth as her lashes flutter, and I am taking in all of the changes in her body like I'm watching a sports match I don't understand.

Again, my treasure. Push!

I extricate one of my hands from her grip to scratch my fingers into her hair, as I whisper a stream of soothing encouragements into her mind. Beads of light travel up and down her torso as monster after monster is born, swims to her breast, and suckles its first meal. With each one, a purple light travels from her heart to the tip of her nipple before disappearing into the baby's mouth.

It's the titan magic, I realize. These monsters are titans. Gods? Demigods? By carrying them, Lillian became like a god herself, her body borrowing their power to sustain itself as she changed to accommodate their growth. And now that they're leaving her body, they are taking that magic back.

Lillian, it's… beautiful, I murmur to her, taken aback by just how incredible a miracle it is. This is Lil: my best friend, the woman I love. The woman who once almost lost herself to a miscarriage, who needed help from the gods to rise out of her depression.

But if she hadn't miscarried, none of this would have happened. She wouldn't have met Erik, I wouldn't have met Dean, and none of these little lives would have come to be.

Phorkys and Erik would have been trapped for all eternity, locked in a zero-sum struggle without any hope of reconciling, and Keto…

Tiffany, my minnow, why did you run from me?!

Fuck. Keto!

She's here! Dean cries from the cave entrance, and Lillian's eyes burst open at the announcement, still hazy from pleasure and pain and who knows what kind of supernatural forces working their way through her body right now. I squeeze her hand, and use the one buried in her hair to turn her face to mine.

Don't worry about Her right now, Lil. Just focus on me. On Erik's tentacles around you, his suckers on your clit. You are a fucking goddess, and you are safe with us.

I have no idea what made those words come out of my brain and into hers, but it seems to do the trick. Her eyes roll back into her head as I see Phorkys redouble His efforts below her legs, cyan eyes wide with innumerable emotions as the procession of monster babies keeps pouring from between her legs.

I'm not even sure if she's pushing anymore. It's almost like now that the process has begun, nothing will stop it until every last titan is free.

The pressure on my hand eases, and I look down to see that Lillian's hand isn't twice the size of mine anymore. It's still larger, to be sure—but it's almost like it shrunk by twenty percent.

In fact... all of her has.

She's shrinking, I realize. *They're taking her power, she's going back to being a human again.*

It is worrisome, a voice I recognize as Erik's responds. *The monsters are getting larger as we go. I worry that her body...*

Agh! Lillian grunts, as the first hitch since her initial contraction breaks into the labor. *Tiffany, Erik... it hurts...*

The monster now suckling her breast is the size of a normal, healthy human baby—easily twice as big as that first little tadpole guy. This one even *looks* a little human: a green, ridged head like something out of an episode of *Star Trek,* sporting little fins on its cheeks and dark freckles across its nose sits above a slender human-like torso and arms with webbed fingers and a split tail like the Starbucks logo. It sucks out its bead of nipple magic before darting out the entrance of the cave with the others.

That's when I see Dean. He's barring the cave entrance, wielding Chris straight out before him while Keto struggles to make it past the onslaught of her own children shooting past her.

I can hear her shouting, but I can't make out the words. I'm too focused on Lillian right now, and the fact that Erik is absolutely right.

Her body is getting smaller, and the monsters are getting bigger.

Kiss me! I shout to her, forcing her neck to turn to me and locking my gaze to hers. *Breathe with me one more time, Lil, together.*

I descend onto her lips, sucking in her exhale before breathing into her open mouth. Her shoulders melt away from her ears as I massage her tongue with mine, nipping and rubbing at the base of her neck while communicating with Erik at her legs. *Keep her feeling good, Erik, distract her from the pain.*

You do not need to tell me twice, he responds, and I can hear the smirk in his voice. When all this is over, I'm going to be very excited to play with our girl together. He seems like he's eager to please, and it'll be way more fun to take advantage of that when all of our lives aren't in danger.

I swallow a moan, and I'm happy to hear that it sounds more pleasured than panicked as Erik and I play with Lillian's body. I can still see the parade of monsters making their way up to her bosom and out of the cave in my peripheral vision. Phorkys's tentacles are holding her legs apart and working her open as gently as he can to facilitate their birth.

You will not keep me from my children!

The words break through our weird, lusty haze, and I break off Lillian's lips to look back at Dean. A terrifying standoff is taking place at the cave's entrance as dozens of tiny monsters swarm behind Dean's back, seeking their escape into the open water.

But Keto is blocking their passage. Her tentacles and tails are spread in a giant web behind Her as She shoves her torso and terrifying head into the rocky opening, the snakes of Her hair swirling and hissing at Dean and Her children alike.

No one is preventing you from them, my mate! Phorkys calls, and the silver of her eyes flickers a moment.

Tiffany, please... Lillian's voice is faint in my head, and I shift my attention back to her face. It's ruddy with red splotches, and the lines around her eyes speak more of exhaustion than pain at this point.

She needs me. But Dean needs me, too.

I... I can't choose between them. Not again.

Tiffany! Suddenly, Erik is right there, his human face floating beside us as his tentacle grips my arm. *I must help Dean. Which means you must stay with Lillian. Phorkys believes there are not many children left, but these will be the largest yet. Please. Help her–* his eyes flash cyan as his voice deepens for the rest of his sentence–**and save them. Only I can calm my lover down.**

I nod at the two entities, dumbstruck. Lillian grips my hand again, and when I look down, I see that she's almost completely back her normal size. The purple glow that was filling the cave has dimmed considerably, the concentration of her magic distributed across hundreds of tiny new gods.

Just a slight glow to her stomach and her irises remains, and even that is limited by the fact that she can barely keep her eyes open anymore.

Tiff... I'm so tired...

I swallow, then try to give her my most reassuring smile. My own pregnant stomach twists in sympathy as I acknowledge all that she's been through—from over a month ago to this moment—and the task that still remains.

I know, babe. But you got this. I'm here, and I'm going to talk you through it, okay?

I pray to every fucking god in Lake Superior right now that everything I learned in my deep dive into Lamaze YouTube back in my first trimester stuck.

Because I'm the only one left who can get Lillian over the finish line.

Good luck, gentlemen, I call out to the three of them one last time. And then I refocus all of my attention back onto my best friend as I lower myself between her legs.

CHAPTER 27
KETO

My children are fleeing. Leaving me. After everything I've done for them.

Phorkys crouches at that human's legs, and her skin glows with magic. *My* magic.

She stole my magic from me.

She stole *everything* from me.

My children. My consort.

Even Tiffany, my last hope, is latched onto Lillian's lusty lips and gazing at her with a hunger she *never* afforded me.

They all must die.

Stop, Keto, you'll destroy your own children!

Quiet, mortal! Son of Perseus, I know your true objective. You would kill every last one of my children if you had the strength!

The man's eyes widen as my truth strikes his heart. Worthless human. He should have perished when he had the chance. Instead of escaping only to shove this holy sword into my throat in the hopes of defeating me.

Please, Keto. I only want to save the women I love. We do not have to fight—

Ah yes,* your *women. You are all the same. You all seek to own every one of us. You just want to own and destroy, again and again, any woman with the power to match you!

No!

His denial is futile. I know the truth. It is unfortunate that he was able to sway Tiffany with his lies.

But why can I not press forward?

All about us, my beautiful children swarm, seeking to escape the nest that is heavy with the cloying scent of magic, blood, and lust.

But they do not recognize me. Not even their own mother.

Their intelligence varies. Some gazes dart about the cave, assessing my face, only to turn and search for another exit. If only they knew that I conquered this entire lake for *them,* as I would have all the seven seas, had I not been banished by this pathetic male and his ancestors!

I lunge toward him, only to be poked by his miserable sword.

Watch it now, missy—only family's allowed in the delivery room!

I am the only family that matters!

My rage is a second skin as I surge forward once more, only to be blocked again. The heady magic of childbirth is enough to make my head spin. It seems to empower everyone in this cave but *me.*

Keto...

The voice whispers in the back of my mind, soft yet powerful. It takes a moment for my eyes to find hers: the purple glow meeting me across the space.

I granted you the gift of childbirth! I lifted the weight

of your grief! And yet, you would seek to bar me from my own children?

Her eyes wrinkle, brow furrowing in an expression I have not seen in millennia. But even in so long a time, it is too soon.

Never would be too soon.

You could have everything you want, Keto. If you just promise not to harm us—

"No!" I screech, claws sharpening, seeking to slice her from sternum to sacrum—only to be blocked once more by a shield of my own flesh and blood. **How dare you turn them against me! How dare you look at me like that. Stop it. Stop it! STOP IT!**

I won't let you hurt them.

"Get out!"

She turns away again, her eyes squinting closed as she pushes. The Son of Perseus, oblivious to our conversation, calls to me again.

Keto! Please, we don't have to continue the fight! We can break the cycle!

"GET OUT!"

Phorkys looks up, his eyes folded with that same look. **Please, my love—is this not what you wanted?**

The same as her. The same as *Him*.

I will not be pitied.

I am not a pitiable creature.

I am the Queen of the Ocean! The goddess of the seas!

You would hide behind this human? The Son of Perseus, who murdered our own daughter? You would ally yourself with these pathetic creatures over me, Phorkys?

Never, my love, my—

"I WILL NOT BE KEPT FROM MY CHILDREN!"

No one seeks to keep you from them, my love. Please,

lower your rage and celebrate this happy day with me! Today is the beginning of our new beginning. Our family. What we've always dreamed of.

But he does not understand. They never do.

Even now, our progeny flees from me. I saw them rocket past as I approached, ignoring my pleas. My greetings. My love.

They do not know their own mother.

They do not know the sacrifices I made for them.

The pain I endured.

The hundreds nipping at my tails seek only freedom. Their sharp teeth and hungry mouths, fresh from suckling their birthright off that mortal's teet, now chew at tentacles. Wanting out.

They will only leave me, Phorkys. They always leave me.

I will not leave you, my love.

But I do not believe him.

For I could not even convince Tiffany to stay. Nor the love of my life, my King. My Poseidon.

I am Queen of the Ocean. I am the goddess of the seas.

And if, in the end, they are only going to leave me, it will not be with their lives.

CHAPTER 28

ERIK

You better know what you are doing.

Phorkys does not respond. There is a barrier between His thoughts and mine, aside from the control He exerts over my limbs to carry us to the entrance of the cave.

Those same children form a thick wall of monstrous flesh we must wade through to reach Tiffany's mate, Dean. Phorkys's will is urgent in my limbs, and I can sense that somehow, He and His mate have been communicating whilst my treasure wails in pain.

I long to speak to her, to hold her head as perhaps I would were this a human birth. But that is impossible, as she is delirious with the warring sensations within her body. And even if she were not, I doubt it would make much difference.

Her existence has been more sensation than thought these past few days. As the babes grew within her, she changed.

I am not surprised. One cannot host a monster without

becoming different than one was. I know this more intimately than most.

Despite the changes, she still looks upon me with love in her eyes when they are able to see me.

I long to hold her again. To make love to her as human mates like we did, what feels like years ago.

As if they are miles away, I hear Tiffany encouraging her. The women of a village band together in these times of birth and death, and even in our circumstances it is no different. I trust this slender woman, whose own belly swells with child. I pray that she is able to remain steadfast as she has thus far for her friend and lover.

As I pray for her mate, Dean.

Brother, I call to him only, in what I hope is a comfort as I wrap a tentacle about his ankle. *What are we to do?*

I don't know man, we're at a stalemate here! She's not listening to anything I say, I can't reason with Her!

Keto is railing, spouting madness that is not worth repeating. She is screaming for Tiffany, for Her children, and reaching for Dean with a fire in her eyes that would have a lesser man crumbling. Even so, I can sense that Phorkys is speaking with Her outside of my consciousness, and the silver light of Her eyes flashes between rage and recognition.

Dean has his curious sword poised at the base of Her throat, and Her snakes wriggle about it in a hypnotizing dance, blocking Her face except for the light of Her eyes. Surprisingly, the snakes are unable to touch the metal of the blade without withering, and Keto herself seems unwilling to swim further forward while it is leveled against Her neck.

What is this blade?

Chrysaor, the Golden Sword of Medusa, he answers. The

names are only nonsense to me. *It's magic, from the gods,* he clarifies.

I scour my mind for similarities. *Sigurd's Sword?*

But Dean does not answer. And perhaps that is well, because two of Keto's tentacles break through past the wall of babes and launch themselves toward us.

My love! Phorkys reacts faster than I am able to, wrestling with the limbs and keeping the goddess at bay. Meanwhile, the tiny babes about us seek to gnaw their way to freedom, chewing upon her numerous tails. ***Please, you must let the children pass!***

"They will only leave me!" She shrieks, and it is like knives against our ears. Even Phorkys recoils, dragging Her tentacles with him, and the point of Sigurd's Sword pierces its tip into Keto's throat. A bead of blue blood floats like ink from the tiny prick, before immediately being gobbled up by one of the monstrous babes. ***"All of you! All of you will leave me!"***

No, my love, my consort–

Her glare turns sharper than the dagger at Her throat, and it is centered entirely on me. My body freezes as if it would turn to stone, but Phorkys's power resists it.

It is then I realize it is *Him* She is angry with. *His* betrayal She resents so strongly.

"I am no one's CONSORT!" She bellows, and Dean's feet drag back in the sand at the force of it. I steady him with what little bit of the monster's form I am able to control.

Meanwhile, more babes have emerged at my back, the last two the size of large human infants, and my heart cries for Lillian. I yearn to look back to her, to return to her side, but I am no match for my host, whose form still fights and twists against its mate.

What is it that infuriates her so? I ask Him, and the terror and confusion and pain that I feel in response is almost as disarming as Keto's scream.

Phorkys is as unprepared for Keto's rage as I am. Which means...

Dean! What is the cause of Her anger?

I don't know! He grits his teeth, fighting to stay upright in the sand against the ever constant push and pull of the water around us. *But She seems to want me dead, ever since She found out I'm... kinda descended from the guy that killed Her daughter.*

This would have been good information to share earlier! I scold, and he grimaces.

I know, okay? If I could start this whole thing over, I'd be a lot clearer about a lot of things!

One more, Lillian, you are doing so good honey! Push!!

Another cry rends the water, and this time, Phorkys and I both turn our head to take it in.

Lillian, my precious treasure, is almost back to her original human size, face twisted with exhaustion and pain and determination as Tiffany reaches between her legs to deliver the final godly babe.

But it gets stuck halfway.

Fuck! Fuck! Get it out, get it out! My love cries in pure agony as the form of the babe blocks its own passage through her birth canal. But it's head is free, and the tiny mouth wails along with its mother—no, surrogate—as Tiffany struggles to free its hips.

I'm trying, I'm trying, it's...stu–OW! She rips her hand back in horror, gaping at the half-born babe. *It bit me!*

WHAT?!

A horrifying laugh bubbles from the monstrous goddess behind us, forcing Phorkys to divert our attention back to

His mate. Keto's eyes flash with victory, with hope, as She sneers at the three of us.

"Yes, my children! If you truly love me, revolt against these false gods! I am your true mother! Fight on my behalf!"

No! Dean cries, chest heaving with the effort of holding Her back. *We're both better than this, Keto! I'm sorry for the actions of my ancestors. I'm sorry for the children you lost. None of us can go back and change the wrongs we or our parents committed—but their actions and intentions don't have to define our future! Our children's future!*

Time seems to freeze as Keto's face morphs into a more open expression. The light in Her eyes dims, and She focuses on Dean.

The sword is still wedged between them at Her throat.

She does not speak, but that in itself is an improvement from Her rage.

Please, Keto, Dean begs, and even the babes seem to still at his urging. *I promise you, I will not harm your progeny. You and your children have just as much a right to exist as I do, as we all do. Please, let's put aside our family's feud and vow today to coexist in peace!*

The only sounds in the cave are my treasure's tortured tears, and my heart feels as though it is shearing in half. There is no hope for any of us if we cannot calm this goddess.

Please, my love...

And then, I hear it. Lillian's final display of strength and courage as she screams, drawing all of our gazes to the miracle within the cave.

Aaaaaaaaaaaaaaah!!!

Open-mouthed, we look on in awe as my mate crunches herself upright and reaches between her own legs.

Tiffany, blessing that she is, clears the path, allowing my treasure to grab beneath the babe's shoulders, freeing its human-like arms and pulling it free to cradle at her breast.

Unbelievably, the tiny monster slips free from her body and follows her urging up and back into the nest. Lillian brushes the child's short, dark hair from its forehead and presses a kiss to its bloody skin, before lowering it to her bosom to feed from her waning reserves of magic.

There you are, she says, as it settles against her, equally tired from its traumatic birth as she is. *We made it, little guy.*

Girl, actually, Tiffany chimes in, before glancing over at Dean. The two of them share a private smile as Lillian's eyes close, and she sinks back into the plants beneath her.

Heat, then. Creeping, uncomfortable heat radiates at my back and stings my tentacles. It's Phorkys who is the first to realize what is going on, and he whips our eyes forward to the cave entrance to prepare for the incoming attack.

"LET GO OF HER!"

The rest happens so quickly, I would have missed it were my senses not enhanced by the titan living within me. But Dean reacts with an otherworldly speed, twisting his feet deep into the lake and thrusting up with his golden sword at the exact moment she pushes forward to steal the babe from Lillian's arms.

The tip slices cleanly through her throat, burying itself into her flesh until it pierces through the other side.

She chokes, wide-eyed, in complete disbelief, before scowling down the length of the blade at her attacker. He twists, and inky blue blood trickles down the metal and dissolves into glowing wisps about the lake.

Then, the hundreds of babes descend upon the body of

their mother, licking up the drops of blood before devouring Her body in a chorus of tiny, monstrous bites.

You, too, shall know the pain of bearing a child that will never truly be yours... The curse rumbles through the cave as her silver eyes glow through the swirling mass of bodies and limbs. The radiant hatred is all that can be seen through the melee, and it pierces us all as Her gaze seems to lock on each of us in turn. ***May you understand... the grief of losing a child to your own... blood...***

With a sickening squelch, Dean wrestles the blade free of her neck at last, and Her head floats off and away into Lake Superior. A dozen wee monsters squeeze free and slither after it.

The body sinks, tentacles and tails splaying in a wide array that's soon enveloped by a torrent of gaping maws. Her torso bends back unnaturally, arcing into a surge of hungry beasts. The mass's slow descent to the lake floor frees the cave entrance, allowing the remaining children to flee the cave and claim their second meal.

It is not long until all that remains of the goddess is a few flecks of green and silver and a pile of bones. Eventually, even the slowest of the babes slink away into the darkness of Superior's waters, exploring their new home.

A tug pulls at my chest as I watch them leave, and I realize it is Phorkys's emotions that I am feeling. A brief glimpse.

It happens, when they are too great for Him to keep from me. I allow my voice to turn inward for a moment.

Phorkys, I...

But what can I say to one who has lost His true mate? Especially after He is responsible for me finding mine.

My children... He answers, and I am surprised by the wonder in His voice. ***Look at how beautiful they are.***

A glance into the open waters is enough to see that the sun has risen: a soft, warm light filters to the lake bed below and illuminates the hundreds of varied creatures gliding through its depths. Babes resembling fish, humans, eels, squids, and hybrids flit about, playing with one another in a language I do not understand.

It is such a strange dissonance: this joy, following such horror. Death begetting life.

But I cannot deny the swell of love in Phorkys's heart as he admires them.

Congratulations.

A long pause, and then: **These children will not know their mother. Yet perhaps, I also did not know her as I thought I did.**

They will know me, though. I swear it.

I wish you well with your family. But I long to return to mine.

Yes. I can now summon the strength to break the curse. It will only require one more sacrifice.

What? My heart stills, panic seeping into my soul. *Have we not sacrificed enough?*

Just one more. From Lillian.

CHAPTER 29

LILLIAN

I drift in and out of consciousness. Somewhere in between wakefulness and sleep, I'm vaguely aware of my body knitting itself back together, some kind of magic medicine healing my ruptured womb, but mostly I'm sore and numb. Tiffany squeezes my hand, and I blink at her.

Hey girl.

She doesn't open her mouth, but I hear her voice. Weird. I open my mouth to answer her, but water floods my mouth.

Oh right. There was something about water recently... I concentrate on remembering what, but it fails me. My mind is a mush of half-memories and what must be dreams, the vast majority of which are weirdly horny.

Like really, *really* horny. With tentacles and a muscly dude with long hair. And Tiffany.

Did we...make out? I manage to ask, and a laugh from nowhere rings through my brain.

Rest now, my treasure. You have done well.

My treasure... my treasure... why does that sound so familiar? Like warmth and light and joy and fuzzies in my belly...

But it all swirls away, and I'm swallowed in black.

"SHOULD WE WAKE HER? Or let her sleep?"

"Are we sure she's even going to wake up? It's been three days."

"Do not say such a thing! Her body has been through an incredible ordeal. She requires rest."

"Yeah, and *food*. If she were in a hospital, she'd have an IV drip. Right now, she's just wasting away."

Hmmm... food sounds good. That lady has a point.

"Is there such a place near here, where she could rest and receive sustenance at the same time?"

The guy talks funny. But he sounds familiar. And like, hot?

Why does he sound hot?

"We can't leave Lake Superior until the final ritual to free Phorkys from your body. But after that, we should absolutely get to a hospital."

"I will need to borrow pants and a tunic. It is frigid in the evenings now."

A few stifled chuckles sound around me, and they are so familiar. Especially the woman's.

"Tiff...any?" The name feels familiar and foreign on my tongue at the same time, and my lips stick together when I first try to speak. It feels like I haven't talked in months.

Oh, fuck!

I bolt upright, eyes popping open like I just woke up from a nightmare. "Tiffany! Dean!"

"Lillian!" A pair of thin arms wraps around me and a mane of thick brown hair blocks my view of the room we're in.

Room.

We're on land!

"Erik?!" I remember suddenly, and a broad chest crashes gently into me from the other side. Two muscular arms encompass the two of us, and I feel myself relax into his hold.

Once the panic recedes, the rest of my senses kick in.

I feel like I've been kicked in the cooch by an enthusiastic bodybuilder, and my throat aches.

"Give her room to breathe," a relieved-sounding voice scolds, but there isn't any anger in it. If anything, a smile hides in the words, and the curtain of brown hair parts to reveal Dean also standing around the bed I'm seated in. Someone stuffs a few pillows behind me, and when I look over my shoulder to see who, Erik smiles at me, placing his big, calloused hand on my shoulder.

"Welcome back, my treasure." His eyes dart to my lips, almost as if he's asking for permission, and I wrap my arms around his neck again, pulling him in. I would never deny this sexy man a smooch.

I'm breathless by the time we're done, stars spinning behind my eyes from trying to take in as much of his musky, woodsy flavor as I possibly can.

"Where are we?" I gasp as we break apart. But within a second of looking over his shoulder, I recognize the place. "Oh shit! We're back at the cabin!"

It's cozy with its rustic log walls and open main room; there's a fire crackling in the little fireplace by the back wall that Tiffany and I have never used in all of our summer vacations here. It's never been cold enough to warrant it.

The light in the kitchen is on, and I see a plate of sandwiches and a couple Party Size bags of Doritos on the table. My stomach growls, and it's all I can do to keep from jumping off the squeaky mattress and pouncing on the modest feast.

"Oh my God, it isn't fish!"

More laughter, and my gaze bounces from Tiffany to Dean to Erik and back in disbelief as Tiff breaks off to put together a plate for me. The three of them look... chummy. Like they're all best friends. Which is weird, because Erik doesn't know Tiffany and Dean. And she and I were...

The memory of the fight comes crashing back a second before she hands me the plate. I glance down at her stomach, so much bigger than I remember it being, before taking in her thin arms and legs poking out of her sundress, and the dark circles under her eyes.

"What... happened?" I say, accepting the plate from her hands.

The three of them exchange glances, and then Dean speaks up.

"Why don't we all grab a plate and eat while we talk?"

I'm on my third bologna-and-American-cheese Wonder Bread sandwich by the time they're done catching me up on the past two months, and I swear it's the greatest thing I've ever tasted.

For some reason, everything after trying to run away back to the shore with Erik is a blur, but a few flashes come back as they describe to me my deal with Keto, my supernatural pregnancy, and the new generation of chthonic deities that inhabit Lake Superior now.

I take a huge gulp of Arizona Iced Tea, eternally grateful

for the fact that Tiffany and I loaded up the cabin pantry with non-perishable goodies from our pre-vacation Costco run before we both got kidnapped. After surviving on nothing but boiled fish and venison for weeks, the influx of salt and sugar has me feeling almost giddy.

I have so many questions. First, I'm curious as to all this weird, sexual tension I'm picking up on between the three of them, as if something happened while I was having all those monster babies—an ordeal that I *still* am not quite convinced actually happened, and wasn't just some incredibly vivid fever dream. Erik's hand is on Tiffany's knee as they talk, and Dean's arm is wrapped around her. But her hand is resting on my leg under the thin blanket covering my lower half, and Erik's other arm is wrapped behind my back, stroking sweet scratches across my shoulders.

I'm also curious about Erik. He's sitting on a rickety wooden dining chair that seems entirely too small for his giant body, and he's been grinning from ear-to-ear since I woke up. Is the curse broken, then? Is he finally just a... man?

"I need to pee," I announce, and all three of them rise before I even put my plate on the nightstand. They all reach out to support me, concern flashing across their faces in unison.

"I'll help," Tiffany says quickly, at the same time as Erik says, "Let me carry you."

I blink at them. "I think I'll be okay, guys. Seriously." The two of them exchange a nervous glance, and I peek around them to catch Dean's eye. "Are they alright?"

He shifts uncomfortably. "Well, the last monster of the...*hoard* was a little violent."

"Violent?"

"She had fangs! And her hips were inflated like a pufferfish. I almost thought you wouldn't get through it," Tiffany explains, a wrinkle furrowing between her eyebrows. "How are you feeling?"

"Um..." I take inventory of my body again. "I'm sore, yeah, but mostly in a bruise-y, achey way. You know? I mean, I'll have to pee eventually. I guess we'll find out if I'm okay sooner rather than later."

I shrug my shoulders, then let Erik help me to my feet. More than my vagina, I'm worried about whether or not I'll be able to walk. It's been a month since I've had to use my legs, after all.

Somehow, we make it to the bathroom, and I shoo away the guys who wait in the doorway as I start to lift my own sundress in front of the toilet. Tiffany closes the door, staying on my side to keep an eye on me.

"Welp, I can't wait until *this* part of my recovery is over," I mutter under my breath as I sink onto the seat with shaky thighs. But the pee comes out, and it only stings a little. Tiffany insists we check before we flush, and though we can conclude from the evidence that I am *severely* dehydrated, we don't see any blood.

"Huh." I push down the handle and the evidence swirls away. "I guess there was a little magic left to speed the healing along." I wash my hands at the rudimentary sink before drying them off with a paper towel.

"About that..." Tiff opens the door again, revealing the men listening in against the door frame.

"Gross! Give me at least a *little* dignity here, guys!"

They avert their eyes guiltily, then help me walk back to the kitchen table.

"There's one more thing we have to take care of before we can go home. Or... wherever we decide to go after this,"

Tiff continues, and the whole vibe shifts back to three-against-one.

I stare at them expectantly. "Alright…"

It's Erik who finally sighs and breaks the silence. "Now that you are healed, my treasure, Phorkys needs the last of your magic to break the curse."

CHAPTER 30

LILLIAN

My face is about a thousand degrees as Erik insists on *carrying me* to the water's edge. The sun has all but set; only a sheen of gray twilight rests above the dark horizon of Lake Superior, a vast black hole sucking the rest of the light from the shore-line and sky.

The moon hasn't risen yet, and only the earliest stars twinkle over us as the four of us sit along the tide line.

"We are ready, Phorkys," Erik finally says, and I watch as the transformation travels up his body, starting with his toes. The tiny digits separate and morph into the tips of tentacles, widening and changing color as the prehensile limbs take over his lower half, then his torso, until his entire body becomes that of a giant Kraken-like monster, completely dispelling the brief illusion that it was all just a dream.

He slithers into the water, submerging completely before circling back and staring at me with His huge, cyan eyes.

"Hey, Phorkie."

"Hello, Lillian."

It's weird being informal with the titan, but it would be weirder to treat this like business. Phorkys has been as much a part of this orgy as the rest of us, after all, and I can't deny that my body still thrills a little at seeing His tentacles unfold in the surf.

Dean and Tiffany shift behind me, offering their support from a few feet back. Part of me wishes they didn't have to see this. But another part—a deeper, secret part that holds memories of the four of us sharing more than just a crazy month underwater together—knows they need to be here for this. That this marks the end of this whole ordeal.

And maybe, just maybe, the beginning of something new.

"I hear you need something from me."

He nods slowly, a subtle incline of His massive head. His eyes maintain their creepy hold on mine the entire time, and it sends a shiver down my spine.

I remember Him from my hazy pregnancy. How gentle He was with my body. The lullabies He sang to His children in my belly. His hunts to keep me fed and nourished as I grew His young.

I'm the closest thing to a mother His children will ever have. And I feel like there's a significance to that, a gratitude that shines in His giant eyes when He looks at me. His posture almost holds a hint of remorse as He asks this final favor, as if He recognizes how much I've given Him and feels bad about asking for more.

"There remains a small portion of magic inside of you. Perhaps you can feel it—I believe it is what healed your body in these past few days.

"Tell me, Lillian... do you still have milk?"

My cheeks burn, and I steal a glance behind me at Tiffany and Dean, who are quick to avert their gazes. But even as I start to deny it, my breasts weigh heavy on my chest. It's as if His closeness, His acknowledgement of the magic still inside me, awakened it.

I stifle a moan as a soft breeze blows, sending goose-bumps up my arms and hardening the peaks of my breasts to firm points beneath the thin fabric of my dress. When I look down, I'm shocked to see two small dark spots there.

I'm leaking.

Oh fuck.

I reach instinctively to cover myself, but a long tentacle wraps itself around my wrist, stopping me.

"Please, Lillian. It is the last thing I need to break the curse. I require the same boon of power that you granted my children.

"Allow me to drink from you."

I swallow, ignoring the pulse of arousal that beats in my still-tender pussy. I hate that the touch of His tentacles on my arm brings back so many erotic memories for me, how my body still responds to His touch with lust instead of disgust.

Do I really, though?

No. No, hate is the wrong word. I could never truly hate Phorkys's body after all we've been through.

A throbbing, sizzling ache settles in my breasts, and the wet fabric covering my nipples feels cold against the sensitive skin. It's a chilly night, and the top of my dress is soaked now. Two more tentacles weave themselves under its hem, lifting it up my thighs to the swell of my hips.

But they pause there, waiting for something. For me, I realize. To give permission.

This is the last thing. With this last little boost to

Phorkys's power, He will be strong enough to give Erik back his body, and we can all go home.

I reach an arm behind me, and Tiffany scoots closer, grabbing it with one hand while she wraps the other around my waist to support me. With her strength and blessing, I reach my other hand back, and Dean wraps himself around me on my other side.

His hands are softer than Erik's—both of theirs are—more slender, but still warm. Still undeniably *right.*

The tentacles under my skirt feel right, too, in their own way. I lock eyes with the monster again, His eyes the main source of light in the cool darkness around us. For the briefest of moments they flicker crystal grey, letting me know that Erik is here, too.

Giving me permission. His blessing. His gratitude.

I close my eyes, and nod.

A sigh escapes my lips as the smooth and slightly sticky pull of the suckers pluck the dress from my skin, handing the excess yardage of the skirt to Tiffany and Dean, who peel the bodice up and over my head, exposing me to the air. I feel the trail of wetness weeping from each nipple as the breeze flits across my skin, before the tentacles crawl up my torso. Two wrap about my sides, and I feel Dean and Tiffany both shiver as Phorkys embraces the three of us, two more tentacles settling about my shoulders as He places His beak against my left breast.

"Thank you, Lillian," He says, before biting down in a hard latch.

"Ah!" I gasp, pain exploding from my left nipple before the titan's thin, devilish tongue licks and slurps away the pain. Heat blossoms within me, soothing the ache as I feel my milk leave my body and enter His hungry mouth. I lean into him, nuzzling my cheek against His head as He presses to my bosom, cradling Him as He cradles me, and in that moment I really do feel like a mother.

It's weird and heady, a mix of different kinds of love swirling through my gut and the rest of my body. Lust, love, affection, and awe fill me as I nourish Phorkys's body as only I can.

This is a blessing, I think to myself. A gift. This is what it means to be a mother, to give of your body to provide life to another.

But being a mother isn't entirely selfless. And it isn't separate from everything else I'm feeling, either. At my back, I know Tiffany and Dean can feel it, too—the dissolution of the idea that intimacy dies in parenthood. I can feel their understanding settle into me, a pulse of heat everywhere our bodies touch, tingling almost, from their skin into mine. I feel Tiffany squeeze my hand against her belly, and it's the reassurance I need to let myself enjoy this.

I didn't think my body would ever do this. And in robbing myself of pregnancy, of motherhood, I also robbed myself of the idea that I could have love or pleasure, too. I'm not sure when it all happened. I didn't even know this was a wound that needed healing.

But all the same, I'm grateful for it.

A slight tingling and a playful lick accompanies a lightness in my left breast, and I realize that Phorkys is about to move to the next one. Already, anticipation is building in my belly at the jolt of pain and pleasure I know awaits me when He latches on—

"Ah!"

An orgasm spirals from His bite on my nipple, through my spine and straight to my clit—my arousal getting lapped up by the tide rippling at my pussy. I can't breathe, the feeling is so intense, as if my body isn't meant to handle it. My insides burn hot, and the water is like ice in comparison, the cold air making my other nipple pebble hopefully, despite the fact that He just finished with that one.

As Phorkys sucks at my breast, I feel Him draw that pleasure up my entire torso, splitting my orgasm from my lower half until the concentration of pleasure travels up my body, behind my belly button, through my sternum, and into the fatty tissue of my breast. A free tentacle wraps about it, suctioning on and giving it a liberating squeeze, and a splash of liquid bursts from my nipple into His mouth.

A warm tingle radiates from my nipple out to my whole body, like a pleasant numbness, as my limbs grow light and limp at once.

And then, the tentacles wriggle back and away from the three of us. I collapse back into Dean and Tiffany's waiting arms, feeling the moist tip of his erection and the warm slick of her pussy against my arms as I fall against them. In a flash of cyan light that turns into a shooting star, Phorkys and his magic rip themselves from the flesh before us, leaving the silhouette of my Viking swaying on his knees in the tide.

"Thank you," the titan cries one last time into the wind as He disappears below the Lake surface. **"I know we'll meet again, someday."**

And then the monster disappears, and Erik collapses into our arms.

CHAPTER 31

TIFFANY

Dean and I drag Lillian and Erik back to the cabin after Phorkys escapes into Lake Superior.

Okay, mostly Dean. I open the door for him and pull back the sheets after we strip them of their wet clothes and tuck them into the two bunks of the cabin. Dean stokes the blaze in the fireplace, then hangs a banged-up kettle on the hook above the coals.

We dry off and change while the water boils. Then I dig around in the cabinets as quietly as I can, although I'm sure Lillian and Erik would probably sleep through a Civil War reenactment outside after all they've been through. If dragging their bare asses up the splintery steps of our cabin didn't wake them, I doubt the sound of me stirring up some hot chocolate mix in mugs is gonna do it.

Dean grabs his sleeping bag from the back of the old couch and nods to the front porch. Typically, we'd have the screens open, letting in the sound of the bullfrogs as we slept through the late summer nights. But with it being closer to Halloween than Labor Day now, it's too chilly to keep the windows open.

The two of us settle into the porch swing with our cocoas, and Dean unzips the padded comforter to spread around us. I nuzzle into him, and then take the biggest fucking exhale in the history of the world.

"You can say that again," he nods, blowing on his drink. His hand around my waist splays across the side of my stomach, which is teetering on the line between "big" and "huge."

I'm almost seven months along now. And I know he's eager to get me back to my OB-GYN for a checkup. Lillian, too, honestly. Part of me is scared to know how much damage we've done.

The other part is just grateful to be alive.

"Is it really over?" I ask. "Now that Erik's free, and Lillian's human again?"

He takes a sip before answering. "Gods I hope so."

I laugh, one of those half-cough, half-honks that threatens to spill the contents of my mug. "Did you have a *sword* at one point, or did I imagine that?"

"Oh, fuck!" Dean's eyes go wide as he straightens, and I grumble at losing my pillow. "I forgot about him!"

"Him?"

He chews on his lip for a second, eyes far away, before settling his arm back around me and shrugging. "Eh, I'm sure he'll be okay. He's a god, after all."

I stare at him. "Care to elaborate on that?"

"Not really. I'd rather just forget about all of this, honestly." He takes another sip, looking down at me as I return to my spot resting in the crook of his shoulder. "Well. Maybe not *all* of it."

I nod. Sip. Turn slightly and peek in through the window behind us at the sleeping forms of Erik and Lillian. "Not all of it."

We sit like that for a few seconds, and then Dean kicks with his foot to rock the swing a little. The swoop tingles in my stomach, and I'm grateful that I don't have morning sickness anymore.

"This is a nice spot. I can see why you two liked escaping here every summer."

"It's peaceful, right?"

"Very."

He squeezes me closer, and takes my mug to set it on the end table when we both drain them. Eventually, our hands wander, twisting around until I'm settled on his lap instead of beside him, his strong hands kneading into my ass as we kiss each other there on the swing.

It starts out sweet. Saccharine, almost: a peck on the forehead, then nose. Followed by a tentative sweep of his lips across mine like a question.

I bite down hungrily, massaging his lips with my tongue before he responds with his own. After facing our own mortality, we kiss like it's our last night on earth—because it almost was. Before I know it, I'm grinding down on his lap, my belly bumping against his abs, his erection thick and hard in his sweatpants, and the sleeping bag is too warm around us.

He moans underneath me, and I need him more than anything. More than air. More than sleep. More than the warm fire in the cozy cabin and its protection from the elements.

It takes some finagling, but when he finally wedges his hands beneath my pregnant stomach and frees his cock from his waistband, I sink down and take him inside me, from tip to base, in one fell swoop.

He stretches me so completely, so fully, I cry out. It feels so good. He shushes me, a laugh in his voice as he does it, and I swallow the sound with another searching, hungry kiss.

"You saved me," I gasp into his mouth when I break for air, rocking back and forth to grind my clit into his pelvic bone. "You saved all of us."

"Lillian did," he grunts, arguing even as his head tilts back and he thrusts his hips up into me, making a little squeak bubble from my throat. "Fuck, Erik and you, too. We all saved each other."

"I could have lost you."

I don't know what makes me say it. Something about the perfect heat spreading through my body as he tops me from below, pistoning his hips and rubbing every spot that matters, bouncing me again and again on his lap. It makes me admit the things I've been afraid to say.

"I wouldn't have let you go."

"She could have died–"

"She didn't!" He grunts, pausing at the top of his thrust and hitting a spot inside me that makes stars explode behind my eyes. Then, with his dick still seated inside me, he lifts us and turns, laying me back against the swing and bending over me, holding my thigh to his chest and resuming his long, determined strokes. "You didn't. None of us did. We're okay. We're safe. We're here."

Every word is like a mantra as he pumps inside me. And suddenly, he isn't close enough. I wrap my other leg around his hip, tilting my head back and arching into him, trying to get leverage and growling as the swing teeters below us.

"I need you closer, Dean, kiss me, please–"

He presses into me, pushing the air from my lungs as his chest flattens into my tits and belly, his neck craning to find my lips again. I meet him, gasping and moaning around his tongue. The whole time, he never lets up, his hips keeping a rhythm like a metronome. Then, somehow, his fingers are there, gathering the slick leaking from around his cock and using it to lubricate their glide across my clit, and the pleasure coiling inside me reaches a breaking point.

"Dean!"

"You're safe. You're safe..." he whispers over and over, in between kisses and in time with his hips and his fingers, and I don't know if it's to me or himself. But I can feel him approaching his climax, and I'm right there with him, climbing a high that feels so right, so sweet, so perfect...

So free of guilt or shame or secrets.

And then I'm coming. My legs straighten and twitch, my back arching with a strength I didn't know I had—some kind of orgasm-induced weight lifting happening up and down my spine as my body clenches down around his length.

He follows me immediately, the fluttering walls of my pussy milking him of his release. It feels so good to know he's filling me up right now, erasing every trace of our entrapment.

My body continues to shake even after he stills and begins to soften. Tears flow from my eyes freely, and it only takes Dean a second to realize I'm not panting from the physical exertion of our sex, but from crying.

"Oh, babe, I'm sorr–"

"Don't!" I shake my head. "Please! No, I need—just, don't leave? Please?"

He searches my eyes, concern melting into understanding as he wraps his arms behind my back and holds me to his chest.

"Of course. Let me get the blanket."

One nice thing about being pregnant? I don't have to

worry about his cum in my pussy as we snuggle up awkwardly on the porch swing, laying half-beside, half-on top of each other.

There may have been a time when we'd have been able to spoon on this thing, but between his broad shoulders and my baby bump, we don't quite fit anymore. Still, he holds me tight against him for longer than we'd normally put up with the discomfort, and I don't try to move him.

I need this. We both do.

At some point, I fall asleep. I don't realize it until I wake up on the pull-out couch a couple hours later to go to the bathroom, still wrapped in my fiancé's deceptively strong arms.

CHAPTER 32
TIFFANY

The smell of cheap gas station coffee and donuts rouses me from my slumber: the drool on my pillow practically choking me as I salivate over the scent of sugar, caffeine, and dough.

"Oh my God, *yes,*" I groan, bypassing the bathroom entirely and walking straight from the pull-out couch to the kitchen table.

Lillian smiles at me, already sipping on her coffee while Erik sniffs curiously at his own, and Dean rises sleepily behind me. "I thought we all deserved a treat."

"Fuck me, are those Bismarks?" Dean peeks over the back of the couch. "Okay, I'm up, I'm up."

"Lillian has said I am not allowed to eat one until all of us are awake," Erik announces. "We have been waiting since sunrise. May I have my pastry now?"

"Yes, my love." She winks at me as he pulls a Long John from the box and sniffs it, his eyes going wide.

When he takes his first bite, his entire face lights up.

"This is extraordinary!"

The Viking has already devoured two by the time Dean and I have gotten our own and taken our first few sips of coffee. Lillian, in a stroke of genius, picked up an entire dozen when she hit up the gas station this morning to catch up on the local gossip and get a few more supplies for all of us.

Thankfully, her SUV still runs and our credit cards all work. She found her phone right in the center console where she'd left it and revived its charge, too, and catches Dean and me up on everything we missed while we were underwater.

"Apparently, the landlord makes his rounds this time of year to lock up the cabins for the winter, so we should head out before then," she finishes, taking a bite of her donut. "The guy at the gas station says he usually comes down from the city on Fridays."

"I'm honestly amazed that he waits this long to check on the rentals. We could have been staying way longer every year if we'd known."

She shrugs. "I guess. Although, someone might have actually reported us missing if he'd checked in earlier."

Fair point. "Did *anyone* know we were missing?" I ask, getting up to find my phone and plug it into its charger.

"I have literally one text from one of the other paralegals in the office asking if I'm sick, but that's it. I haven't checked my voicemails yet, though. I'm kinda scared to, to be honest. I'm sure they fired me weeks ago."

Lillian bites her lip, and Dean puts a hand on her shoulder.

"What is a voicemail?"

The three of us stare at Erik, whose beard is dusted in powdered sugar. He hasn't touched his coffee since his first tentative sip, which made him scrunch up his face in disgust. He's been silent aside from some appreciative moans whenever he tries a new flavor of donut, letting us catch up on the modern world together without asking for clarification.

But his question reminds us of just how crazy our situation is. My job is nothing special, and I'd been about to claim maternity leave in a few months. But hearing about Lillian's law firm, I realize we've likely *all* lost our jobs while we were at the whims of Keto.

We'll be lucky if we even still have our apartments when we get back.

Erik seems to realize that none of us are going to answer his question, and he picks up another donut.

"There's something else we need to talk about before we handle any of that," Dean says, setting his coffee down.

My stomach flips at that.

Last night, with Dean holding me in his arms and kissing away the tension of the past weeks, there was a part of me that wondered if it was enough to erase everything that was laid bare between the four of us during this little *vacation*. If, maybe, now that he and I had had our moment together, and Lillian wasn't under some weird supernatural sex trance and leaking magic milk from her titties, the sexual tension between us all would sort of... poof away.

I realize now that was silly. The second he says it, Lillian's face turns pink from her neck all the way to her forehead, and Erik stares expectantly at each of us in turn, his gaze far too transparent for my liking.

Lillian and I lock eyes for a moment, and I can almost feel her lips on mine. Her naked body collapsing back into Dean and me on the beach, as the last remains of our own titan magic flowed from our bodies into hers. The heat between our bodies, our mouths, our hands.

I don't remember when exactly it happened, but our gills have all disappeared since we returned from the beach. Just a few rows of thin, pink scars line each of our necks above our collarbones now—a mark of what we've all endured together. Seeing them in the bright light of morning, it's hard to believe I could have ever thought we'd be able to sweep it under the rug and return to something resembling normal.

"I love you, Lillian," I say, breaking the tense silence. "I have since college, actually. I never knew how to tell you. And I never stopped—even after meeting Dean. I was so afraid of losing both of you. Terrified. But it had been going on so long, I didn't realize just how much my anxiety was ruining our friendship until..."

"It was too late?" Lillian finishes for me.

I nod, shame pinching my lips closed. She bobs her head in acknowledgement, then looks over at Erik and reaches to take his hand before responding.

"I'll admit, I never picked up on any of that. But, I mean, I wasn't exactly the best after you and Dean got together, either. I was jealous. Of you, mostly, I thought at the time, because you got this perfect guy who was super nice and smart and rich–" Dean snorts, and Lillian rolls her eyes at him before smacking him on the shoulder with her free hand. "Well, compared to *us* you were rich, okay? Mr. I-Work-With-Computers." She laughs a little, and he grins at her. "But *you* were also getting to spend so much time with *my* best friend, so clearly I was jealous of you for taking Tiff away from me.

"But after meeting this lug," she nudges Erik with her

shoulder, and he tilts his head, a confused look on his face. "It's a term of endearment," she assures him. "I realized just how obsessed you can become with a person when you fall in love. So now, I kinda get it. But... I never stopped being obsessed with you a little bit, either."

"Same." Admitting it feels like a weight off my chest. I don't remember how much of what I said to her in her underwater nest she remembers, but hearing her say these words is so important to me right now. It's an acknowl-edgement of all of the things we never said to each other. "That's exactly it. I'm obsessed with Dean. Who wouldn't be? He's adorable. But I never stopped being obsessed with you."

She and I stare at each other, both getting a little misty-eyed. She reaches her free hand across the table toward me and I take it, and feeling her fingers warm against my palm gives me butterflies.

It's like that feeling of discovering your first crush in middle school likes you back. Only, it's Lillian. Lillian likes me back. *Me.* Tiffany.

Lillian like-likes me.

We're grinning across the table at each other like idiots, and Dean finally shakes his head. "Well, Erik, I guess our girlfriends are girlfriends now."

"My treasure can have as many lovers as she wants."

That makes Lillian's jaw drop, and she breaks her gaze away from mine to gape at him. "Wait, are you for real right now? How many *lovers* do you expect me to have?!"

The Viking shrugs, as if this whole discussion couldn't be less monumental. "In my village, all men and women of a certain age had multiple lovers. Is this not common where you live? We all had many children, and raised them together as a village, because it was safer and easier than attempting to sequester ourselves and rear them on our own.

"You are a beautiful lass. In my village, you would have been desired by dozens of warriors. As would you, Tiffany."

He meets my eyes, not a hint of dishonesty or flattery in their crystal grey depths.

My stomach flips for a whole new reason.

Dean clears his throat.

"Ah yes, you too, Dean, although you are a bit slight to be a warrior yourself."

I cackle at that, and Dean blusters. Lillian slaps Erik's arm. "Excuse you! That *warrior* killed a power-hungry titan and saved all our lives!"

"Thank you, Lillian," Dean mutters, eyes darting to Erik. "We can't all be Captain America, you know."

"Who is Captain America?"

At this point, Lillian and I are both trying and failing to hold in our laughter as we observe the standoff between my red-faced fiancé and her earnest Viking. Eventually, Dean realizes that it's no use holding resentment towards the man when he meant no harm, and he sighs.

"I have a confession to make, too," he says. And the three of us sober. "Lillian, I also think you're beautiful. I always have. I've... kinda wanted you and Tiffany to hook up since we started dating. Not in a pervy way! Well, I mean, maybe a little in a pervy way..."

He's positively scarlet now, and I pat his knee in sympathy as he rubs his hand down his face. "I just mean, well, *I'm* one of the warriors who desires you, too, I guess, is what I'm trying to say. With Tiffany, or with Erik, even, if you both would be up for that. I mean, you're both very attractive and I..."

He trails off and after a second, Lillian closes her open mouth to smile at him graciously.

"I had no idea you felt that way about me, Dean."

"I mean, who wouldn't?!" He bursts out, staring between the two of us. "When I first met Tiffany, and she took me back to her place and introduced me to her gorgeous, funny roommate, what guy *wouldn't* have fantasized about the two of you together? Come on, Erik, back me up here!"

For a moment, the other man doesn't say anything, just glances back and forth between the three of us. Then understanding dawns on his face.

"Am I to understand the three of you have not had sex?"

We all blink at each other for a minute.

"Before being captured," he clarifies. Another pause. "Ah. The three of you were *not* lovers. I believe I misunderstood."

"I think we all did," Lillian mutters under her breath.

"So, wait." I stare at Dean, still processing his admission and not even truly grasping Erik's question. "You're bi, too?"

"You didn't realize that?"

"*No!*" I shout, and suddenly I'm standing at the kitchen table, my spindly dining chair tumbling to the floor behind me. "How did I not know that?"

"Well, you never told me *you* were bi, so I assumed we just both knew that about each other and didn't need to talk about it?"

"What is bi?" Erik whispers to Lillian, and she whispers an explanation in his ear. He nods, then bangs his fist on the table, making us all jump.

"I am also bi!"

He says it like an announcement, clear and completely

devoid of embarrassment or shyness. And I gotta say, I'm beginning to understand what Lillian sees in the guy. Aside from his muscles and the fact that he saved her life and looks at her like the sun shines out her ass.

Lillian also bangs her fist on the table, grinning from ear-to-ear. "I have an idea! Why don't we all have sex?"

CHAPTER 33
LILLIAN

The three of them stare at me long enough that I begin to wonder if my isolation in an underwater sex cave with a Kraken shifter may have made me incapable of reading social cues.

It's possible, I suppose. I mean, I've apparently been misreading Tiffany for the majority of our friendship, and I even misread my own sexual identity for longer than I care to admit.

But if being trapped on a deserted island and bartering my womb to an ancient fertility goddess in exchange for my friends' freedom and a month of orgasms has taught me anything, it's that life is too short to stan purity culture.

So, I double down.

"That *is* what we're building up to here, right? We're all attracted to each other, have feelings for each other, and want to bang?"

Surprisingly, it's Erik who speaks up first.

"My treasure, you are my salvation and a blessing from Odin. I will love you until the end of my days on this earth." He squeezes my hand, doing that thing where he looks into my eyes with so much intensity my insides feel like a bottle of champagne. Then he takes a deep breath and turns to Tiffany and Dean. "Were it not for both of you, my dearest Lillian would not have survived her labor, or Keto's attack. For that, I will be grateful for all eternity.

"My short time with Lillian has reminded me that sex is not something to be ashamed or afraid of—not anymore. My body has been both prison and slave to the whims of a monster for so long, I do not remember how it feels to give into my own desire without fear. I would be honored if you, Tiffany, and you, Dean, would join us in celebrating that freedom."

"Sorry," Dean wheezes, all traces of the warrior who defeated Keto with an Olympian sword evaporating. "I need a minute to process this."

"What's there to process?" I ask. "Didn't you just say you've wanted this for years?"

"Yeah, hence the minute."

I look over to Tiffany, who's slumped back into her chair and closed her eyes. "What do you think?"

"I think," she says, eyes still closed, "I need to take a mental snapshot of this moment so I can come back to it whenever I start to feel self-conscious. Three hotties at once, all wanting to have sex with me." She lets out a breath, then opens her eyes, a dream-like smile sneaking across her lips.

Her very kissable lips.

I reach for her, letting my arm cross the small distance through the weightless air, glorying in just how much easier it is to move on land than it was underwater. My fingers graze her thigh, and the softness of her skin is a revelation. Each individual hair on her leg stands at attention as goosebumps swell under the surface, and before I know it, my hand has traveled up her body to cup her hip.

I scootch my chair closer—close enough that it's easy to just lay my head onto her shoulder and breathe in her scent.

Scent.

Gods, it's a *gift,* to be able to smell the buttery warmth of her skin. The fresh grapefruit and basil of her shampoo. To stroke my knuckles across the peach fuzz on her cheek and tilt her lips to mine with zero resistance as I dart my tongue out to taste the traces of bitter coffee and buttercream on the corner of her mouth.

I've been without my sense of smell for weeks, and now that I have it back I swear I'll never take it for granted again.

Her whole body shivers, and I *feel* it. It's like I've been numb for a month, and the cool autumn air has woken up my skin again.

And I want to feel her over every inch of it. Her, and Dean, and Erik... all of them. All of them at once.

Her breath is stilted as it ghosts across my lips, and she swallows.

"Is this really happening?"

Her voice is a whisper—barely audible. I smile, and my cheek presses into hers. "Yes."

A large, calloused hand skims down my back and squeezes the curve of my ass, making me gasp. Then Erik's whole, firm body is behind me, his lips kissing down my neck before he playfully nips the meat of my shoulder.

I moan, and Tiffany echoes it.

A screech breaks the heady silence of the cabin, making us all jump. Dean has crossed the room to where the two rustic, wooden twin beds are separated by a nightstand.

Correction: *were* separated. Faster than I've ever seen

him do anything, Dean has yanked the nightstand in front of the cabin door and is pushing the one bed from the corner right up against the other one. Their headboards now touch side-by-side along the far wall, creating an inviting surface that's big enough for all of us.

Suddenly, Erik hoists me into the air with one arm under my knees and the other against my back and yeets me onto the combined beds. I yelp as my plus-size body legitimately flies through the air, the sound morphing into a girlish giggle as the butterflies in my stomach take off in flight.

He's so strong!

It's *so* stupidly hot.

But I have hardly any time to process my giddiness, because Dean's hands replace Erik's. He climbs up between my splayed legs before I have a chance to close them, fisting his fingers into the hair at the nape of my neck and crashing his lips to mine.

Oh.

Where Tiffany was soft and questioning, Dean is desperate and commanding. I can taste every day of the three years he's apparently yearned for this, feel it in the way he kisses me, the enthusiasm at his chance to play with Tiffany and me together. I barely register the weight of her body and Erik's sinking into the mattresses beside me as Dean's tongue spears past my lips, searching and sucking and pinning me between his grip and his mouth.

It's overwhelming in the best way.

I kiss him back, battling my tongue with his while I spread my legs wider. I can feel his erection pressing against my tummy, already so hard despite the suddenness of all of this. His thigh is pressing against my mound, and I grind into him, suddenly aware that we're all wearing way too many clothes.

I gasp, breaking the kiss, only to see Dean's thirsty expression taking me in like I'm an oasis in the desert. I start to ask if we can take a break to disrobe, when Tiffany grabs Dean's shirt and yanks his face to hers.

He falls willingly, bracing one arm against her head while the other skims up my waist. His hand gropes at my breast, and I moan when his fingers dig into the soft flesh— a sound that's mirrored back in stereo as one rumbles in his throat and Erik's eyes grow hungry watching us.

It's a helluva sight. Even just watching Dean and Tiffany make out is enough to make me wet, and when Erik and I meet eyes over their entwined bodies, the heat in my core blazes.

Dean's thumb scrapes across my nipple through my shirt. My back arches into it, and Erik slides an arm beneath me for support. My head falls back on a groan, and the Viking takes advantage, slipping his lips around my bottom lip and sucking it between his teeth.

We are a mess of limbs and hands and tongues, and I'm briefly disoriented as the four of us grapple hungrily for each other. This isn't slow or organized, like I guess a part of my brain assumed it might be. There's no seductive bass playing beneath a sultry saxophone, no silken sheets and pouting lips. This isn't a candlelit, seductive moment.

No, this is what happens when four humans escape a battle with the gods and live to tell the tale. This is a celebration of life, of air, of breathing through our noses and mouths and feeling through our skin: light and smell and taste. This is an all-you-can-eat buffet of sensation and unrepressed sexual freedom, and we are filling up our plates as fast as we can.

"Fuck. *Fuck,*" Dean rasps as he comes up for air. "I can't breathe. I need–"

"I know. It's so good," Tiffany pants, and I look back to see her arms splayed above her head, one hand fondling blindly at Erik's lap beneath my shoulder. "God, Erik, how big are you?!"

He rolls his hips under me, seeking the friction of her hand, and her eyes go wide. I can't suppress my laughter at her reaction.

It's just all so... *fun.*

I'm fucking around with my best friend and our sexy boyfriends. And I cannot wait to find out just how good we can make each other feel.

"Why don't you take off his shorts and find out for yourself?" I say, sitting up to tear off my pajama shirt. My breasts swing free, and three pairs of eyes zero in on them like homing missiles.

"Oh fuck," I breathe as all of them pounce on me in unison.

Tiffany grabs at the waistband of my bike shorts, shoving down the spandex like they owe her money. I let out an *oof* as the twisting mass of bodies knocks me off balance, and I fall back into the pile of pillows at the headboard.

That, of course, only makes it easier for her to wrestle the fabric down my legs and straddle one freed leg. She reaches through the curly hair covering my mound, poking one finger into my slit and ghosting the tip across my clit.

It happens at the same moment Dean and Erik each latch onto one of my nipples, and the triangle of tingles formed between the three erogenous zones makes my head go fuzzy. I gasp, then groan, my stomach jiggling as my breath grows shorter and shorter as they work me up into a tizzy.

I would feel self-conscious, but Erik splays his thick fingers across my middle, squeezing into the soft flesh with lusty affection. A warm glow spreads from his fingertips, meeting up with the tingling in my chest, and the combination of sensations is almost enough to believe we're back underwater—I'm *weightless* in their arms.

"Do you know," he growls in his powerful baritone, and *fuck* is it a sexy sound, "How jealous I was of Phorkys for getting to taste your milk?"

"*Fuck*, right?" Dean agrees, lapping and swirling his tongue in tantalizing circles around the swollen bud. "God, it was so sexy. So fucking hot."

"Will you drink *my* milk, Lillian, when it comes in?" Tiffany coos, and my clit twitches in her hand. "Or will you just watch as these two clean up after feeding time?"

"Oh God, oh God, *oh God!*" I moan, each repetition raising in pitch as her devilish fingers work me up to a fever pitch. I'm *soaked* down there, so wet I can hear the sloppy noises of her fingers slapping back and forth, and the contrast between the slide between my thighs and the dry scrape of Erik's fingers on my stomach and breast is *heaven*.

Fuck, to be wet and dry at the same time!

My leg feels wet, too, underneath Tiffany's seat, and when I look down I see her rocking her hip into my thigh. I close my eyes, plucking out the textures of her sex: the scratchy lace of her panty seams, the coarse stubble of her hair, the slick suede of her juices lubricating the slide of the cotton gusset cupping her pussy... *fuck*. Her body is a symphony on mine, and it's working me up to a crescendo.

"Get yourself off on me," I whimper, rolling my hips up

to try to meet her thrusts. "Fuck, I want to feel *all* of your cum covering my body.

"*Fuck*, Lillian," Dean mutters, shifting to wedge a hand between our bodies so he can palm his cock. "I would love to paint your tits in my cum."

"I want to save my seed, my treasure. I want to fill one of your sweet cunts with it, and watch the other lick it clean."

Fuck.

At that, Tiffany mewls above me and dips two slippery fingers into my cunt, and it's the last thing I need to push me over the edge. I'm crying out as I come, Dean sucking off my nipple with a *pop* as he sits up and strokes himself to completion. Erik straightens a little, pushing my tits together to make a welcoming surface for Dean's cum, and the sight of him spurting across my chest sends Tiffany crashing, too.

"I'm coming!" She shouts, bending forward with the force of it, her face scrunched up in pleasure. I reach my hand between Erik's body and mine to pull her down on top of me, tasting the soundless cry on her lips as she rides out her aftershocks.

Our bellies press together, Dean's cum sticky between us, the smell of sex heavy in the air. But I don't care. It feels so nice to have her body smothering mine, her lips nipping and pinching my own between them as I massage my fingers into her scalp.

"Oh, that *is* a beautiful sight," Erik murmurs, his voice farther away than I remember.

Our mouths break apart, and Tiff and I both look over her shoulder to see Erik towering behind her bent body, stroking his massive cock as he takes in the view of her ass.

"So hot, right?" Dean strokes a hand from the middle of

her back down over the curve of her cheek, before pulling back and delivering a satisfying sounding *smack!* The strike rings out in the tiny cabin, and Tiffany moans again, arching her back and sending her pregnant belly squishing into mine and her ass higher in the air.

"Please, may I have another?" She asks breathlessly, and despite the fact that I just came, I am instantly hornier than I have ever been.

And remember, I've had sex with a literal tentacle monster.

But hearing Tiffany beg so pretty like that while my Viking boyfriend rubs the head of his cock up and down through her folds?

Fuck.

"May I fuck you, Tiffany?" Erik asks, as calmly and politely as he would ask someone at the dinner table to pass the salt.

But instead of answering him, she looks to me. We lock eyes, and a shiver of heat passes between us as she raises an eyebrow. "Well, Lillian? What do you say? Is it alright if your boyfriend fucks my pussy with his massive cock?"

"I'd be offended if he didn't." I give her a shit-eating grin, and she smacks my arm.

"Just for that, I'm gonna stay on top of you while he does it."

"You asked for it, then," I say, wiggling under her until I can snake an arm between us and just barely tickle her clit with my middle and ring fingers. She gasps, and my smile grows wider. "Tit for tat, you little minx."

"Yes, my treasure, play with her button while I take her cunt," Erik groans, sliding inside slowly, inch by inch, until his balls press into the back of my hand.

"*Fuuuuuuck,*" Tiffany exhales, eyes fluttering closed. I

feel her clit jump beneath my fingers as she presses back, fucking herself in little pulses on Erik's cock. He steadies himself by grabbing her hips.

"Odin's beard," he hisses, "the gods have blessed us, Dean, to have such perfect women to fuck."

"You can say that again."

My gaze flicks to Dean, who's stroking his half-hard cock as he watches us, face still beaming like a kid on Christmas who got everything on Santa's list. I turn my head to the side, letting Tiffany rest her forehead against my shoulder as I flick my fingers back and forth over her clit and Erik slowly starts to pump his hips.

"Dean," I say, body feeling delightfully numb as I support the weight of my boyfriend and my best-friend-turned-lover, "why don't you let me suck that tasty cock of yours?"

His hand stutters. "Really?"

"Mm-hmm."

Tiffany moans, and Erik's face glows with heat and pleasure as he watches me part my lips around Dean's cock. It's smaller than Erik's, but the tip flares to a delicious girth that spreads my mouth wide before I notch my lips under the head. Dean groans, weaving his fingers through my hair and holding himself still in my mouth as I swirl my tongue around and around, flicking it against the notch in the head below its opening until the shaft swells to full mast once more.

"*Fuck*, Lillian your mouth feels so good."

"You should feel his," I breathe around his length, pulling back a little to look into his eyes. He shoots a nervous glance at Erik, who waggles his eyebrows before pulling back and spearing himself into Tiffany again.

"Oh God!" she cries, and I latch around Dean's length

again, taking him as deep as I can go. "Fuck, Dean, you better be fucking that smart little mouth of hers."

"Yeah, shut me up, Dean," I bait, knowing that Tiffany's sweet, golden retriever boyfriend isn't the type to shove himself down someone's throat.

But then he proves me wrong.

His fingers curl against my scalp, tugging at my blonde strands until my head tilts back, stretching the front of my neck. Then he pistons his hips as hard as Erik just did, thrusting himself across my tongue and blocking off my airway.

I gag in surprise, but he pumps through it, until my mouth slackens and my eyes water and drool leaks from my lips.

"Mmmm," I gargle, pinned between his body and Tiffany's, pushed and pulled with both Erik's thrusts and his, trying desperately to open my throat and breathe through my nose and keep my teeth from closing on his thick cock.

It's so good, though.

Fuck, it's *spectacular*.

"Mmm, mmmm!" I hum around him as I start grinding on my own forearm, still wedged between me and Tiffany and flapping at the wrist as I rub furiously against her swollen clit. I'm so goddamn aroused from all of them using my body like this that I can feel an orgasm coiling inside me, winding tighter and tighter and priming my core like a spring.

"That's right, Lil, you take that fat cock," Dean grunts, head tilting back as his hips start to lose their rhythm. "Are you gonna swallow my load for me? Are you alright with that, with tasting me all the way down your tight little throat?"

My hum turns to a rumbling groan of affirmation as his dirty talk revs me *all* the way up. It's such a contrast from Erik's polite requests and worshipful praise. It's demeaning and sloppy and *amazing*.

I have it all. I am having every kind of kinky, delicious sex at once, and it's the greatest thing I've ever been a part of.

"Are you close, baby?" Tiffany gasps, her breath puffing across my shoulder. One of her hands squeezes around my breast, wrapping around us and trapping my arm even tighter between our bodies, even as she shifts her shoulder back to free my nipple so she can pluck at it with her thumb. It makes me groan again, and I redouble the efforts of my fingers at her clit, reveling in the sound of her little gasps and whines of pleasure.

"So close, babe. Are you?"

"So close."

"I am going to fill you with my seed, Tiffany," Erik says, voice tight and husky. "While Dean fills Lillian with his."

"Oh, *fuck!*" She cries, and I wish I could see her face. Her voice is so goddamn sexy, so carelessly breathy and whiney and high-pitched like I've never heard her before, letting go in a way that's so new and beautiful and sexy.

And I can't take it anymore.

I come, my pussy pulsing around nothing but leaking like a motherfucker. Tiffany isn't far behind, I know, because she literally bites my shoulder in an attempt to muffle her cries. The pain just adds to the electric pulses skittering across my body, providing an anchor point that makes it even headier.

I'm drunk on her pleasure as she quakes on top of me, giddy with the sound of Erik grunting his own release into her fluttering pussy, high on the taste of Dean's semen splattering the back of my tongue and coating the inside of my mouth. I lose myself to the overwhelming pleasure, the press of perfect bodies, and the sounds of ecstatic release.

This is what it feels like to be alive.

To be safe.

To have cheated death with the three most important people in your universe, and carry on to squeeze every ounce of pleasure from the time you won back.

WE WAKE up to the sound of an angry fist banging on the wooden door.

"Hello? Hello? Are you girls still in there?"

"Shit!" Tiffany hisses, bolting up quickly before remembering that she's seven months pregnant and her body doesn't do *anything* quickly anymore. "Lil! It's the property manager!"

I'm already racing to grab a coverup, a dress, a robe— literally *any* article of clothing that will fit around my body. "Just a minute!" I call out, settling for an oversized t-shirt and my bike shorts from last night, which are still coiled into a tight-spun circle of fabric from being rolled down my thighs by Tiffany the night before.

I shake them out and pull them up my legs, glancing around in a panic as I see the state of disarray we left the cabin in last night.

You really can't blame us for fucking like rabbits the entire day, seeing as we literally fought a titan a few days ago. Shit, I had *kiloplets*.

Milliuplets? What would you even call a pregnancy with a thousand babies?

"Hide!" Tiffany whispers, poking at the men.

"Five more minutes..." Dean mumbles, only for her to shove him onto the floor with a crash.

"What's going on in there?!"

"Shit, Erik, Dean, get in the bathroom," I whisper, throwing one of the rustic, cozy quilts that came with the cabin over Tiffany's still naked body. "I need to talk to the landlord."

Ten frantic seconds, and then I'm finger-combing my hair and stepping out the door, which I open just wide enough to squeeze through. "How can I help you?"

"Lot's closed for the season." A short, grumbly man in a fleece-lined plaid button-down shirt and a baseball cap says, scowling at me. "You all were supposed to be gone weeks ago!"

"I am so sorry, sir—we are so grateful to see you! You see, we just got back to get our stuff, we got lost hiking along the trail..."

Fifteen minutes later, the man is ambling back down the path to his truck, having believed my bullshit story of getting lost in the woods, only to be shuttled back to the city by the kind people who found us, and only now getting back to gather up our camping supplies.

It's threadbare at best, and would have been blown wide open if he'd been the *actual* owner of the property. Apparently, this is not the first time he hasn't received an email about a renter asking for an extension on their stay.

Still, when I see him typing out a text message on his way back to the truck, I know it's time for us to get the hell outta dodge.

We pack up our belongings into my SUV and Dean's pickup in record time, plugging our phones into our chargers and setting course for the closest Denny's for us to get a bite to eat.

We worked up an appetite over the past couple months.

Tiff and Dean take his truck down the dirt road to the highway, and I take one last look around the property to make sure we aren't leaving anything behind. When I determine we're good to go, I find Erik standing by the lake in a pair of Dean's trunks and my "Smut is for Lovers" t-shirt that pulls across his broad body, showing off every line of muscle definition in his back.

"Hey, honey," I say, pressing a kiss to his shoulder. "It's time to go."

He stares out into the water, brow wrinkled into an anxious expression that I've never seen before.

"I do not understand this world anymore, Lillian. How am I going to survive in one of your modern cities?"

Oh.

I think for a moment, rubbing his back and standing quietly with him before I answer. It isn't an easy question. He's been divorced from society for almost a thousand years, and he's right. He doesn't know enough about the modern world, doesn't understand how it works or how to survive in a place like Chicago.

"You're going to lean on me," I answer honestly. "Me and Dean and Tiffany. We're going to help you through it, just like you helped me survive on that island out in the middle of the lake."

A swallow bobs down his throat, and he purses his lips, nodding tightly. I grab his hand. Our fingers lace together so naturally, it seems impossible that we won't be able to make this work. After all, we fought literal gods to win his freedom. Surely we can survive filling out some paperwork and teaching him to drive a car?

"Will you miss it?" I ask as we gaze out over the giant blue expanse before us. This inland sea that we were trapped in. Caught in a web of fate and bargains, castaways of destiny.

"It is the only life I've known in this new land. Bound to a god, trapped and alone…until I met you."

"It wasn't your life, Erik. Not really." He squeezes my fingers, and I squeeze back, cherishing the little bite of pain as his knuckles dig into mine. "Now you have the chance to start living for yourself."

He nods again, then looks from the lake to our entwined hands, to my face.

"With the four of us, I've no doubt it will be an adventure worth living for."

I smile at him, understanding his meaning. We were willing to die for each other: him, Tiffany, Dean, and me. We loved one another enough that we were willing to pay the ultimate price.

But there's isn't only work in dying. There's work in living, too. In starting over. In paying bills, in going to work, in learning to read. In building a family.

I think of Tiffany, about to bring a new life into the world. What it will take to figure out the family dynamic with the four of us, to face the world knowing that we're different from everyone else. That we've fought gods. That we survived a new titanomachy. And even the other, more human things that make us different: we're bisexual, we're polyamorous, we're not a traditional-looking American family.

But knowing how good it can be when the four of us let go of our pretense and decide to live honestly with each other? How much joy and pleasure and hope we're capable of?

I'm willing to do the work.

"Come on, Erik. It's time to go home."

EPILOGUE

DEAN

"Are you... family?"

The ultrasound nurse blinks at the hulking Viking man standing in the doorway of the doctor's office, seeming altogether too large for the modern world. She has to tilt her head back to look him in the eye, and I hide a chuckle with a cough into my elbow.

"Can't you see the resemblance? He's my brother," Tiffany says, which doesn't make it easier to keep from laughing. Even Lillian covers her smirk with a hand as she catches my eye over the nurse's shoulder.

"And I'm her best friend," Lillian adds, dragging her boyfriend by the arm despite his obvious reluctance to enter the tiny room. His eyes are wide as he takes everything in, as if every object lining the counter is filled with hazardous waste that he could unintentionally knock over.

"We want them here."

The nurse looks back at Tiffany one last time to confirm, then nods, waving Erik and Lillian inside. The stirrups are folded back down now, the pelvic and cervical exam having gone as smoothly as we could have hoped, and all that's left to check is the baby's vitals.

Erik pulls at the collar of his borrowed polo shirt, the only item of clothing I had in my duffle bag that was able to stretch over his massive pecs. Even so, it's obvious that it's two sizes too small for him, and way too fucking short—the waistband of his (my) sweats is just visible under the hem.

Lillian beams at Tiffany as the tech squirts goo on her belly, and I know she's aching to squeeze her hand. So I grab on with both of mine to compensate.

"There he is. A nice, healthy heartbeat, too!" The tech smiles a practiced, toothy grin, eyes on the screen with the rest of us, the blurry image just barely showing a silhouette of a tiny hand and arm before flickering with a head and blobby body. We breathe a collective sigh of relief. "Wait. You *did* say it was a boy, right?"

I blink and tilt my head. "Ye-es... why, what's wrong?"

"This is a girl. A girl with...um..." The woman's face pales, and her eyes go wide. "Uh, sorry, this can't be right. If you'll just excuse me."

Tiff and I exchange a quick glance, before the four of us all bounce our focuses around the room.

"A girl?" My fiancée finally says. "That's... surprising."

I've never heard of a gender changing in utero. Not that having a girl would be a problem; we'd be happy with any gender our child identifies with.

But this is the first appointment we've been able to get for Tiffany since we left for what we've decided to refer to as "the vacation". And seeing as the nurse just ran out of here looking like she'd seen a ghost, I find myself reaching for my phone to Google what it might mean when a tech leaves the room in the middle of an ultrasound.

Erik leans over my shoulder as I search—something I've become accustomed to in the three days since we've all gotten our technology back. At first, it was off-putting having him gape at my screen every time I pulled out my phone, but we've all decided that exposure therapy is probably our best course of action when it comes to introducing Erik to modern society.

Meanwhile, Lil grabs the wand and runs it over her stomach, trying to assess what might have made the nurse panic.

"Don't do that!" Tiffany hisses, reaching over her stomach to swat Lil's hands away.

"She just left us here! I might as well—oh shit."

"What? *What?!*"

The four of us lean in to look at the screen, and none of us are quite sure what to make of it. First, because looking at an ultrasound is not something any of us are particularly skilled at, and Lillian isn't a trained tech.

Second, because we all have seen what human babies' feet are supposed to look like. And that's *not* what's on the screen before us.

We all see the head. Then some fingers pop up, almost like the baby is waving at us, and I can't help but squeeze Tiff's hand when I see the little munchkin on the screen in black-and-white. But then we get to the lower half. And it's...

A lot.

As in, a lot of *limbs*.

"Please tell me I'm dreaming."

None of us answer Tiffany as we gape at the screen. Well, Lil and I gape. Erik squints at it, I think still waiting for somebody to explain what we're supposed to be surprised by.

"Is that... is it just me, or do those resemble..." Lil trails off, voice weak.

"Tentacles." I swallow. "They look like tentacles."

"What are those bumps?" Tiff asks in a whisper, pointing with her finger at the widest part of the baby's body, which just so happens to be its *hips* instead of its head.

"I do not know exactly what is going on," Erik cuts into the ensuing silence. "But if I am correct in *picking up on context clues—*" this is a phrase Lillian had taught him over the past three days to be a nicer way of telling Erik to try to figure something out on his own— "that woman may have just discovered that Tiffany's baby has tentacles."

Lillian nods, placing the wand back into its holster and grabbing a paper towel to wipe Tiff's belly. "Break something on the machine first."

Tiff and I stare at Lillian, alarmed.

"Lil, we support Planned Parenthood, we can't break their machine–"

"She's probably checking to see if it's broken, guys," she explains quietly while gathering Tiffany's clothes and handing them to her. "Right? What would you do if you started seeing tentacles in ultrasounds? You'd assume it was some kind of like, weird artifact or something, right? Dean! You work with tech. Download a virus on it or something!"

"I'm not going to–"

I'm cut off by the sound of Erik slamming one of the cabinet drawers shut. Then he grabs one of the many wires coming out of the back of the machine and slices it with a scalpel.

The screen flickers, and dies.

"Will that suffice, my treasure?"

"Perfection, my love. Thank you." She kisses him on the cheek, then grabs Tiff's bag and sandals. "Now just drop that knife in the red bucket over there with the yellow triangle on it, and let's get out of here!"

Twenty minutes later, the four of us are sneaking across the parking lot of Planned Parenthood in the outskirts of Chicago, having thankfully avoided the ultrasound tech and hopefully covered our tracks.

"Well. That was fun. What now?" Tiff asks.

What now, indeed.

Our return to Chicago has been a bust. Our first stop when we got back from the cabin was mine and Tiff's apartment in Lakeview, only to find a big, red eviction notice taped to the door and the locks replaced.

Fortunately, the mail key still worked. We opened our cubby to find it stuffed with notices from our landlord, work, and utilities companies informing us that we were both now jobless and homeless, and that all of our stuff had been relocated to a storage unit. Supposedly, we had until the end of last week to claim our stuff or it would be auctioned.

Lillian's apartment was even worse. Her car had been towed, and there was a new person living in it when we went to check the status.

I guess we shouldn't have been surprised to lose our jobs, apartments, and health care after we'd been missing for two months, but it still stung for that to be our first greeting when we returned to town. Exhausted from driving the eight hours back home, we ended up staring at each other from across a sticky booth at a truck stop

Denny's at one AM, wondering whose parents it made sense to call.

Lillian's were in Ohio and, as it was normal for her to go months without calling them, she didn't even have a text from them waiting for her when we charged back up our phones. She doubted they even knew she'd gone missing, and wasn't too keen to inform them.

Tiffany, of course, was estranged from her parents after being emancipated when she was 17. She didn't talk to them anymore, and I didn't blame her.

Which left my mom and dad. They would be the only ones we could tell (at least partially) what had happened up at the Lake, but I still wasn't sure if I was ready to return home.

On the one hand, Dad might actually, finally, be proud of me when he learned I killed a real, honest-to-gods titan.

But did I care about his approval anymore?

I'm not sure if I ever want to go back. Especially not now that we knew there were hundreds, if not thousands, of other titans or gods—monsters, he would say— swarming the Great Lakes.

How long could I keep it secret from him? And how soon after it eventually came out would he insist on me going back there, hounding me until every single one of Phorkys's children were dead?

"He doesn't need to die, too, does He?" Lillian asked as we discussed our options.

"I do not believe He will kill without needing to," Erik said, looking pensive. "There are plenty of fish and deer to sate His hunger, and that of the babes."

I wondered how long that would last. If I could trust the delicate peace we seemed to leave behind us on the beach.

But if I'm honest with myself, I don't think I have it in

me to kill any titans. I meant what I'd said to Keto back in the cave, when I pleaded with her to leave the demands of our families behind us and start fresh. I'm tired of carrying the weight of my ancestor's expectations.

"I've got some money saved away," Lil volunteered. "Not a ton, but something. An emergency fund. What do you guys have?"

"I have no money from this land."

"We know, honey." Lil patted the Viking's knee. "We'll cover you for a while, okay?"

I had a moderate savings and some stocks from working at start-ups for a couple years, and Tiffany said she didn't mind using the wedding account to float some expenses for a while. We settled the tab (thankfully, no one had stolen our wallets from the campsite while we were underwater), and decided to stay in one of those sketchy, short-term rental motels until we could get Tiffany into a clinic to make sure she was okay. The three of us went to the cops to file a report that we'd gotten lost hiking while we were on vacation in Michigan, so we could at least have some kind of record and explanation for the gap in our resumes.

I'd been hoping that once we got Tiff checked out and knew the baby was healthy, I could call work and try to get my job back. Then find an apartment. But knowing what we know now...

"So... what do we do?"

It's Lillian who breaks the silence as we climb back into my car, Erik's head bumping against the roof in the backseat.

"I do not understand. Why do we not return to the lake?"

The three of us look at Erik, none of us sure how to explain just how fucked we are. The guy's been an absolute champ as we drag him around the midwest, fielding his questions about literally *everything* he sees. But with the stress of calling utility companies, reporting our absences to work, and all of the other modern paperwork and bull- shit we have to deal with, we didn't always have the patience to answer him. I could tell there were a million things he *wasn't* asking bouncing around his head.

"Honey, that's not how things work anymore. We don't own the cabin we were staying at, and the owner doesn't rent it out in the winter. We need a place of our own. But we need money, and jobs to get approved for a place, and we need to provide proof of identity and get references and all sorts of things to get jobs... it's complicated."

"I was able to live alone on the shores of Lake Superior for hundreds of years," he argues. "Could I not build us a shelter in the woods?"

"Before winter?" Lillian presses. "You're not half titan anymore, Erik. That's an impossible amount of work to do in a month, even for you. And I'm not exactly eager to go back to our little lean-to on the island. Now that we're back in the real world, I don't want to give up electricity and grocery stores and donuts."

He nods slowly, face serious. "It would be a tragedy to give up *donuts*."

He says the name of the treat like he's still amazed such a thing could exist.

"Well, he might have a point, actually." Tiffany says. "There are hunting cabins people rent in the winter all the time—far enough out for privacy but close enough to civi- lization for supplies. Certainly we could find something like that we could afford for a bit while we sort everything out."

"Maybe even a vacation rental," I say, picking up Tiffany's thread. "Not in Chicago, but somewhere we might be able to lay low for a while. Somewhere on the lake, in case..."

My eyes glance to Tiff's stomach, and there's an uncomfortable silence as we all refuse to acknowledge the elephant in the car.

"We'll never fully be able to forget it, will we?"

"I don't think so, hon," Lil says, reaching over the front seat to squeeze her shoulder. "But you aren't alone."

"We are family now," Erik says, inclining his head in agreement.

"And we're going to keep all of us safe. Even if it means we need to get a little...unconventional," I tell her, patting her knee. "Lil, get out your phone. It's time for another roadtrip.

~

TWO MONTHS LATER

I'm chopping wood for the long winter ahead when Lillian runs out of our cabin on the north shore of Minnesota, sprinting across what will eventually be our vegetable garden to find me in the edge of the forest in our backyard.

"Dean! *Dean!* It's happening!"

The axe falls from my hands and I run up to meet her, immediately pressing a hand to her lower back to lead her up the porch stairs, through the open kitchen/dining/living room and right into the master suite bathroom, where Tiffany is going into labor.

I know, I know. Look, we didn't initially *plan* on doing a home water birth, okay?

But it's not like we can have this baby in a hospital.

I have to admit, I was skeptical when Lillian first found

this place for sale: a rustic two-bed, two-bath fishing cabin just off a state forest on the coast of Lake Superior.

But the owners hadn't known what to do with the place for years. It rented out well enough in the summer, but with only a wood stove for heat, and rudimentary electric and running water, it wasn't particularly popular during the rest of the year. And it was isolated enough from the rest of society, being secluded from the main road by the woods and a long, dirt driveway, that not many people had been interested in snatching it up.

To Erik, of course, it was positively luxurious. And with him helping us manage the fire for heat and my survivalist knowledge, we had just enough know-how to get it ready in time for winter. And with the money that Tiff, Lillian, and I had squirreled away in savings, the owners were happy to let us take it off their hands for cash.

Eventually, we'll get it fixed up enough that Erik can manage most of the property and I can get a job again. But for now, Lillian makes enough as a paralegal in Duluth to supplement the last of our savings for a few months.

After all, we're a little more comfortable with roughing it than we were when we lived in Chicago. But in times like this, the isolation is more than a little scary.

My heart thuds in my chest at about a thousand miles a minute, and I almost crash into Erik at the edge of the antique clawfoot tub.

"You okay, babe?" I ask breathlessly, reaching for Tiffany's hand and letting her squeeze it.

"That's five minutes," he says, staring at a stopwatch that Lillian must have shown him to use during our baby drills. "Should I call Him?"

"I thought we decided against that!" Tiffany grunts,

already looking sweaty and tired. "We've read every book we could. Lil's got a doula on standby. Can't we just–"

"We can't bring a human doula in here, Tiff. You know that. Phorkys has magic, He can help us. He owes it to us."

"You mean to *you*."

"Okay, well, yeah, maybe to me," Lil huffs, giving me a desperate look. The kind that says, *hey, husband, talk your wife off the ledge, wouldja?*

I squeeze her palm with my fingers, dipping my hand into the warm tub water and wiping away the flyaways from her forehead. "Hey, it's okay, we talked about this, remember? He'll be right outside unless we need him. It's just in case, alright?"

She glares at me. "I want you to get a vasectomy after this. You too," she adds to the Viking, who's eyes widen as if to ask *who, me?* "We're not going through this again. After this, these uteri are closed for business, understand?"

Lil shushes her, walking around the freestanding tub to rub Tiff's shoulders as she peeks out the window that looks out onto the northwest coast of the lake. She gives Erik a nod, and he runs out of the room to call on our titanic friend.

"Fuck, fuck, it's another–*argh!*" Tiff grunts, and Lillian grabs the stopwatch off the windowsill and hits the start button.

"You got this girl, breathe with me. In..."

It's like deja-vu all over again.

"She is a beautiful child. Reminds me of one of my daughters," Phorkys says, almost wistfully, cradling our little monster as He lounges with her in the tub. The titan barely fits, even shrunk down to His smallest possible form.

But He graciously offered to help with the first twenty-four hours—after a little magic from His tentacles got Tiffany healed up from the lengthy labor.

"Thank you for saving her."

My voice is hoarse. My hands are still shaking, although I'm not sure if it's from adrenaline or exhaustion.

Tiffany is resting now, Lillian and Erik tucked beside her in our giant bed and seeing to her needs. I'm taking first shift with the baby, which means I'm also sharing the duty with Phorkys. Without whom, Tiffany might not have survived.

"There was a debt between us. It has been paid." He rocks the little girl with two tentacles woven like arms, while another brushes a wispy, blonde hair from her forehead. Her own tentacles, eight in total, splay from her hips much like Keto's did, draping over the side of his arms. At her waist, the heads of six puppies snore softly, eyes closed and toothless mouths twitching in response to six separate dreams. Her own mouth is open slightly, breathing the air as easily as she breathes in water.

"I could raise her with the others," Phorkys suggests, seeing the anxiety written in the wrinkles on my forehead. **"She need not know who her parents are."**

"Even you know who your parents are."

"And I wonder if it wouldn't have been better if I hadn't."

I think about that, the pressure one can feel when they know they're descended from the gods. How it changes a person, forms them into someone slightly removed from their peers.

"Would you ever give up yours? Knowing the pain of them being taken from you?"

The monster stills at that, bright blue eyes staring unseeingly at my daughter. *"No."*

Of the four of us: Tiffany, Lillian, Erik, and I, we've had three interactions with Phorkys since He sucked the last of Lillian's magic from her breasts. One when we first moved into the cabin; Erik walked to the shore and called for Him to inform Him that we would be neighbors. The second occurred when Lillian asked Him if He would be available to lend his magic for Tiffany's delivery.

And third, when I opened the bathroom window and screamed for Him to come and help, when our baby's hips got stuck in Tiffany's birth canal.

We've all had time to process since "the vacation". Once the initial shock and gratitude that we survived wore off, once we had a place to live and realized that we were going to somehow still participate in society, our bodies reminded us of the trauma we endured. I am still grateful for my partners: we take turns supporting each other when one of us is having a particularly bad day. Erik, especially, having lived with his trauma the longest, has been a rock of understanding for each of us when we've needed it.

But he still cries in his sleep. He mourns losses of a different kind, ones we can't fully understand, as he takes in the world of today and compares it to the world he was born into. We could not have carved a home for ourselves here without him, just as he could not have survived here without us.

Tears fill my own eyes as I become overwhelmed with just how grateful I am for all of them. And Phorkys, too. I do not blame Him for Keto's sins. He is also a victim of Her cruelty, in His own way. I didn't hear all the things She said to Him in that final battle, but I can recognize the sadness in His monstrous face when He looks at my daughter, and remembers all the children he will never see again.

I take the healthy baby girl from Phorkys's grasp, our own little monster, and He lets her go willingly. I offer gratitude that, thanks to Him, my wife is *also* healthy, her womb knit back together with His magic, her labor eased by His generosity. Because of Him, my partners can sleep soundly tonight, and we can begin to learn what it means to co-parent a tiny little demigod.

"What will you name her?"

"Priscylla," I say without hesitation. I'd been thinking about it since the moment I saw the hazy outline of her form in the ultrasound. Since I first heard her cries mixed with the mewling of her puppy hips.

"A beautiful name."

"It is." I press a kiss to my daughter's forehead, my love for her still permeating every cell in my body. "She's beautiful."

And I believe it. Despite the fact that every time I look at her, I remember Keto's curse. Despite the fact that she will remind us everyday of the torture we endured at the bottom of the lake. Despite knowing that she will never go to school, or meet our neighbors, or belong to the world of her parents, I believe she's a beautiful, *beautiful* girl.

Just as I believe without a doubt that her four parents will raise and love her with everything we have.

You can't choose your children. You can't choose your parents. Just like you can't control how many limbs you have, or what you look like, or who you love.

But you can choose to love with all your heart.

And that's what I intend to do.

THANK YOU FOR READING

If you aren't ready to leave these characters behind just yet, you can download a spicy bonus epilogue for free when you sign up for my newsletter at www.cassandramedcalf.com/subscribe!

And there's always more spice, bonus scenes, new stories, and NSFW art on my Patreon! Get new chapters weekly, plus my ebooks & audiobooks for free when you subscribe at www.patreon.com/cassandramedcalf .

AUTHOR NOTE

Thank you so much for reading *Bride of the Kraken!*

I have so many more monstrous stories planned for you. Please take a moment to leave a review so I know which scenes were your favorite!

Your honest review will help future readers decide if they want to take a chance on a new-to-them author. In a world full of beautiful, diverse stories, it can be hard to find the book that hits all the right buttons. So if this one tickled your fancy, recommending it on Storygraph, Goodreads, or social media can help you find more stories it!

And if you want more awesome book recommendations, consider joining my book club on Discord! We have monthly book chats, bingo, prizes, accountability and more —completely free!

All that and more can be found on my website, www.cassandramedcalf.com.

Hope to see you soon,
Cassandra

ACKNOWLEDGMENTS

With every book I write, this list gets longer. And that's a wonderful problem to have!

First, my partner, Andy. Herner, you are the absolute light of my life. My biggest cheerleader, my support system, and my best friend. I love you and the puppies more than I will ever be able to put into words (and considering I'm a romance author, that's saying something!). Thank you for putting up with my early mornings and late nights as I claw my way into a *hopefully* successful author career.

I am so fortunate to have a supportive family, even if I'm never letting them read this book. Mom, Dad, Kelley, and yes, you too, Sue (since I APPARENTLY HAVE TO CALL YOU OUT BY NAME NOW)—you all have always been my biggest fans, and I am so grateful for you.

So many authors are an inspiration to me (you can check out the list in Kraken's Castaway for more), but I would be remiss if I didn't mention Kathryn Moon and the worlds she creates. They are my happy place, and I love disappearing there.

I'm also lucky to be part of an amazingly supportive writer's group called The Bi+ Book Gang, led by the incredible Bailey Merlin. Y'all kept me writing through some of my toughest times this year, and the book wouldn't have gotten done without you. Thank you so much!

And finally, my readers! A few of you go above and beyond to support me on Patreon, and I cannot tell you how grateful I am. This year has been a tight one for me, and there have been months where Patreon has kept the puppies fed. So thank you. Thank you, thank you, thank you SO much for supporting me and reading along as I write my monster smut:

Danielle S

Gennifer N

Bryce N

Jess T

Kitt3n Bree

Terri V

And my beta readers, without whom I would not have been able to release this book:

B.M. Light

Kaiidth

Taylor

THANK YOU SO MUCH!

ABOUT THE AUTHOR

Cassandra Medcalf is a writer, narrator, audio engineer, food enthusiast, wine taster, do-it-yourselfer, and an amateur film critic (despite barely having seen any movies). She lives in Duluth, MN with her adorable husband and their even more adorable dogs. You can follow her and her family's hare-brained schemes and lofty pursuits on her website, cassandramedcalf.com (or, if you're just here for the smut, on Instagram @CassandraMedcalfVO).

Also by Cassandra Medcalf

STAND-ALONES

Fowl Play, A Small Town Sports Romance

FIXER UPPER SERIES - LGBT SMALL TOWN ROMANCE

Betting on the House

Betting on the Bird

Hot Rod Hookups

Here Comes the Bride

FOR THE LOVE OF TITANS SERIES - LGBT PARANORMAL ROMANCE

The Kraken's Castaway

Bride of the Kraken